### "I have to fire you."

"What happened?" Grayson asked. Because something did between the time Harlow left his house and now.

"Anthony was waiting for me when I got home. He said that if he found out I was cheating on him, whoever it was, they'd never find his body."

Grayson laughed.

"It's not funny. He's killed before and gotten away with it. We know that."

"Honey, your ex doesn't have a clue who has your back. You've got three highly skilled men behind you."

"I know, but—"

"It's more than just that. A normal person would say they have your back. When we say it, it means we'll give our life for yours." At hearing her gasp, he wanted to slap his forehead. It did mean exactly that, but he shouldn't have said it. That was what she was worried about, why she wanted to fire them.

"No, Grayson. Just no. I can't let you and your friends risk your lives."

"Harlow. You can. It's our job."

Dear Reader,

Writing the first book of a new series always excites me. A new world, new characters, new problems and challenges. In this series, The Phoenix Three, three high school boys are kidnapped for ransom. That event changes their lives more than they could have imagined at the time. The Phoenix Three men have dedicated themselves to saving children—no matter the cost.

If you've read any of my previous books, you know I love the idea of a band-of-brothers theme. Brothers don't have to be related by blood. It is the bond among a group of men that brings them together, that makes them a team. These men aren't looking for love, but when they find it, they fall hard. They are protectors—it's in their DNA—and they will do anything to keep the women they love safe.

Harlow Pressley has been robbed of her confidence and self-worth by her ex-husband. When Grayson Montana meets Harlow, he likens her to a shy mouse who dresses in granny clothes to hide herself. As the story unfolds, he is thrilled to have a front-row seat to watch a beautiful butterfly emerge from her cocoon and find herself again.

Before they can have their happily-ever-after, a villain must be vanquished, and Grayson must do what he does best—protect.

Happy reading!

*Sandra Owens*

# DANGEROUS SECRET

## SANDRA OWENS

**Harlequin**

**ROMANTIC SUSPENSE**

# Harlequin®
## ROMANTIC SUSPENSE™

Recycling programs for this product may not exist in your area.

ISBN-13: 978-1-335-50275-9

Dangerous Secret

Harlequin Enterprises ULC
22 Adelaide St. West, 41st Floor
Toronto, Ontario M5H 4E3, Canada
www.Harlequin.com

**Printed in Lithuania**

MIX
Paper | Supporting responsible forestry
FSC® C021394

**Sandra Owens** lives in the beautiful Blue Ridge Mountains of North Carolina. Her family and friends have ceased being surprised by what she might get up to next. She's jumped out of a plane, flown in an aerobatic plane while the pilot performed death-defying stunts, and ridden a Harley motorcycle for years. She regrets nothing. Sandra is a Romance Writers of America Honor Roll member and a 2013 Golden Heart® Finalist. Her books have won many awards and she is an Amazon bestselling author.

### Books by Sandra Owens

### Harlequin Romantic Suspense

#### *The Phoenix Three*

*Dangerous Secret*

Visit the Author Profile page
at Harlequin.com for more titles.

I'm dedicating this book to you
because you're reading my book and you're awesome!

# *Prologue*

Grayson Montana was good and buzzed. Wasn't that the goal of spring break? A pretty girl in a bikini passed, and he turned, walking backward as his gaze locked on her cute ass. "That's what I'm talking about." He was in South Florida for the sun, the surf, the weed, the beer and the girls. So far, he'd crossed off everything on his list but the girls. That was okay, there was plenty of time for a hook up.

He'd be eighteen in two months, and he meant to go home not a virgin. It was his first time in Fort Lauderdale, and for a pampered boy from South Carolina who'd never been let loose on his own before, he was wide-eyed and lit.

His father—who owned eleven luxury car dealerships throughout the Southeast—had asked what he wanted as a graduation gift. Grayson was sure his dad had been expecting to hear that a Porsche or Dodge Charger muscle car was on his son's bucket list. Nope. Grayson wanted to go to spring break in Florida. Besides, he already knew he was getting the Charger as a graduation gift.

The reason he'd asked for the trip was simple. His friends were going to Fort Lauderdale for spring break. He turned in a circle. Where were his friends? They'd been with him only minutes ago, but he'd lost sight of them on the crowded beach. "Dudes, where are you?" he yelled.

"What dudes?"

Grayson narrowed his eyes at the guy staring back at him. "My friends. I lost them."

"Lost mine, too." The guy gave him a drunken grin as he lifted a red Solo cup. "And they have the beer. Not cool. I'm Cooper."

"Grayson. I got some weed."

"Even better." Cooper glanced around. "Let's go up there." He pointed to a nearby parking lot. "More private."

As they walked across the hot sand, Grayson wondered why he'd shared that he had weed. He didn't know Cooper, so why should he share? He only had the one joint on him, and he should have saved it for himself, especially if he couldn't find his friends.

"Where you from?" Cooper asked.

"Myrtle Beach. You?"

"Hotlanta." He waggled his eyebrows. "Home of the best baseball team in the world. I'm gonna play for the Braves one day."

Grayson laughed. "Lofty goal there."

"It's gonna happen. I'm good. Got a full-ride scholarship to college."

"That's impressive. What position?"

"Pitcher. You play sports?"

Grayson couldn't resist messing with his new friend. "Yeah, I'm my school's top-ranked badminton player." He snorted when Cooper sputtered, trying to find something to say.

"Ah, really?" Cooper finally managed.

"No, man. Just messing with you. Track and field's my thing."

"Grayson…" Cooper studied him. "What's your last name?"

"Montana." Grayson grinned when Cooper's eyes widened.

"Damn, dude. You set new records in the sprints at Nationals."

"Yep." His father was counting on him going to work at the dealerships, someday taking over. Grayson was torn. He didn't want to disappoint his dad, and he did love cars, but…his secret wish was to become a teacher and coach. He was damn good at track and field events, one of the country's best. He dreamed of teaching kids how to be as good.

He considered it a blessing that even though his dad would be disappointed if Grayson didn't go to work at his dealerships, he would still support his son's decision. His future could wait until he got home, though. For the next three days, he was going to have fun and not think about tomorrow.

Cooper pointed to the far end of the parking lot. "Let's go over there."

They stopped behind a pickup truck, and Grayson lit the joint. He took a deep drag and managed not to embarrass himself by coughing. He handed it to Cooper.

"You ever do any hard stuff?"

Grayson shook his head. "Nah, man. I work too hard to keep my body in shape to mess around with stuff like that. Truth, I don't even smoke weed at home. I gave myself permission to enjoy my week of freedom. Smoke some pot, drink too much beer, meet some hot girls. You?"

"Same. My body's my temple and all that shit."

Grayson laughed so hard that he plopped down on the truck's bumper. Was that even funny? He stared at the half-smoked joint Cooper handed back to him. He was buzzing good now, that was for sure. "I'm thirsty."

"I'm hungry." Cooper looked around. "Wonder what's to eat around here."

"There's a taco truck down the street." Grayson took another drag before passing the joint to Cooper. "I want a beer." He took the fake ID from his pocket and waved it in front of Cooper. "Let's find us some beer, then we'll load up on tacos." He also needed to find his friends…or not. He was doing fine without them.

"A man with a plan. I like it."

Cooper handed the joint back, and Grayson pinched off the end, then stuck what was left in his pocket. They were walking toward the street when a white van turned into the lot and came to a stop next to them. Expecting to be asked directions to someplace, Grayson was surprised when the side door slid open and two masked men pointing guns at them appeared.

"Get in," one of the men commanded.

"No way!" He was faster than most people on earth, and he wasn't going to stick around for whatever the men had planned for them. "Run," he shouted at Cooper.

"You take one more step, Mr. Montana, and I'll shoot you in the back. Then I'll blow your friend's brains out."

Grayson froze. Terror slithered down his spine. They knew his name? He turned, and his stomach lurched at seeing the gun held to Cooper's head. Fear shimmered in Cooper's eyes, but he didn't beg Grayson to stay, even though it was apparent that Grayson was their target. What was going on?

"Get in the fucking van, Mr. Montana," the man said.

Since the second man had his gun pointed at him, Grayson didn't feel he had a choice. Both men's eyes were cold and menacing, and if he tried to run, he didn't doubt they'd shoot him and then Cooper. He got in the van.

As soon as he was inside, they pulled Cooper in, then slammed the sliding door closed. There weren't seats in the back, and before Grayson could decide if he should try to fight back, he and Cooper were handcuffed. Knit hats were put on their heads and pulled down over their eyes. Grayson had never been so scared in his life.

"What's going on? How do you know my name?"

One of the men kicked his hip hard. "Shut up."

He shut up. Hands patted him down, and they took his phone, wallet and hotel room key. And the joint. He should have smoked the rest of it. He almost laughed at the absurdity of regretting not finishing a joint when he was being kidnapped by men with guns.

"Cooper Devlin, from Atlanta," one of the men said.

They must be going through Cooper's wallet.

"You rich, too, boy?"

*Rich?* Was that what this was, a kidnapping for ransom?

"Hey, I'm talking to you, Devlin."

"Oomph," Cooper said, his body jerking against Grayson's.

Grayson winced. They must have kicked Cooper.

"I'm nobody," Cooper said.

"We'll find out how valuable you are soon enough."

Grayson was beginning to hate that cruel voice. He tried to get a sense of the direction they were going, but the driver was making a lot of turns, and he had no idea how far they'd traveled from the beach.

If this was for ransom, which it sounded like it might be, then that was good, right? They just wanted money and wouldn't kill him and Cooper. His father could pay whatever they demanded, but could Cooper's? He wished there was a way to ask his father to save Cooper, too. It wasn't his new friend's fault that he was in the wrong place at the wrong time with the wrong person. He wanted to tell Cooper he was sorry, but he didn't want another kick to his body.

He had no idea how long they'd been driving when the van came to a stop. Rough hands dragged him out and pushed him into a house. The sound of the door ominously closing behind him put the horror movies he and his friends liked to watch in mind. The monsters always won. He prayed that he and Cooper wouldn't die by a monster's hand.

# Chapter 1

*Ten years later*

It was the anniversary of their rescue, a date the three of them were celebrating at a Myrtle Beach bar. Cooper Devlin and Liam O'Rourke sat across the table from Grayson. They were also celebrating Cooper finally coming onboard The Phoenix Three, the security company they'd founded that specialized in rescuing missing and kidnapped children.

Grayson settled back in the booth as the waitress set three shot glasses each in front of them. He and Liam had opted out of the military a year ago, but Cooper had stayed with his Army ranger team until recently.

"Here's to those assholes rotting in prison," Liam said. He poured the contents of the first shot glass down his throat.

"Fucking A." Grayson downed his.

When he and Cooper had been locked in a room with another boy who'd been kidnapped a few days before, the three of them had bonded during the time they'd been held prisoner. Turned out the kidnappers had only planned to snatch him and Liam for ransom. As for Cooper, he didn't come from a wealthy family, so Grayson didn't even want to think of what would have happened to him if they hadn't been rescued.

And rescued they were. Instead of the millions the kidnappers had demanded, they'd gotten a long prison sentence.

"Here's to your father," Cooper said, raising his second shot glass toward Grayson.

It had been Grayson's father who'd hired the men who'd rescued them. Both his and Liam's fathers had immediately agreed to pay the ransom, but when the kidnappers had decided that had been too easy, they'd demanded more. Daniel Montana, a former SEAL, decided he wasn't going to mess around with his son's life and had called in some favors. In sending a team to rescue his son, Liam and Cooper had benefited, the team also getting them out of that house.

"May he rest in peace," Grayson quietly said, then downed the contents of the shot glass. It was still hard to believe his father, a man who'd always been larger than life to Grayson, was gone.

"Amen," Liam and Cooper said in unison.

"Here's to finally having Cooper join us," Liam said.

Grayson pointed his empty shot glass at Cooper. "'Bout time." When one was kept in a dirty room with two other boys—barely fed, a bucket for a bathroom, and not knowing if they were going to live or die—it was no surprise that a lifelong bond was formed. They weren't blood brothers, but they were brothers all the same.

"I know." Cooper twirled his shot glass in a circle. "Things weren't good with my team, and I couldn't just walk away."

"Well, you're here now. The Phoenix Three are finally together. Oorah," Liam said, giving the US Marines' battle cry.

"Hooah." The Army's battle cry from Cooper.

Grayson gave the Navy's. "Hooyah." He glanced at the

two best men he knew. "Did you really think when we were still just boys and made a pact after we were back in our cushy lives that we'd actually make The Phoenix Three happen?"

The name had been Liam's idea. He'd said they'd risen from the ashes. They'd kept in touch after being rescued, and for each of them, settling back into their privileged lives no longer fit. On a group text one night, Grayson had asked the question that had changed their futures.

Do you think there are other kids out there who need rescuing but don't have parents with the money to ransom them, or the connections to bring in badass men to save them? Kids like Cooper would have been if not for having been abducted with two rich boys.

Cooper: Maybe we should save them.

How? That from Liam.

Almost instantly, the answer appeared in Grayson's mind, and his heart had raced—in a good way—as the whole picture was laid out in front of him. Grayson had always been fascinated by his dad's stories from his SEAL days. That was probably why he could see the answer so clearly. His fingers flew over the keys as he texted his vision.

We learn how to plan missions, how to stage rescues, how to fight. Then we come back together and start a company that saves children who don't have the kind of families we do or the money to rescue them.

Liam: Again, how do we do that?

Cooper: We join the military.

Grayson grinned at how fast Cooper saw the same answer. Exactly.

And that's what they did. Grayson joined the Navy, becoming a SEAL. Liam enlisted in the Marines, becoming a Marine Raider, an elite Special Forces unit. Cooper became an Army ranger. As afraid and hungry as Grayson had been during those weeks in that room, it had brought these two men into his life and a mission that gave him immense satisfaction. They'd made an impossible dream come true, and he wouldn't change a thing.

"To The Phoenix Three," Cooper said, holding up his third shot glass.

Liam held up his. "To the children we'll save."

"Especially the children," Grayson said.

The next afternoon, Grayson was in The Phoenix Three office by himself. Cooper was taking a few days to get settled in the apartment he'd rented, and Liam was tracking down a fifteen-year-old runaway.

He glanced out the window, and as it always did when taking in the view, his gaze settled on the ocean, visible over the rooftops. Back when he'd told his father their plans, as expected, his dad had been disappointed that his son wasn't coming to work at the dealerships, but that hadn't stopped Daniel Montana from giving his support. Cooper had thought Atlanta would be the best place to base The Phoenix Three, especially since it was close to a major airport. Liam hadn't cared where they settled on as long as it wasn't in Kansas and anywhere near the father who'd disowned him.

Grayson's father, however, meant to keep his son close and had made them an offer they couldn't refuse. He'd buy a building in Myrtle Beach and charge them a hundred a month. And there was a perfectly good airport in Myrtle Beach.

The ocean was Grayson's happy place, and he'd been relieved when both his partners agreed to base their company in Myrtle Beach. His father had bought a building three blocks from the beach. The Phoenix Three offices were on the top floor, giving Grayson a view of his beloved ocean. The bottom three floors were rented out to other businesses.

They owned the building now thanks to his father. Grayson had inherited his father's dealerships, and in his will, Daniel Montana had gifted the building equally to the three of them. Grayson was happy that his father had gotten to know Cooper and Liam, had come to love his two best friends. Damn, he missed his dad.

He walked to the window and stared out. Since he was a year old, it had just been him and his dad. The loss of his father was still fresh, and his throat closed and his eyes burned as he lifted his gaze to the sky. "Hey, old man. You better be happy up there. I'm counting on you getting reprimanded by God for flirting with the pretty angels."

A soft bell sounded, indicating that someone had pushed the elevator button for the fourth floor. The early warning that someone was coming up to their floor was one of the first security measures they'd installed.

His appointment was on her way up. Over the phone, Harlow Pressley had sounded meek as a mouse with her soft voice that he'd had to strain to hear as she reluctantly answered his preliminary questions. He'd tried to form a picture of her, but all he could see in his mind was…well, a little brown mouse trying to hide in the shadows. She'd sounded desperate, though. Something to do with her son, and he'd agreed to see her.

They hadn't hired a receptionist yet, so he walked out to the lobby to meet her. A minute later, the elevator door opened, and she froze at seeing him. He hadn't meant to scare her. Realizing the door was closing, he put his hand out to stop it.

"Miss Pressley?" She'd said she needed help with her son but had refused to say over the phone what that help was, and she'd only said her name was Harlow Pressley. He didn't know if she was married or single, so he went with the Miss.

She nodded.

"I'm Grayson Montana." Along with softening his voice, he smiled, hoping it would put her at ease. "You're right on time." He stepped back to give her plenty of room to walk past without touching him.

As for his image of a shy mouse, he'd nailed it. She scurried by him, then seemingly at a loss as to where to go, she stilled. Her back was to him, and his gaze took in her hair in a tight bun, the brown print dress that looked at least a size too large that covered her from her neck to an inch below her knees, the beige knit sweater and the brown soft-soled shoes. From the brief glimpse he'd had of her face, he guessed her to be in her mid to late twenties. Why would she dress like that?

He moved around her. "My office is down the hall." She didn't respond, just followed him in those quiet old-lady shoes. He walked behind his desk, then waved his hand at one of the chairs facing him. "Have a seat. Would you like something to drink? Water, coffee, a soda?"

"No thank you." She sat, fussed with the hem of her dress, making sure that it covered her knees, and then pulled her sweater tight around her chest.

He took the opportunity to study her while she was getting settled. She didn't wear any makeup, not even lipstick, and her skin was pale, as if she never let the sun touch her face. Her hair was honey blond, and he imagined it was pretty when not coiled in a tight ball. It was her eyes that had him blinking in surprise. They were the bluest eyes he'd ever seen. They put him in mind of the sea around the Virgin Islands. Almost turquoise. They were beautiful and unique.

With her dress and sweater fixed to her liking, she stared down at her hands where they were clasped tightly on her lap. Instinctively, he knew he was going to have to treat her with kid gloves. She was pretty, would maybe be beautiful if she wasn't trying so hard to fade into the woodwork. He couldn't imagine that she'd always been like this, and he wanted to have a word with whoever had turned her into a scared little mouse.

"Before we start, I need some basic information. Full legal name, address, home and cell phone numbers, and your email address."

"Why do you need all that?"

"Because you're asking for our help, so I need to know all the ways I can contact you. I'm not going to show up on your doorstep unannounced, if that's what you're worried about."

"I'm sorry," she said to her knees. Then, still not looking at him, she rattled off all her information.

"Thank you." From the way she meekly apologized, he guessed she was used to being sorry for something. That didn't set right with him. He picked up one of his business cards and, after writing on the back, slid it across the desk to her. "I know you have the office number, but my cell phone number's on the back. You can reach me anytime of the day or night. Now, you mentioned that you needed help with your son," he said, still keeping his voice soft. "Let's start with his name."

"Tyler." She tucked the card into her purse.

As he had on the phone when she'd called to make an appointment, he had to strain to hear her. He rested his elbows on his desk and leaned toward her. "How old is Tyler?"

"Five."

They were going to be here all afternoon if she was only going to give him one-word answers. "What is it you need from The Phoenix Three?"

For the first time, her eyes met his, and there was a fierceness in them that surprised him. "I need you to help me get custody of him, Mr. Montana."

"Grayson." Getting her to use his first name was one way to get her to start trusting him. "Where is your son now?"

"His father has full custody."

Oh, boy. The last thing he wanted was to get in the middle of a custody battle. The Phoenix Three specialized in finding children who'd been kidnapped or abducted or were runaways. They did not get involved in family disputes. "Miss Pressley, I think you need a good lawyer."

"No! You don't understand, Mr. Montana. I had a good lawyer. It didn't help."

"Grayson." Had she been declared an unfit mother? If so, there was nothing he could do to change that. He should send her on her way, but the desperation in those pretty blue eyes was impossible to turn his back on. He'd talk to her for a little, maybe give her some advice before apologizing for not being able to help her.

"Why don't you explain your situation." Ah, hell. There were tears in her eyes now.

# *Chapter 2*

Refusing to let this stranger see her cry, Harlow willed her tears away. She wasn't sure how she even had any left. She hadn't seen or touched her little boy since Anthony had been given full custody seven months ago. Her ex-husband couldn't care less for his son now. He only saw Tyler as a means to an end. The first, to punish her for daring to leave him, and the second was to keep Tyler under his control and, when he was a few years older, to train her sweet little boy to step into the Pressley shoes. God forbid.

"Miss Pressley?"

She startled. What must he think of her, that she could get lost in her head and forget there was someone else in the room? She hadn't been herself for years, and she didn't know how to explain it to this man with the soft voice and pity-filled eyes. She hated that his pity was directed at her.

There'd been a time when she was a confident woman, happy in her own skin. Then along came Anthony, and… No, she wasn't going there. Not with this man's intelligent eyes on her, no doubt thinking she was a doormat. The sad thing, that was exactly what she'd become under Anthony's thumb.

"I… I'm sorry, what was the question?" Anthony's voice filled her head. *How is it possible for one woman to be so stupid?* There was a time when she didn't believe she was stupid, but she wasn't sure about that anymore.

"You were going to explain your situation. I gather your relationship with your ex-husband isn't a good one?"

She snorted, then wanted to crawl in a hole. *Ladies don't snort, Harlow,* Anthony said in her head. She blew out a breath. "Um, I don't know where to start."

"At the beginning is always good."

"Do we have a limited amount of time?" Like did she need to condense everything into a half-hour time slot?

"You have as much time as you need, Miss Pressley."

"Harlow." If her son didn't bear the last name of Pressley, she would have taken her maiden name back after the divorce.

He smiled. "Harlow. Pretty name."

"Thank you." She liked how her name sounded when he said it in his soft voice. "My greatest wish is to have nothing to do with the Pressleys. Unfortunately, Anthony…that's my ex-husband, uses Tyler to punish me." And to try to still control her even though they were divorced.

"He also lives in Faberville?"

"Yes. The Pressleys own the town. If you ever go there, it's best to just keep going." At his raised brows, she said, "Everyone in Faberville knows of the Pressleys, and everyone with any sense tries to stay under their radar." Well, she knew that now. "After graduating high school, I went to Clemson."

"Go Tigers."

Before she realized she was doing it, she smiled. There was something about this man that put her at ease in a way she hadn't been since marrying Anthony. "That time in my life was some of my happiest. Anyway, I returned home after graduating. I thought I got really lucky when I landed a job as the manager of marketing and events at the Pressley Resort and Golf Club. That was where I met Anthony." If there was one thing she could do over, she would have never taken that job.

She glanced out the window. "You have a beautiful view." Yes, she was stalling. It was embarrassing to have to tell this man how gullible she'd been. "I wish I lived closer to the ocean. There's something soothing about the sound of the waves."

"Would you like to take a walk on the beach?"

Surprised by the offer, she wasn't sure what to say.

As if sensing her hesitation, he smiled. "The beach is my happy place. I'm always able to relax even if I'm just walking along the shore. If you pull one more thread, your sweater's going to fall apart. Just thought a walk along the beach might help you the way it does me. We can talk while we get our feet wet." He shrugged. "Up to you."

She stilled her hands and glanced down at the long thread wrapped around her fingers. He was too observant. There was something about the way he looked at her that made her feel exposed, as if he could see through all her walls and defenses.

"The beach?" he said.

"I think I'd like that." And if they were walking side by side while she told her story, she wouldn't have to see the pity in his eyes.

"Great. It's only three blocks, but we can take my Jeep. I have no way to lock it, so we'll need to leave our shoes and your purse here. I'll lock your purse in my drawer."

This was a strange meeting, she thought, as they rode the elevator down, both of them barefoot. He kept surprising her, but in a good way. It had been a long time since she'd been interested in much of anything except getting her son back. It wasn't that she was interested in Grayson as a man she'd like to date, or hook up with, or whatever man-woman label applied. She didn't like men. Didn't trust them. She used to, but Anthony had cured her of that idiocy.

According to the article she'd read about him, Grayson had been a SEAL. Knowing that, she wasn't surprised that he wore his blond hair military short. After his smile, his brown eyes were his best feature. Except they weren't the more common dark brown. His were the color of her favorite candy...caramel. If she'd met him before Anthony, she would have definitely been interested in him. But she wasn't that girl anymore.

"Wait here," he said when they stepped out of the building. "The pavement's hot. I'll bring the Jeep around."

She grinned when he tiptoe-hopped across the parking lot. He jumped into a Jeep that had no top and no doors, which explained why he'd said he couldn't lock their things up. This day was turning out to be nothing like what she'd expected.

When he stopped the Jeep with the passenger side closest to her, she managed to climb in without losing too much of her dignity. Minutes later, he turned into a driveway of a house on stilts right on the beach.

"Um, is it okay if we park here?"

Amusement flashed in his eyes as he glanced at her. "I know the owner."

"That roof is awesome." It was a tin roof that was a copper-and-green patina.

He glanced up. "Yeah, it's pretty cool. Hang tight for a minute."

Already, sweat dripped down her back from the heat. After a moment of hesitation, she slipped off her sweater. Her sweaters—a shield even in the summer—were so much a part of her now that she felt naked without it. She almost put it back on, but it would be ridiculous to walk on the beach bundled up as if it were winter.

He reached into the back, bringing out a pair of flip-flops. "These will be big on you, but they'll keep your feet from burning until we get down to the water."

"What about you?"

"I'm used to walking on hot sand."

"Thanks." She slipped them on, and they were definitely big. As they headed to the shoreline, she chuckled.

He glanced at her with raised brows. "What?"

"I feel like I'm walking in clown shoes. How big are your feet, anyway?" As soon as she asked the question, she cringed. Would he think she was making fun of him? Conditioned to expect criticism or a sarcastic reprimand when she said something inappropriate, she hurried to say, "I'm sorry. That was rude of me."

He frowned at that. "It was?"

"Yes. I shouldn't have made fun of your feet." Sometimes she hated herself. Things that shouldn't be voiced came out of her mouth before she thought better of it. Then when she did, she loathed that she instantly turned into a doormat. A kicked puppy. That was what she was. Afraid of being kicked again. Her gaze snapped up to his when he chuckled.

"My feet are pretty big." He wiggled his toes in the sand. "Size thirteen, by the way."

"Oh, okay." He must think she was a ninny.

"You can leave the flip-flops here," he said as he rolled up his pants legs when they were a few feet from the water. "We'll pick them up on the way back."

"What if someone steals them?"

"They won't, but if Bigfoot strolls by and decides he wants them, I'll buy another pair."

She laughed. He was silly. After she slipped them off, they walked along the water in silence for a few minutes. The ocean was cool on her feet, and the sea breeze swirled the hem of her dress around her legs. An odd sense of calm that she hadn't felt in a long time washed over her. She should make the hour drive to the beach at least once a week.

"So," he said, breaking the silence. "Tell me your story."

How much did she need to tell him to get him to help her?

# *Chapter 3*

The idea to take her out of the office where she was uncomfortable had been a spur-of-the-moment decision, made when she took in the view from the window with longing in her eyes. Grayson likened handling Harlow Pressley to that of gentling an abused animal.

He still wasn't sure he was willing to put The Phoenix Three in the middle of a custody dispute, but he was coming around to the idea that hers wasn't a typical he said/she said case. From her wary eyes and the way she'd flinched a few times, she'd been the victim of her husband's abuse. That was his impression at this point, but he could be jumping to conclusions and she was just a good actress. If he was right, he was going to love teaching her ex a thing or two.

"So," he said after they'd walked along the shore for a few minutes. "Tell me your story." Her steps faltered, and she lowered her gaze to the water. If he was reading her right, she was debating what and how much to tell him. "You need to not only be honest with me but to tell me everything. I can't help you if you don't."

"I know. It's just that I'm embarrassed by what I let him turn me into. It's hard to admit that I didn't leave when I should have. The me you see here now isn't the me I once was."

"Would it be easier if I just asked you questions I need answers to?"

"Yes, I think it would be."

"How long were you married?"

"Six and a half years. Six years longer than I wanted to be." She kicked at the water as if she were angry at it.

"I assume you stayed because of your son?"

"Yes. I found out I was pregnant when we'd been married for six months. I was going to leave him and file for divorce, but that changed everything." She sighed. "The thing I want you to understand is that I loved my husband. Well, I loved the man he pretended to be when we were dating and for the first month of our marriage. He was all that a woman wanted in a man. Kind, thoughtful, loving. Then a few weeks after our wedding, the real Anthony began to make an appearance. Suddenly, I couldn't do anything right. I dressed to entice other men's attention. I said stupid things that embarrassed him. I wasn't attentive enough to him. It started as mild criticisms disguised as loving suggestions on how I could be a better wife. He had a way of making me believe I was in the wrong and I'd apologize. Over and over."

"And you tried to be that better wife, I'm guessing."

"I tried so hard, but in doing so, I lost me."

One of his cousins had been involved with a man who'd been controlling and mentally abusive. He'd watched the light fade in Leah Ann's eyes during the year she'd been with the asshole. Fortunately, she wised up before marrying the man. He'd never understood why she stayed as long as she had, and he'd asked her that very question after she left him.

"You have to understand," she'd said. "With a master manipulator like that, it starts with little things. And you think, I love him, and I want to please him, so you try to be what he wants. As the digs and criticisms grow harsher, you begin to believe that he's right, that you're the problem, so you try even harder. Somewhere in there, you lose yourself, which was his goal all along. You can't leave him because he has you believing that you're not strong enough to make it on your own."

"But you did, and I thank God for it. Did you just wake up one day and realize you couldn't go on like that anymore?" he asked.

"Pretty much. One morning, I looked in the mirror and wondered who that sad, beaten-down woman looking back at me was. That was the moment I knew I had to leave. Honestly, it would have been easier, and I would have left sooner if he'd physically abused me. I never would have put up with that. But his mental abuse was subtle, and men like that have the ability to make you believe it's you, not them."

Grayson thought about that conversation with his cousin before asking Harlow his next question. "What finally motivated you to leave him?"

"The day I walked in on him kissing Tyler's nanny. Tyler was sitting on the floor at their feet, playing with his toys while they were sucking face. I fired her on the spot, and they looked at each other and laughed. He said, 'This is what happens when my wife is a cold fish.' He was right about the cold fish part. By that time in our marriage, I couldn't stand for him to touch me."

"Good God." The man wasn't just a manipulator, he was downright cruel. "Whether you were or weren't, there is no excuse for him to carry on an affair in your home, and especially no excuse for kissing another woman in front of his son. Or kissing another woman anywhere while he's married. Tell me that's when you left."

"Not that minute. I waited until he left that night to go see his mistress." She chuckled, but it sounded off, like a sarcastic chuckle. "Yeah, he's had several mistresses over the years. After he left to go see her, I packed up some things for myself and Tyler. I checked us into a hotel. The next day, I saw a lawyer to file for divorce."

"How did your ex-husband come to have full custody?"

"Because his family owns the town."

"Explain."

"The judge, the police chief, literally anyone Anthony can use to his benefit is in his back pocket."

If that was true, things were going to get interesting. "I have to ask. Is it so bad that your ex has custody? You get visitation, right?" Just because Pressley was a bad husband didn't mean he was a bad father.

"Anthony couldn't care less about Tyler at the age he is now. He never spends time with him. The only reason he hired a nanny was because he didn't like me giving attention to Tyler and not him. He sees Tyler as a nuisance until he's old enough to begin his training as the heir. He'll teach our son to be just like him, and I can't allow that." She lifted pleading eyes to his. "I just can't. Please help me."

As much as he wanted to promise he would, he couldn't. Not yet. "That's all the questions I have for now. Before I can agree to take this further, I have to do some background research." She was emotionally exhausted. He had more questions, but they could wait.

"But you'll help me?"

"If everything you've told me checks out, yes. You should know that I'll not only investigate your ex and the Pressley family, I'll look into you, too."

"Okay. I have nothing to hide."

He hoped not. "If you can without being obvious, record your conversations with him."

"That's a good idea."

"I have them occasionally." He smiled, and as he'd intended, she smiled back.

Later that evening, he was still in the office when Cooper came in. "Thought you'd be out surfing."

Grayson rolled his eyes. "Dude, it's dark out there. Can't see the sharks."

"Since when is a big, bad SEAL afraid of a fishy?" Cooper dropped into the chair across from Grayson's desk.

"Since that fishy has big, bad teeth. You never saw *Jaws*, did you?"

"That one scared the shi—"

"Did I miss the memo that we had a meeting tonight?" Liam said, walking in, then lowering himself onto the chair next to Cooper's.

Grayson leaned back and grinned at his not-by-blood brothers. "Nah, Cooper's just trying to give me a hard time."

"About what?" Liam elbowed Cooper. "Tell me so I can join in."

"Grayson's afraid of sharks."

"Didn't you see *Jaws*, man?" Liam said. "Sharks are about as badass as it gets. I'm with Gray on this one."

"Yes, but we aren't scary SEALs. Aren't you dudes supposed to be afraid of nothing?"

"I'm afraid of being a midnight shark snack," Grayson said. "There, I said it."

His brothers laughed. "Good to know you're human," Liam said. "You had an appointment today, right? How'd it go?"

"Not like I expected." He told them about Harlow. "I've

been looking into the family. No one is that perfect. It's almost like no one dares to say a bad word about the Pressleys."

"Maybe they are perfect," Cooper said.

"I don't think so. I found an archived newspaper article from several years back, an interview with a woman, Etta Jankowski, claiming the Pressleys stole her house."

Liam frowned. "How do you steal a house?"

"She swore to the reporter that she paid her property taxes, but according to the tax records, she didn't. Jankowski also claims the same thing was done to one of her neighbors. The reporter didn't name the individual because he's been unable to contact the person to verify Jankowski's claim. The article did say that two liens were sold in a private sale to Pressley LLC, so we can do a search for the name. Here's the thing, though. That the tax collector held a private sale is questionable." He air quoted the word *private*.

"There should have been a public announcement that there would be a sale but there wasn't. Also, the homeowner should have been notified and given a chance to pay the tax. Apparently, that didn't happen. And guess what?"

"I'm on the edge of my seat here." Liam glanced at Cooper. "Right?"

"Just missing the popcorn to go with this story."

"Both of you are clowns. Here's the interesting part. The next day, there was a retraction in the paper."

Liam shrugged. "So? They made a mistake."

"My gut tells me they didn't. The two plots of land were the last pieces the Pressleys needed to build a shopping center on, so a dirty tax collector? I need to find Miss Jankowski and the other homeowner."

"I'm settled into my apartment, and I've got nothing going on," Cooper said. "Why don't you let me do that?"

"That'd be great."

Liam raised his hand. "What about me? I found the kid and he's back with his family, so I'm available. Anything I can do to help?"

"Not that I can think of." Unless… "Actually, there is something right up your alley. How would you feel about nosing around Faberville for a few days? See what intel you can pick up on the Pressley family." Liam had a talent for blending in or impersonating anyone from a bum to a billionaire.

Liam grinned. "I do love sneaking around. I'll head over there tomorrow." He gazed up at the ceiling for a few seconds. "Is there a golf course in Faberville, do you know?"

"Yep. It's a resort owned by the Pressleys."

"Perfect. I'll check in, horn in on some golf games. You'd be surprised at what you can learn playing a few rounds with the locals."

Grayson didn't doubt it.

"Now that we have our assignments, let's grab some dinner," Cooper said. "Know of a beach bar that has good beer and burgers?"

"I sure do."

Later that night, after a shower, Grayson got in bed with his laptop. It didn't take long to find the engagement announcement of Harlow Grainger to Anthony Pressley. He'd assumed that she hadn't dressed like someone's great-grandmother back then, but he was stunned at seeing her photo.

"Wow," he murmured. Her honey-blond hair was shoulder length, the soft curls framing her face. And what a face. Smoky eye shadow highlighted her distinctive turquoise-blue eyes, drawing attention to them. Creamy skin, high cheekbones and full pink lips made for a beautiful woman. In the photo, she wore an off-the-shoulder pale blue dress that fit her perfectly and showed off her figure.

He studied Anthony Pressley. He was what women called tall, dark and handsome. He wore an expensive suit, and a pale blue handkerchief that matched Harlow's dress was tucked into the pocket. It was the man's eyes that Grayson was most interested in. Where love was shining from Harlow's eyes as she looked up at her fiancé with a soft smile on her face, Grayson didn't see the same from Pressley.

"You got yourself a trophy wife, didn't you?" he said to the photo. There was something cold and calculated about the man, and Grayson doubted that Pressley had the capability to love any woman.

The next photo he found was of their wedding, and again, Harlow was stunning. Her gown was simple and classy, a strapless, maybe satin body-hugging dress. There were no beads or crystals on it, no fancy ribbons or other adornments. It took a back seat to the woman wearing it, and Grayson smiled, knowing that was exactly what she'd intended.

As in her engagement photo, she was all soft smiles and hearts in her eyes for her new husband. Grayson wished he could tell that girl to run away as fast as she could. He'd downloaded the security footage from their building's inside camera, and he found the feed of her riding up in the elevator. Seeing the difference in her from then and now was heartbreaking.

He saved the engagement and wedding photos to the file he'd created, then continued his search. There were pictures of the couple at numerous galas and charity events. The most noticeable thing as he progressed through the years of their life together was the change taking place in Harlow. The light in her eyes dimmed and the smiles faded. He was able to follow the change in her appearance from that of a stunning, well-dressed woman to that of a woman who was using clothes and no makeup to hide from the world. It was one of the saddest things he'd ever seen.

As he sent her an email, he crushed the thought that he was looking forward to seeing her again, granny dress and all.

# *Chapter 4*

When Harlow turned into the parking lot of her apartment complex, Anthony's BMW XM was parked in her assigned space. She gritted her teeth as she drove several buildings down to the visitor parking. She'd asked him repeatedly not to park in her space, but did he care about what she wanted?

It wasn't good that he was here, and she considered driving right out of the complex and going somewhere. Anywhere he wasn't. But that would only delay dealing with him. Remembering Grayson's advice to record her conversations with Anthony, she set her phone to Record, then held it in her hand, the face hidden against her palm. She walked as slowly as possible, but she still ended up next to his car sooner than she was ready.

His car windows were down, and he was texting someone…probably his mistress. Not that she cared, she just wanted him to say why he was bothering her and then be on his way. He knew she was waiting because he'd glanced at her, but he continued to ignore her as he kept his attention on his phone. She knew him well, and knew his intention was to teach her a lesson.

She wanted to walk away, go inside her apartment and lock the door against him. He'd just follow her, though, and demand that she let him in. Not happening. A few more minutes passed, and heat burned her neck as her blood pressure rose. She was tired of his games, so very tired.

*Screw it.* She wasn't standing here a second longer. As if he realized he'd pushed her to her limit, he set his phone on the dash, then stepped out of the car. There'd been a time when she'd thought he was the handsomest man she'd ever seen, but all she saw now was a spoiled, selfish man who thought he was entitled to take whatever he wanted no matter who it hurt.

There were things she hadn't told Grayson. Things that could ruin the Pressley family. It wasn't what she wanted to do, but Anthony was going to push her into doing just that. They were dangerous secrets, and she didn't know quite what to do with them. One reason she'd turned to The Phoenix Three.

"I've been waiting for an hour," Anthony said. "Where were you?"

*None of your business.* But if she said that, he'd make it his business to find out where she was. And there was no way he'd sat for an hour waiting for her, not Anthony. "I had some errands to run. What do you want, Anthony?"

"You need to come back to work."

That meant Sherri, whom he'd promoted to director of events because she was young and pretty, never mind that she wasn't qualified, was messing things up. Harlow could have told him that would happen, not that she'd felt like bothering. She'd resigned via email the day after catching him kissing the nanny, so what happened at Pressley Resort and Golf Club was of no concern to her.

"I'll come back if you promote me to vice president of marketing, retail merchandise and events." Had she missed anything she could attach to that title? She couldn't think of anything, so she named her acceptable salary. "At four hundred thousand a year."

There was no way they'd give her that title or pay her that much, and even if they did, she was not now or ever coming back to work for the Pressley family. And look at her! She'd never stood up to him before. It felt freaking good.

He sneered. "Have you lost your mind?"

"I did once. When I married you." Done with this conversation, she turned to leave.

He grabbed her arm, digging his fingers into her skin. "We're not done here."

"Says you, but I don't agree. Get your hand off me."

"I should have never agreed to the divorce. I only did to teach you a lesson, but you've had your little spat. It's time to come home where you belong."

"Let go of me. I'm not coming back." The only reason he'd agreed to the divorce was because she'd threatened to tell anyone who would listen that he'd had a mistress the entire time they'd been married and that she'd caught him kissing their son's nanny. The Pressleys cared greatly about their image. Her threats had worked at the time, mainly because he was sure that by taking Tyler away from her and isolating her that she'd come crawling back. Never going to happen.

"Your son misses you. You're his mother, yet you don't seem to care that he cries, wanting to know when you're coming home."

It was a low blow, and he knew it. Tears burned her eyes thinking of her little boy missing her, but she refused to let them fall. She would not give him the satisfaction of knowing how much she hurt.

"I want to see him. Please." She hated begging, but she

would for Tyler. What she would not do was return to that house that was a prison.

"You can see him when you come home." He leaned his face close to hers. "You belong to me, Harlow. That's a fact you need to remember."

The smell of his cologne—a scent she used to love— made her want to gag. She jerked her arm free. "Go to hell." She walked away, leaving him seething with rage.

As soon as she stepped inside her apartment, the tears she'd managed to hold back streamed down her face. The thing she could never let Anthony know was that she'd almost gone back several times just so she could be with Tyler, where she could touch him and hug him. She could put up with all the abuse in the world for her baby.

What always stopped her was her fear that he'd learn to be cruel to women, to use them the way his father did. If he grew up watching his own mother being treated like dirt under his father's shoe, he would never learn to respect women. She couldn't bear to think of him growing up to be another Anthony, so she stood strong, refusing to let her longing to be with her son be the reason she went back.

Instead, she would do everything in her power to take Anthony down. If The Phoenix Three wouldn't help her, she'd find another way. In the far reaches of her mind, she had a desperate plan. If all else failed, she would run away with her son. She prayed it wouldn't come to that.

"Miaow," Einstein grumbled—that particular sound meant feed me this second or I'll starve and die—as he made circle eights around her legs.

The first week after she'd moved into her apartment, she'd been so lonely and sad from missing Tyler that she'd thought she'd lose her mind. It had been too quiet, no little-boy giggles and chatter. No questions wanting to know why the sky was blue or where bugs came from.

Impulsively, she'd gone to the local shelter intending to adopt a kitten, something she could talk to even if it didn't talk back. And they'd had so many cute ones. But it was the nine-year-old gray-and-white longhair cat quietly observing her that caught her eye as she gushed over the babies. Her first impression as he watched with intelligent green eyes was that he had too much dignity to beg for attention like the little ones. Instead of a playful kitten, she'd ended up with a talkative, opinionated cat that woke her up at six in the morning by standing on her chest and loudly demanding his breakfast.

When she was home, he followed her around like a puppy, talking to her about the birds outside the window, his empty stomach and the best napping spots in the house. That he was a chatterbox had surprised her since he'd been so quiet at the shelter. She found herself talking back, telling him about her day, her worries and her hopes. He knew all about Tyler and how much her heart ached from missing him. Sometimes she was sure that Einstein understood her.

"One day you're going to trip me, and I'm going to fall on you and smash you," she said as he wound around her legs on the way to the kitchen.

After she gave him fresh water and a few treats to tide him over until his dinner, she went to her bedroom and changed into leggings and a T-shirt. Since walking away from her job, she had managed to build a little business designing and maintaining websites, writing advertising copy and handling social media for authors.

Just recently, she had contracted with three indie authors to run ads on Amazon and Meta for their books and tweak or write their book blurbs. She hoped that they would like

her work and refer her to other authors. She was in nego-
tiations with a well-known baseball player to handle his
social media. If she could make that happen and he was
pleased, he'd hopefully talk her up to his friends. It would
be another avenue to pursue.

She got her laptop and her phone, taking them to the
sofa. Between the money she'd saved over the years—which
Anthony didn't know about—and her little business, she
was doing fine. The rent got paid on time, there was food in
her pantry and, as long as what The Phoenix Three would
charge to help her was reasonable, she was okay financially.

That she was gave her a great sense of satisfaction considering that Anthony had told her when she'd left him that
she couldn't make it without him and would come crawling back before a month was out. Ha! She'd shown him.

"You ready to get some work done?" she asked Einstein
when he jumped on the sofa and curled up next to her.
Along with being a chatterer, his grumbling purrs were
so loud that his body vibrated with them. She smiled as
she scratched him behind his ears, which always revved
up his motor.

When she removed her hand to log in to her laptop, he
put his paw on her arm and tried to pull her hand back to
him. "Gotta get some work done, sweet boy." Having said
that so many times since bringing him home, he understood his ear massages would have to wait for later. He
gave a wide yawn, then pushed his nose against her leg
and went to sleep.

She opened her email and the first thing she saw was
one from The Phoenix Three. Her breath caught, and she
hovered her finger over the key, almost afraid to open it.
"Please," she whispered. "Say you're going to help me."

As she clicked on the email, her heart pounded in her

chest. It was from Grayson telling her to call him. She blew out the breath she'd been holding. Was that good or bad? Was the call to let her down personally?

Einstein stirred next to her. His eyes opened and, as if sensing her anxiety, he meowed softly. "What do think, Einstein?" Apparently, Einstein for once didn't have an opinion since he yawned again, closed his eyes and went back to sleep.

Well, she wouldn't be able to get her work done until she knew what Grayson's answer was. She appreciated that he'd included his phone number in the email, and she didn't have to disturb Einstein to get her purse. After another little prayer that she was going to get the answer she wanted, she picked up her phone and called him.

"Grayson Montana speaking."

"It's Harlow." She crossed her fingers.

"Thought you'd like to know we're going to help you."

*Yes!* She made a fist pump. "Thank you so much. You said *we*?"

"I did. You get the three of us. I'll explain everything to you. When are you available to meet again?"

"As soon as possible." The sooner they started, the sooner she'd have her son back. And yes, she was going to 100 percent believe that was going to happen.

"Tomorrow morning, then? To keep you from driving all the way back here, Conway is halfway between us. There's a diner that serves a great breakfast. That work for you?"

"Sounds perfect."

He gave her the diner's address, and they agreed to meet at eight. For the first time since Anthony had taken Tyler from her, she had hope. It was a wonderful feeling. If Anthony managed to find out she'd hired The Phoenix Three, he would make her life miserable…more miserable than it already was. She'd just have to make sure he didn't find out.

She got up and went to the room she had ready for her son. When he saw it, he was going to love it. Tyler loved three things: picture books, robots and dinosaurs. Her gaze scanned the room. She'd painted three of the walls a pale blue, and the fourth wall was a chalkboard. The bedspread was cute cartoon dinosaurs. There was a bookcase filled with picture books, and shelves with robots and dinosaurs waiting for him to play with.

"Soon, baby. Soon."

Without thought as to what to wear, Harlow dressed for her meeting with Grayson. She stuck the last pin into her bun, and then she froze as she stared at the woman in the mirror. How had she become so…dowdy? Well, she knew how, but why was she still dressing like someone's great-grandmother? She no longer had to bear Anthony's jealous rages.

Anthony had, without reason, accused her of dressing to catch the attention of other men so many times that she'd started to dress more conservatively. Over time, when his jealousy continued, she'd gone to the extreme, becoming the woman in the mirror. That her frumpy appearance embarrassed him secretly pleased her. He couldn't have it both ways.

Even his contemptuous criticisms hadn't swayed her to give up her too-big dresses and hair buns. It was the one thing she'd stood fast on because she found she liked embarrassing him. It had the added benefit that he stopped requiring her presence at many of his functions.

She searched her closet for something that didn't look as if she'd escaped from a cult. She changed into black pants and a white blouse she found in the back of her closet. Definitely better. She added a black-and-silver belt she couldn't remember owning, but it helped bring her outfit into the modern world.

She needed to go shopping.

Even though she was five minutes early, Grayson was already seated at a booth in the rear. He had his back to the wall, giving him a view of the diner's interior and entrance. She did enjoy her romance books, and she especially liked military ones. Harlow smiled to herself that those books had taught her that these alpha men wanted their backs to the wall where they could watch for danger.

His gaze tracked her from the moment she'd walked in. She slid onto the seat across from him. "Good morning."

"Morning, Harlow." He raised a hand and a waitress scurried over as if she'd been just waiting to serve him.

Although he hadn't commented on how she looked, Harlow thought she saw approval in his eyes, making her glad she'd decided to stop hiding herself. She took the opportunity to study him while the waitress filled their coffee cups. Of course, she'd noted he was one heck of a good-looking man when she'd met with him yesterday, but she'd been too nervous and sick at heart to really notice how seriously hot he was. How well built he was. Wowza!

Not that she was eyeing him as a potential anything, but there was nothing wrong with appreciating such a fine specimen of a man. In the here and now, though, she only had one goal. Get her son away from Anthony.

"I want to thank—" The waitress handed them menus, and Harlow peered over the top of hers. "To thank you for agreeing to help me. You have no idea how much this means to me."

"No thanks necessary. It's what we do. Let's have some breakfast, then we'll get down to business."

She was too nervous to eat anything heavy, so she only ordered toast and scrambled eggs. When he ordered the hungry man special, she found it on the menu. Three eggs, bacon, sausage, toast or biscuits and grits or hash browns. She lifted wide eyes to his. "That's a lot of food." Why couldn't she keep her mouth shut? He was going to think she was making fun of him.

He laughed. "Growing boy and all that."

Okay, she hadn't offended him. He wasn't Anthony. She relaxed and smiled. "If I ate half of what you ordered, you'd have to roll me out in a wheelbarrow." Look at her not being afraid to tease him.

That she could joke with a man without fearing a verbal lashing made her want to giggle. Somehow, she managed not to.

# Chapter 5

"I don't normally eat like this," Grayson said as he pushed his empty plate aside. "It's usually a protein shake to start my morning." He nodded for a refill when the waitress came by with the coffeepot.

"My eggs and toast were good. I think they make their own jams."

"Probably." He leaned forward and rested his forearms on the table. "Ready for some serious talk?"

The first thing he'd noticed when she'd entered the restaurant was the change in her. Her black pants and white blouse were a vast improvement from yesterday's clothes. Instead of the tight bun, her hair was in a low ponytail. Another improvement. He wanted to compliment her but was afraid it would make her uncomfortable.

What he liked most, though, was that her eyes were brighter today. She didn't look quite as defeated, and that made him want to do whatever he could to keep the light in those pretty eyes.

"Before we go any further, I need to make sure I can afford you. Do you have an estimate of what it will cost to hire you?"

"It depends on how long this takes, of course. How about we agree on a retainer, and then we can evaluate as we go.

I'm hoping to be able to give you enough ammunition to get the custody arrangement overturned, or at least get a more equitable agreement, in no longer than two weeks. Let's start with two thousand. That work for you?" It actually should be more, but apparently, he was a softie. He'd do it on the side and for free if he had to because he was going to make sure she got her son back.

"Yes. I actually thought it would be more than that."

"It might be in the end, but that's good enough to get started."

"Thank you. I'm ready for your questions."

"My first question. I asked you about visitation yesterday, but we got sidetracked and you didn't answer. What are your visitation rights?"

"I'm allowed supervised visits at Anthony's discretion, which he hasn't seen fit to allow unless I move back in with him." Tears filled her eyes. "I haven't seen my son since the divorce was final. Haven't been able to touch him, to hug him. It's killing me."

"So, he's using Tyler to try and force you to do something you don't want to." What kind of man used a child as a weapon? Grayson's loathing for Anthony Pressley was growing with each of her revelations.

"Is there a reason he's trying so hard to get you back other than that he loves you?"

She made an unladylike snort. "Anthony doesn't love anyone but himself. He sees me as his property, nothing more than that."

"Has he ever physically abused you?"

"No. When he's really angry, he'll grab my arm hard enough to leave bruises, but he's never hit me."

"Did you take pictures of the bruises?" Any time a man

left bruises on a woman it was abuse. It would help to have proof.

"I never thought to, but I will if he does it again. He was waiting for me when I got home from meeting with you yesterday. It's like he somehow knows I'm doing something he doesn't like."

"Does that happen often?"

"Yes. It's a little spooky, really. Like he has some kind of radar. I know he has people who report my whereabouts to him if they see me somewhere, so I guess that's why."

Or he was sneakier than she suspected. "Unlock your phone and let me see it." She handed it over, and it only took a minute to find the tracking app. "How long have you had this phone?"

"This one, a year. He gave me my first phone when we got engaged. Said he put it on the family plan so I wouldn't have to keep paying for the one I had. He replaces it every time a new model comes out."

"This isn't going to make you happy. There's a tracking app in here, and dollars to doughnuts he's put one on every phone he gave you from that first one."

"The rat bastard." She slapped her hand on the table. "Take the app off."

"I have a better idea. Be right back." He went to his car and got the burner he kept in his middle console.

When he slid back into the booth, she was staring daggers at her cell phone. He pushed it back to her. "Here's what I want you to do. If you're going to the grocery store, your hairdresser, someplace mundane like that, take your phone." He entered his cell phone number to the contacts, then handed her the burner. "This is a burner. You know what that is?"

She nodded.

"Good. Keep it with you at all times. When you're going someplace you don't want him to know about, especially when you're meeting me, leave your phone at home. Let him think that's where you are. If you need to make a call during those times, use the burner. Always use it if you need to talk to me."

"This is so cool. I feel like I'm in a spy movie." Amusement danced in her eyes. "Maybe we need secret code names."

He grinned. "Sure. What's yours?" He was more curious than he should be as to what she'd come up with.

"Let's see." She tapped her lips with her index finger. "Cat Mama!"

"How about we shorten it to Cat?" He liked playing a part in her having fun.

"Okay. What's yours?"

He shrugged. "You tell me." Her finger tapped her lips again, drawing his attention to her mouth. It was a kissable mouth. *Don't go there, Montana.* She wasn't a woman you played with and then moved on.

"Got it," she said. "Snoopy."

"Snoopy?" He snorted. "Seriously? I thought you'd give me something fierce or savage. Like Cougar or Viper. Cobra would be good."

"Nope. Snoopy. That way I'm a cat and you're a dog. Plus, you're snooping, so that fits."

"Snoopy it is." Why did that man at the counter keep glancing at them? "You have a mirror and lipstick in your purse?"

"Um, I have a mirror and ChapStick. Why?"

"Listen, don't turn around. A man just came in and he glanced around until his gaze landed on you, then he took a seat at the counter where he can see you. He seems to be paying us more than casual attention. Take out your mirror and put on the ChapStick. While you're doing that, you can use the mirror to see if you recognize him. His head is shaved, and he has on a dark blue Henley."

"Why don't I just go to the restroom? I can look at him as I walk by."

"If you do that, he'll know you're checking him out. You're a spy, and you need to identify the villain. Use the tricks you learned in spy school."

"Oh, this is fun." A smile tugged at the corner of her lips. "Sneaky's the word."

He managed not to drop his gaze to her mouth as she applied the ChapStick. He epically failed at not thinking about those kissable lips. Would they be soft when pressed against his? Would they... He gave his head a mental slap and his brain a warning. *Stop it.* That was easier said than done, but he was a highly trained warrior, and discipline was his middle name. He would not think of her in any way other than a client who needed his help.

Her face paled. "That's Don Delgado, Anthony's... I guess you'd call him Anthony's right-hand man. He followed me here?"

"Appears so. What will you say if your ex questions you about being with me?"

"That it's none of his business. And although that's true, he won't rest until he finds out who you are."

"Tell him I'm your new client." In his research on her, he'd learned that she was freelancing, doing an assortment of things for people, one of them being designing websites. That would work for a reason to give her ex if he asked. "The Phoenix Three needs a decent website. Cooper slapped one up for us, but it's not great."

"Okay, that's believable since that's what I do."

"Actually, I'm serious about you doing that for us. We need it, and we can do some trade, which will cut down on what this is going to cost you." He was telling the truth about needing a professional website, and by the relief in her eyes, he was glad he'd impulsively made the offer.

"Thank you. I'll do whatever it takes to get my son away from that family."

"Did you not get any alimony?"

"No, and I didn't ask for any. That would have just been another thing Anthony would have fought me over, and he would have won."

The Pressleys were worth millions. It didn't sit right with him that the man who supposedly cared enough about her to want her back didn't care enough to make sure the mother of his child was able to pay her rent and buy groceries. The man was a manipulating bastard, and if Grayson had anything to say about it, Anthony Pressley was going down.

"I should probably go," she said, gathering up her purse. "What's the next step?"

"Keep the burner on you. I'll call and text you on it." It occurred to him that if Pressley was tracking her, he might be spying on her in other ways. He needed to figure out how to get into her apartment without Pressley knowing and check for cameras or listening devices.

Their waitress appeared with the check and Grayson handed her his credit card. Delgado, at seeing Grayson was paying the bill, stood, and walked out.

"Thank you, Grayson. I feel a little less lost now."

"I'm glad. I know it's hard to be patient but hang in there. I'm going to do everything in my power to reunite you with your son."

The trembling smile on her face had him wanting to wrap her in his arms and be the man who gave her anything she asked for. He didn't know why, but she called to something in him. He wanted to be the hero in her story.

*Enough of that, Montana.* All he needed to *want* was a thank-you after this was over. He signed the credit card receipt when the waitress returned it to him. "I'll walk you out." He wanted to make sure the man didn't bother her.

She nodded as she slid out of the booth. As she walked ahead of him, he tried and failed to keep his eyes from roaming over her, from the long ponytail swaying with her steps, down to the curve of her waist and then the flair of her hips, on down over her mighty fine ass. He mentally slapped his head. Again. Maybe he should have Cooper or Liam take over, remove himself from temptation.

He should, but he wasn't going to.

# Chapter 6

Why wasn't she surprised when she arrived home to find Anthony's car in her space again? It made sense, though, now that she knew he was tracking her. Not up to dealing with him, she drove right back out of the complex. She needed to go grocery shopping anyway.

At the grocery store, she groaned when Anthony stopped his car behind hers, blocking her in. Guess she wasn't going to be able to avoid him after all. She reached for her phone and set it on Record. As she had before, she kept it in her hand with the face against her palm.

Dread settled like a rock in her belly as she stepped out of her car. She refused to walk to him, so she stood next to the door. She didn't speak or smile, just waited. Two days ago, she would have cowered under the rage in his eyes, but she was done with that. She straightened her shoulders and stood tall. It was time to stop letting him intimidate her.

"Who was that man you were with?"

"Hello, Anthony. How are you today? I have no idea what you're talking about. Goodbye." The urge to scream at him for sending Don to spy on her was so great that she bit down on her cheek to keep from revealing they were onto him. She moved to step around him but wasn't surprised when he blocked her.

He stepped into her personal space. "Who was he, Harlow?"

That was his command voice, the one he used when he expected to be obeyed. She hated that voice. She could keep acting clueless, but then he'd never leave, not until he got an answer. "Not that it's any of your business, but he's a client I'm building a website for."

"That better be all he is. If I ever catch you with another man, you won't like the consequences."

"Do you not understand what a divorce means? I don't answer to you, and you have no say so over who I talk to, see or sleep with." Did she really just say all that? She almost cringed at the rage in his eyes. But she wasn't that girl anymore, and she refused to cringe.

"Your smart mouth isn't attractive. I taught you better than that." Suddenly, he smiled. He brushed her cheek with the back of his fingers. "We were good together, babe. We can be again. Let me take you to dinner, spend some time with each other."

"No thanks." She didn't trust that smile, not at all. As for his eyes, they were as cold as ever. Jekyll and Hyde. One minute a monster, the next charming. This time when she stepped around him, he let her go. Not that she believed she'd gotten through to him or that he'd leave her alone.

She managed to hold it together as she shopped, but inside, she was shaking with anger. Why couldn't he leave her alone? What kind of man punished his son by keeping his mother from him out of spite? She hadn't lied when she'd told Grayson that Anthony didn't love her. That wasn't the reason he wanted her back. She was just another piece of property that he owned...or believed he did. And Anthony always kept what was his.

Back at her apartment, she stared at the bunch of bananas she pulled out of one of the bags. She didn't like bananas, but Tyler did. She didn't remember putting them in her cart. In another bag, she found a jar of cherries she didn't remember buying.

Tyler loved cherries, and she'd always kept a jar on hand. Was Tyler's nanny making sure there were cherries for him, or was she too busy sucking face with Anthony to care about seeing that smile on Tyler's face when he got to have a cherry?

"Damn you, Anthony. Damn you to hell," she screamed as she threw the jar across the kitchen. The jar broke, and red syrup dripped down the wall, looking like a freaking crime scene.

She collapsed onto the floor and buried her face into her hands. How had her life turned into this mess? She couldn't even shop for groceries without Anthony showing up.

Einstein wandered into the kitchen, and she grabbed him before he could walk through the broken glass and cherry syrup. "I made a mess, didn't I?" She got his container of treats out, put more than he usually got in the corner, then set him down. "You stay over here."

After she got her mess cleaned up, she finished putting the groceries away. Once that was done, she decided to dust. Then she cleaned the bathrooms. Next was vacuuming. Three hours later, she'd run out of things to clean. Her sheets were washed and put back on the bed, the towels washed and her clothes were clean, folded and put away.

If nothing else, her meltdown had resulted in a sparkling apartment smelling of lemon oil. She got her laptop and tried to work for a while, but she couldn't concentrate. It was too quiet, so she turned on the TV. After fifteen minutes of scrolling through the channels and finding nothing she wanted to watch, she turned it off. She needed to hear a human voice. A kind one. Someone who wouldn't talk down to her. Someone like Grayson. She chewed on her bottom lip. Should she?

Grayson would want to know that Anthony was waiting for her when she returned home, that he'd asked who Grayson was, that he'd followed her to the grocery store. Before she could talk herself out of it, she went to the kitchen counter where she'd dropped her purse. As she was reaching for it, she noticed the bruises on her arm from Anthony digging his fingers into the skin. She used her phone to take a picture of her arm before she called Grayson. Then she took the burner phone to the sofa.

"Is it okay to call him?" she asked Einstein when he joined her.

"Mrruh."

"That's yes in cat talk, right?" If Einstein thought it was all right, then it must be. He continued to chatter while she made the call.

"Hello, Harlow."

She frowned. "How'd you know it was me? I thought burner phones were untraceable."

He chuckled. "They still have a number assigned to them, and I know the number to this one."

"Oh. Is it okay that I'm calling you?"

"Absolutely. I told you that you could. Is everything all right?"

"Yeah...no, not really. Anthony was waiting for me when I got home today."

"What did he say?"

"He threatened me. I recorded it."

"Good job on remembering to record it."

Jeez, she was really needy if his mild praise filled her

with warmth. "Well, you're probably busy, so I'll let you go. Just wanted to tell you about Anthony showing up."

"I'm not busy. In fact, I was going to call you later."

"Oh. I guess I should have waited to hear from you."

"Harlow, never hesitate to call if you need to tell me something." He paused. "Or if you just need to talk."

"Thank you." He had no clue what that meant to her.

"What's that noise?"

She glanced around, wondering what he was hearing. The only sound was Einstein's chatter. "That's Einstein, my cat. He's a talker."

"He got anything interesting to say?"

She smiled at the amusement in his voice. "He thinks so. Right now, he's grumbling because I'm not giving him enough attention. You said you were going to call me later?"

"I'd like to check out your apartment. Make sure there aren't any cameras or listening devices."

"You think there might be," she whispered, afraid now that Anthony might be hearing every word she said. Her gaze bounced around the room, looking for... Well, she had no idea what to look for.

"I hope he hasn't gone that far, but I'd feel better knowing for sure."

"Believe me, so would I. How do I check?"

"Will you be home in the morning?"

"Yes." She was pretty much home all the time. How much more boring could she be?

"At ten, a plumber will show up to clear up your stopped-up drain."

"I don't have a...oh." She rolled her eyes at herself. "Right."

"Don't say anything else until we know for sure that no

one is listening to your conversations. For now, we'll assume the worst. Write this number down."

She grabbed her laptop and opened Notes. "Go."

After he gave it to her, he said, "In thirty minutes, call that number using your own phone and request a plumber to unstop your drain."

"On it, Snoopy."

He chuckled. "I think it best that we hang up now, Cat."

"Okay." But it wasn't. She wanted to stay on the phone with him. Talk all night. She forgot to be lonely when talking to him. When the thirty minutes were up, she called the number he'd given her.

"Acme Plumbing. This is Wile speaking. How may we assist you today?"

She laughed, then slapped a hand over her mouth. It was Grayson speaking with a British accent. Wile didn't speak with a British accent, did he? "Yes, Mr. Wile, I seem to have a stopped-up drain."

"Oh, dear girl. That is dreadful. Would tomorrow morning at ten be convenient for us to take care of your drainage problem?"

"That would be perfect." She gave him her name and address when he asked for her information, and then, she reluctantly disconnected. Grayson would be in her apartment in the morning, and she couldn't stop grinning.

Later that night, she went to sleep with a smile on her face.

# Chapter 7

Grayson put his feet on the railing and tipped his chair back. The night was balmy, only a sliver of a moon, so stars glittered in a black velvet sky. A storm was brewing in the distance, stirring up the ocean. What he loved most was the sound of the waves crashing on the sand.

As soon as he'd opted out of the military and returned home, he'd gone house hunting for a place on the beach. The minute he'd seen the two-story, pale green-and-white house on stilts with a copper-and-green tin roof, he'd fallen in love with the outside. The landscape was natural to the beaches of South Carolina…sand, a dozen palm trees scattered on the lot, sea oats and swamp sunflowers. It was a low-maintenance landscape, just what he wanted.

He'd been disappointed at the inside, which was outdated, but no problem. A great contractor who got his vision for the interior, eight weeks and a few bucks…and voila! He had his dream beach house.

"This is the life," he murmured as he took a sip of his beer. Except he was sitting on his deck by himself. He bet Harlow would love it here. Maybe he'd invite her over one day. The impression he had was that she didn't have much of a life. Did she have any close friends or family?

He'd had a date tonight that he'd canceled. Wasn't in the

mood. Not just that, but it wasn't fair to take one woman out when his mind was on another. He sighed as he lifted the bottle to his mouth.

Why her? His type of woman was outgoing, ready to have some fun and no more interested in having a relationship than he was. Yet, here he was, unable to stop thinking of a woman who was as timid as a mouse, delicate, maybe a little needy and carried a whole lot of baggage.

If she knew the things he'd seen, the things he'd done, she wouldn't look at him with those soft, innocent eyes again. He didn't like the idea of her being afraid of him, and she would be if she knew what he was capable of. The faster he got her reunited with her son, the faster she could move on with her life, and he with his.

His phone buzzed, Cooper's name coming up on the screen. "Yo."

"You home?"

"I am."

"Great. I'll be there in five."

"I'm around back." After disconnecting, he went inside and got two beers and a large can of mixed nuts. He was kicked back in his chair when Cooper came around the corner of the house.

"Honey, I'm home." He jogged up the steps.

"All is right in my world now," Grayson muttered.

Cooper eyed the table next to the chair he plopped onto. "Knew I could count on you, sweets, to have a beer and snack ready for me." He let out a contented sigh. "Can I live on your deck?"

"No, you cannot, *sweets*. It would be like having a puppy I'd have to feed and pet."

Cooper laughed. "Well, at least I'm house trained."

"Still a no. Tired of your apartment already?"

"Not so much the apartment but there are people."

"There are people? How very odd." But he understood. After the life they'd led, having people in your face was the last thing you wanted.

"Hardy-har. I took the month-to-month rental thinking it would be okay for a while, until I was ready to find a house. I didn't think I'd be ready the first week I moved in. There's an elderly woman on my floor who wants to set me up with her granddaughter. The dude next door wants to be buddies. I went down to the pool the other day, and before I could blink, three bikini-clad women were competing for my attention."

"Oh, the horror."

"Right?" Cooper dug his hand into the can of nuts and grabbed a fistful. "I didn't think I'd want to live on the beach. There's sand, and it gets into everything. But sitting here, listening to the waves, and with the breeze cooling my face, I think I could overlook a little sand. Want to help me find a house?"

"Sure. I have a great Realtor I'll set you up with."

"Cool. So, I found Miss Etta Jankowski, and we had an interesting talk."

"I'm all ears."

"We bonded over tea, and I was given permission to call her Miss Etta. I hate hot tea."

"Your sacrifice is noted. What did Miss Etta have to say?"

"She was born in that house eighty-seven years ago and still sharp as a tack. Her children grew up in that house, her husband died in his sleep in that house, and all she wanted was to live out the rest of her life where all her memories were. She got out a Bible, put her hand on it and swore that she mailed her property taxes the year the tax office said she didn't. I believe her."

"Me, too, and that's just wrong."

"She told me the name of her neighbor who she swears had the same thing happen to him. George Pickens. She said they were both taken advantage of because they're seniors and neither have families to look out of them."

"We need to find Pickens."

"I plan to. After that newspaper article, Miss Etta received anonymous letters warning her to shut up about her house being stolen from her or else. She told me that it was dangerous for her to be talking to me about all this, but that they could just take their 'or else' and shove it where the sun don't shine. I really like her. She's got spirit."

"Where's she living now?"

"In an efficiency apartment in a not-so-great part of town. It's all she can afford, and even that's a stretch. The sad thing is, her house was paid for, and the property taxes on it were minimal. Because the house was seized, she didn't get anything for it. I sneaked a peek in her fridge when she went to get her Bible, and, Gray, it was about empty."

"What can we do to help her?" Even though they hadn't cheated her out of her home, they couldn't stand by and not do anything.

"I was thinking about that on the way over. What if we buy a small condo in Faberville in a better part of town as an investment and convince her we need a caretaker?"

"Funny thing, I'm in need of an investment."

"Even funnier, so am I, and I bet Liam is, too."

"No doubt. How about you find a place that actually is a good investment, then convince her to move into it?"

"On it. I also want to look into the tax office, see what

I can dig up. Someone there made their checks disappear, and I want to know who."

"I'd like to know that, too," Grayson said. "If we can prove it and connect them to the Pressleys, we can go to the state's attorney or maybe the FBI."

"On behalf of Miss Etta, I'd love nothing more than to see that happen. What's the latest with your client?"

"*Disturbing* is the best word I can think of. Her ex has a tracking app on her phone, and he shows up at her apartment whenever she goes somewhere he finds suspicious. Which is any place outside of the grocery store or… I don't know. Probably anywhere else." He was getting angry again just thinking about Pressley showing up and getting in her face.

"That's called stalking."

"Yep. I'm going to her apartment in the morning disguised as a plumber to check for cameras or listening devices."

"Why don't you take me along as your assistant. It would be a good idea for her to meet me so if she sees me around somewhere, she'll know I'm from Phoenix Three."

It was a good idea, and his disappointment that he wouldn't be alone with her was a warning that the last thing he needed was to be alone with her. "Okay. I'm borrowing a van from the dealership. We're from Acme Plumbing. I'm Wile, and you're—"

"Elmer."

Grayson snorted. "I was thinking Sylvester, but fine, let's go with Elmer."

"I love Elmer. He's a hoot."

"Let's just hope you're not as clumsy with your gun as Elmer."

Cooper slapped his hand over his heart. "Dude, you wound me."

Of the three of them, Cooper was the best shot, but Grayson wasn't about to admit that. "We'll leave at nine."

Grayson parked the borrowed van in a visitor's space at Harlow's complex. He and Cooper both wore ball caps pulled low and sunglasses, but since Pressley's man had seen him, Grayson had also added a fake mustache to his disguise. While picking up the van at his Myrtle Beach dealership, he'd also borrowed uniforms from two of his mechanics who were close in size to him and Cooper.

"We look like the real deal," he said as they walked toward her apartment with toolboxes, also borrowed.

Cooper eyed him. "You look like a cartoon villain with that mustache."

"I think *debonair* is the word you're wanting."

"If you say so, Wile."

They both scanned the area around them as they ambled along, two workers in no hurry to work. He didn't see anything suspicious. When they reached her door, he knocked, and apparently, Harlow was standing on the other side, as it immediately opened.

"I understand you have a blocked drain, ma'am," he said, then winked.

Her eyes widened as her gaze slid over him, and a little giggle escaped before she pressed her lips together.

"You're from Acme Plumbing?"

"Yes, ma'am. I'm Wile, and this is my apprentice, Elmer." They were standing outside her door, so he wasn't worried they could be overheard if she was bugged.

There was that little giggle again as her eyes shifted to Cooper.

"Elmer at your service," Cooper said with a bow.

"Nice to meet you." Her gaze returned to him. "Please tell me you have a Sylvester working at Acme."

"Sure do, but he's the boss's son and as lazy as a cat. We don't allow him on a job." It was the silliest conversation he'd ever had, but if it made her laugh and kept that light in her eyes, he'd be silly all day long. "May we come in?"

"Of course." She stepped back.

As he walked past her, he caught her scent, which was interesting. Before today, she hadn't had a scent, but now she smelled like vanilla and lavender. He wanted to bury his nose against her neck and breathe her in.

From what he'd learned and observed, he bet she'd stopped wearing any kind of perfume or scented lotions around the time she started hiding herself. This morning, she wore a pair of skinny jeans—which happened to be his favorite style of jeans on a woman—and a turquoise T-shirt that made her eyes pop, and her hair was in a high ponytail. She'd said she lost herself, and it seemed to him that she was beginning to find herself again. That made him happy.

"What drain is blocked?"

"Um…the bathroom drain?"

"Elmer, how about you check that out."

"On it."

Grayson leaned his mouth next to her ear. "We're going to check for cameras and bugs."

"Okay, I'll be in the living room."

Not liking the idea of Cooper being in her bedroom, he went there first. "Mistake," he muttered at seeing her bed and imagining her in it. What did she wear to sleep in? If he'd asked him that question the same day he met her, he would have guessed a granny nightgown, one of those flowery cotton ones. Now though? Maybe something cute like those boy shorts women liked and a camisole. He shook his head to clear it from thinking of her in bed.

Her room was as opposite from what he would have guessed as could be. Three of the walls were painted a cheery yellow. The one behind her bed was a deep, matte red. He never would have put the colors together, but it worked.

The bedspread made him think of an abstract painting, a hodgepodge of yellows, reds, greens and black. On one wall was a photograph—enlarged to take up half the wall—of a woman with long honey blond hair holding the hand of a little boy, their backs to the camera as they looked out at acres of sunflowers. The woman had on a red-and-yellow sundress, and the boy wore red shorts and a yellow shirt.

Grayson tore his eyes from the photo to take in the rest of the room. She'd taken the colors from the picture of the woman and boy to decorate her room. On the opposite wall were dozens of framed black-and-white pictures, and he walked over to them. They were all photos of Tyler from when he was a baby up to maybe four or five. The kid was cute.

He was here to work, not pry into her life, so he turned away from the photos. It only took a few minutes to scan the room with his bug detector. It was a good thing for her ex that there wasn't a camera or a bug in her bedroom. If there had been, Grayson would have been paying the man a visit tonight. Her bathroom was bug free, too, and he forced himself to not spend any extra time in there thinking of her in the shower.

The apartment was a three-bedroom, and he poked his head into the one closest to Harlow's. Cooper was in there, running his bug detector over the furniture. Grayson marveled at the room she'd obviously decorated for her son.

"I want a room like this," Cooper said.

Grayson chuckled. "Of course you do. I'll get you a dinosaur bedspread for Christmas. You get the other room yet?"

"Yeah. It's her office, and I scanned everything twice to make sure it was clean. Got the guest bath, too."

"Good. You take the kitchen, and I'll get the living room." He hoped the rest of the house was clean so he didn't have to tell her that Pressley had been spying on her.

"Who's your friend?" Cooper said, glancing down at the cat chattering away as he rubbed his face against Grayson's leg.

"Pretty sure this is Einstein. He's been curious about the goings-on in his house this morning." Curious and talkative. Like nonstop.

"He seems to have a lot to say." Cooper bent over and tilted his head as if listening. "What's that? No, sorry, I don't have any catnip on me." He stood and widened his eyes. "I think I've just been cussed out by a cat."

Grayson hid his amusement as he shook his head. "Go finish up. We need to leave before we're here so long that it looks suspicious."

"Roger Dodger."

"I seem to have picked up a familiar," Grayson said on returning to the living room with the talking cat shadowing him.

"Aw, he likes you."

She was sitting on the sofa with her legs curled under her and her laptop resting on her upper legs. When she smiled at him, his heart skipped a beat. That was not good. "We're almost finished." He circled the room with the bug detector.

"Find anything?"

"No."

"Me, either," Cooper said, coming into the room. "You ask her yet?"

"Ask me what?"

Grayson moved to the sofa and perched on the edge of it. "Would you be okay if we put in a camera that was only pointed at your door? We can hide it in the A/C vent. I'd be more comfortable if we could monitor your entrance. It will be connected to my phone, but I won't be able to hear anything, and all I'll be able to see is anyone coming or going." He glanced at Cooper. "Show her how much space will be in view of the camera."

Cooper walked to the door, opened it and stepped into the apartment's hallway. "From here, to…" He came about three feet inside. "…to here. That's all."

"You really think Anthony might break in?"

"I hope not," Grayson said. "But the more I learn about him, the more I wouldn't put anything past him." He needed to ask her about Miss Etta, if she knew anything about that, but they'd already been in her apartment too long. If anyone was watching, they'd be getting suspicious about now.

"You're right to not trust him." She sighed. "Yes, put the camera in. I'd feel safer with you watching my door."

He was relieved he didn't have to push her to let them install a camera. It didn't take long to install a Ring camera, and as they were leaving, he said, "I have something else I want to talk to you about. I'll call you tonight if that's okay."

"Of course."

Unable to resist, he went to her, reached for her hand and gently squeezed it. "Everything's going to be okay, Harlow. I promise."

She peered up at him with those beautiful blue eyes. "I trust you."

A lot of people had put their trust in him. His dad, his

SEAL team, his Phoenix Three partners, his employees at the dealerships, but hearing her saying it, well, that was something else entirely. It was as if her trust in him was something sacred and fragile that he needed to protect at all costs.

He leaned in closer, his gaze locked on hers as he cupped her face and brushed his thumb over the soft skin of her cheek. When a throat cleared behind him, he dropped his hand and stepped away from her. Eff him. He'd almost kissed her, and he was sure she would have let him.

"Talk to you later," he said, then strode out of the apartment without looking back.

"You didn't tell me how pretty she was," Cooper said as they drove away.

"Don't be getting any ideas, Elmer." If Coop dared to touch her, he'd have to kill his friend.

"You've got the hots for her."

"Do not, so how about shutting up."

Cooper just chuckled.

# Chapter 8

Harlow stared at the door that Grayson had hightailed it out of as if he couldn't get away fast enough. What was that about? For a moment there, she'd thought he was going to kiss her. And she'd wanted him to, and that was a surprise.

She'd thought Anthony had ruined her for wanting to ever kiss another man. Apparently not, because Grayson stirred something inside her that she hadn't felt in years. She admonished herself. She couldn't be thinking of Grayson and kisses. The timing was all wrong. She had one mission, and that was to get her son back.

Einstein jumped on the sofa, his ever-present chatter filling the silence. That was one reason she loved him. When the silence without her boy threatened to lay her low, Einstein was there to demand her attention. He never allowed her to wallow in her misery. How could she when he parked himself on her lap and told her about his day? She was pretty sure this conversation was all about Grayson. He'd seemed fascinated by the man, and she couldn't blame him.

"I know you're a guy and you probably don't notice these things, but Grayson's pretty hot. Even more appealing, he's really nice."

Einstein meowed in agreement.

Of course, she'd thought Anthony was nice at one time,

and look how that had turned out. Her judgment couldn't be trusted and her confidence in herself was shot. Before she even considered letting another man into her life, she had to finish what she'd started…finding herself again.

Grayson and his partner had been fun with their Wile and Elmer names and their jokes. The apartment seemed empty without them in it in a way it had never felt before. Thankfully, they hadn't found any bugs or cameras. That would have really creeped her out.

She wished she had a friend to talk to, someone she trusted enough to share what was going on in her life. Maybe talk about Grayson a little, but Anthony had cut her off from her girlfriends. Why had she let that happen?

*So, fix it.* Were her old friendships fixable, especially with Lena, who'd been her best friend since fifth grade? They'd been similar enough in appearance—with their blond hair and, although Lena's were darker, they both had blue eyes—that people sometimes asked if they were sisters.

*Call her.* Where were those thoughts coming from? She'd have to think about calling Lena. For one, she was embarrassed that she'd shut Lena out without any kind of explanation. How did you explain to your best friend that you'd let your husband bully you into cutting all ties with anyone he didn't approve of, which was everyone from her life before him?

For another, would Lena even be happy to hear from her after years of silence? *Only one way to find out.* Maybe she would. Later. After she thought of what to say to the woman who'd been her best friend. But first, lunch. *You're delaying.* Yes, she was. It was a positive step to even be thinking about repairing old friendships, so… "Give me a break, voice in my head."

"Meowooow."

"Don't get your knickers in a wad." She tapped Einstein's nose. "I wasn't talking to you. How about some lunch?" She chuckled. The old boy could move fast when one of his favorite words was uttered.

After lunch, she actually managed to get some work done. Her baseball player had emailed with some questions, and after responding, she'd created and scheduled ads for several of her authors. That done, she worked for a while on the website she was designing for an up-and-coming country singer out of Nashville. Designing websites was one of her favorite things to do, and she got lost for a while in the work.

Her stomach growled, and when she glanced up, she blinked at realizing the sun was setting. She set her laptop aside and stretched. What did she want for dinner? She ended up making one of her favorite easy meals: slices of assorted cheeses, artisan crackers, a few feta cheese-filled olives, grapes and some walnuts. She took the plate and a glass of pinot grigio out to her balcony. She set them on the table, then went back inside and got both phones and her Kindle.

One of the things that helped keep her mind off missing her son and sinking into a depression was reading, so when she wasn't working, she read a lot. She took a sip of wine as she scanned the lake for the swan couple. She'd picked this apartment because it looked out on Lake Painted Turtle, named for the resident painted turtles. Then when she'd walked out on the balcony when first viewing the apartment and seen the swans floating in the lake, she'd thought of how much Tyler would love watching them.

It would happen. She had to believe that she'd have her

little boy back. Believing was the only thing keeping her going. She'd been close to despairing that he'd never be with her again when she'd seen the newspaper article. It was a story about The Phoenix Three and the twelve-year-old girl who'd been kidnapped by a pedophile on her way home from school. Grayson had been the one who'd found her and returned her to her parents.

Although the article had named the three men of The Phoenix Three, along with their photos, she'd wanted the man who hadn't given up on finding that young girl. Maybe it wasn't fair to him that she was putting all her hopes on him, but she didn't know what else to do.

It also wasn't fair that she hadn't told him the secret that could put Anthony in prison. It was a dangerous secret, and she had to know that she could trust Grayson before she shared it. She didn't know that yet.

She'd just finished the last of her grapes when Homer and Marge floated by, and as she always did when she saw them, she sighed. Even though they were swans, she liked to think they were proof that love existed.

The burner phone buzzed, and she smiled. Grayson had said he'd call tonight, but she hadn't expected him to. She shouldn't compare him to Anthony, though, who never did anything he said he was going to.

"Hello."

"It's Grayson. Did I catch you at a good time?"

He could catch her anytime he wanted. Okay, that was a wild thought out of nowhere. "Um, yeah, now's good. I'm just sitting on my balcony watching Homer and Marge."

"You like that show?"

"Never watched it. Homer and Marge are the swans that live on my lake. Right now, they're facing each other with their foreheads touching. So sweet." She doubted he was interested in her swans. "You said you had something you wanted to talk to me about."

"Yes, do the names Etta Jankowski or George Pickens mean anything to you?"

"I don't think so. Why?"

"It appears that the real estate side of the Pressley business cheated them out of their home."

"That's terrible. How did they do that?" As he told her the story, something she'd overheard back when she and Anthony were dating nagged at her mind. What was it?

"We're working on finding out who in the tax office helped the Pressleys."

"Dale Jenkins would be my guess. He heads up the tax office. Anthony's had him over to the house on occasion. Do you think they've done this to anyone else?"

"We've only learned about these two, but it's always a possibility."

True, especially knowing what she did about the family. She was going to have to tell Grayson soon. It was just that if the secret wasn't handled right, Anthony would suspect it came from her, and *revenge* was one of his favorite words. He excelled at retaliation.

"Homer and Marge still sucking face?"

She laughed. "No, they floated away. What are you doing?" Was that okay to ask? She really liked talking to him and didn't want to hang up.

"Sitting on my deck. You'd love it here tonight. There's a storm in the distance, and the waves are crashing on shore. The sky above me is still clear, so there are thousands of stars."

"I love the beach when it's storming. I just have my little lake, so I'm jealous of your ocean."

"You should come over sometime."

Was he asking her out on a date?

"We need to talk some more about the Pressleys and how to proceed, and this is as good a place as any to do that."

Not a date, then. There was no reason to feel disappointed, yet she did. Even if he did ask, she'd politely decline... She was pretty sure she would. The last thing she needed in her life right now was a man. "Okay. When's good?"

"Up to you."

"The sooner we get things rolling, the better," she said. "Does tomorrow night work?"

"Sure. I'm going to pick you up."

"You don't have to."

"I'd prefer it. I want to make sure we're not followed."

"Oh." She shouldn't have to worry about being stalked.

"I want you to leave by the rear of your building. Carry a bag of trash to the dumpster. I'll pick you up there at four. That'll give us time to get back to the beach and have a drink before dinner."

"Okay." She hated this cloak-and-dagger stuff, and it rankled that she had to be secretive even though she was free to go wherever she wished with whomever she wished. She wanted it over.

"Do you like seafood?"

"Love it, why?"

"I'll throw some shrimp on the barbie," he said with an Australian accent.

He needed to stop making her smile.

# Chapter 9

Grayson was relieved they hadn't been followed from Harlow's apartment to his place. Interestingly, she hadn't commented on the Jaguar he was driving. It was a demo, the latest model, and he'd wanted to check it out.

The only vehicle he actually owned was his Jeep Wrangler. Why spend money on a fancy car when he had luxury cars at his fingertips? Not once had he considered selling the dealerships. They were his father's pride and joy, his sweat and tears during the hard years. But Grayson didn't want to take over, so he'd promoted Sam Cohen to CEO of the company, and left the day-to-day running of the dealerships in Sam's capable hands. Sam had worked for his father from the day the first dealership opened. He'd been a SEAL teammate of Daniel Montana's, and Grayson trusted Sam with the business. Hell, he'd trust the man with his life.

"Are we going to your friend's house?" she said when he came to a stop in his driveway.

Why would she think that? "No, this is…" Right, he'd told her he knew the owner the last time he'd parked here with her. "This is my house."

"Oh. I guess you really do know the owner, then." She grinned as she opened the car door. "I want the VIP tour."

She bounced up the steps to his porch ahead of him.

Tonight, she wore a blue-and-white-striped sundress and white flip-flops with crystals on the straps. Through photos, he'd seen her go from a beautiful, happy woman to a wary mouse who hid herself in ugly clothes. In front of his eyes, she was shedding her mouse skin and transforming back into the beautiful, vibrant woman in the pictures of her.

He followed her up the porch stairs, doing his best not to notice the sway of her hips. His eyes refused to obey. She was taller than the average woman, maybe five-eight or so. He told himself he would not imagine those long legs wrapped around his but imagine he did. He sighed in defeat. He was attracted to her, more than he'd ever been attracted to any other woman.

It was what it was. What he was going to do about it was the question. She was still fragile, and he didn't think she was ready for a man like him. It was up to her whether she ever wanted another man in her life, but if and when she did, he was beginning to think he wanted it to be him.

He opened the door after unlocking it and stepped aside to allow her to walk past him. What would she think of his house? He loved it and normally didn't care if anyone else did, but he found himself wanting her to love it.

"Oh, wow," she said as she turned in a circle in the middle of his living room. "This is amazing."

A warm feeling settled in his chest. His gaze followed hers as she took in the great room. The ocean side was all floor-to-ceiling windows and French doors. A bitch to keep the salt off on the outside but worth it. A massive white stone wall featured a long and narrow fireplace with the biggest TV available above it. Facing the TV and fireplace was an oversize, off-white leather sectional. Blue-and-white-striped pillows in assorted shapes and sizes added color to the sofa. On the wall behind the sectional was a large painting of a sailboat on the ocean on an azure-sky day.

"I love this room," she said.

"Yeah, I'm happy with how it turned out." The shiplap ceiling was painted white, and the floor on this level was the palest gray ceramic tile that he could find.

"Ooooh." She headed for the kitchen. "I covet your kitchen."

It was a great kitchen.

"Do you cook?" she asked as she stared at the six-burner range with a built-in grill.

"I do. It was just me and my dad growing up, and cooking dinner together was something we enjoyed. He was better than me, but I can hold my own."

"That's really cool. I always thought it would be romantic for a couple to cook together, but Anthony..." She shook her head. "Nope, not talking about him until I have to. Show me the rest of your amazing home."

"There's a powder room here if you need one," he said, opening the door to the right of the sectional. "There are three bedrooms and an office upstairs." He led her to the second floor. His bedroom was on the ocean side with a balcony off it. Where he'd used off-white and pale blues downstairs, he'd gone with gray carpets and a dark blue and gray color scheme for his room.

"I love that you have a fireplace in your bedroom." She peeked into his bathroom and squealed. "You have a claw-foot tub and a shower you could throw a party in. I'm just going to move into your bathroom."

He chuckled. "No problem. I won't even charge you rent." He'd commissioned a claw-foot tub that was half the size larger than a normal one, plenty big enough for the two of them. He might climb into it with her if she was living in his bathroom.

"You think I'm kidding?" She trailed her fingertips over the edge of the tub.

His eyes followed her fingers as she caressed his damn tub. "Uh, the sun's setting in a few minutes. Let's go out to the deck." Before he pushed his way between those fingers and his tub. And before she noticed his pants were tenting.

By the time they reached his kitchen, he had control of himself again…barely. If you'd told him the little mouse who'd walked into The Phoenix Three would have him reacting to her like a randy teenager, he would have laughed. "Not laughing now," he muttered.

"Pardon?"

"Would you like a glass of wine?" She stood too close to him, and her vanilla scent wafted to him. He was toast.

"That would be nice."

He'd uncorked a bottle earlier, and he poured them each a glass. "That's a pretty dress," he said as he handed her one. He wanted to tell her she made him think of a beautiful butterfly emerging from its cocoon. That was a little much, so he settled for complimenting her dress.

"Thank you. I went shopping today."

Hopefully, she bought a whole new wardrobe. "Let's go out to the deck before we miss the sunset." This wasn't a date, but it felt like one. He'd spent the afternoon prepping dinner, and he might have gone a little overboard, but she deserved something special.

The sun was low over the ocean, painting the sky in shades of pink and orange. They settled into the cushioned chairs, sipping their wine, and watching the sky turn dark. They didn't talk while enjoying nature's display, and it wasn't uncomfortable.

"I hope you don't mind, but I invited my partners to dinner." He'd done that because the purpose of her being here was to discuss her case, and she needed to be comfortable with Cooper and Liam since they were working for her, too. Now, he wished he hadn't. He didn't want to share her.

She leaned her head against the back of her chair and tilted her face toward him. "Tell me about them."

"You met Cooper."

"Elmer?"

"Yes. He grew up in Atlanta. Liam's from Kansas City. I met them both when we were in high school."

"How did you meet two boys from different parts of the country?"

That was a question he wasn't prepared to answer, not the full truth. "Spring break in Fort Lauderdale. We connected, kept in touch and decided to start The Phoenix Three together."

"Just like that?"

Not even close to *just like that*. "It's a complicated story for another time. I'm curious. Why us, The Phoenix Three?"

"I saw the article in the newspaper after you found and rescued that girl from that pedophile. Her parents said that you refused to give up on finding her. I mentioned the article to my great-aunt, and that I was thinking of hiring you. Ester told me she'd babysat your father. It seemed like a sign."

He smiled. "It's hard to think of my father as little enough to need a babysitter. In my eyes, he was larger than life."

"You speak of him with fondness."

"He was the best man I know…" He cleared his throat. "Knew." It was still hard to believe he was gone, a heart attack five months ago while standing on the floor of his

Myrtle Beach dealership. He was gone before the first responders arrived.

"I had dinner with him the night before he…before we lost him." He still couldn't say *died* when speaking of his dad. "Dad owned luxury car dealerships throughout the Southeast. Although he was disappointed I didn't come to work for him, he told me that night how proud of me he was." He would always treasure those words, and he'd forever be thankful that his father hadn't reacted like Liam's and disowned him.

"What about your mother, if you don't mind me asking."

"She died when I was a baby. Breast cancer. She was too young to worry about getting mammograms. By the time they caught it, it was too late to save her. I don't remember her, but Dad said she was an amazing mother. I have pictures of her holding me, and she always looks so happy in them." It was hard to miss someone you couldn't remember. He did wish he had memories of her.

"It sounds like you were close to your father."

He smiled. "Very much so. Enough about me. What about your parents?"

"Single mother. Never met my father. He split when she told him she was pregnant. Said he was too young to be responsible for a baby."

"What an ass. How old was your mom when she had you?"

"Sixteen. She's amazing, but sometimes a bit much. Finished high school, then got her degree in sociology, and now works for the Welfare Department. Volunteers all her spare time to her cause of the month. I'm a bit of a disappointment in that I'm not a vegetarian, not on a crusade for social justice or whatever. I'm also not into yoga, which might be my worst sin, along with eating meat."

She rolled her eyes, making him laugh. "She sounds… uh, very busy."

"You don't know the half of it. But she loves me in her own way. I decided at an early age, about the time I was sneaking fast-food burgers on the way home from school, that I didn't want to be like her."

"Good for you. How does she feel about your ex?"

"She said she has more third-world problems to worry about than the mess I've made of my life, that there are people going hungry or being homeless that need her help. She doesn't understand why I left a good thing, that I wasn't homeless and hungry, and that Anthony didn't abandon me when I got pregnant like my father did her."

He didn't know what to say to that.

"Left you speechless, hmm?"

"I've always heard that if you can't say something nice about someone, then don't say anything at all. I think I'll leave it at that." She'd grown up without a father, and he'd grown up without a mother. Same but different. The real difference was that his staunchest supporter, the most important person in his life, had been his parent. Even more significant, he'd been the most important person in his father's life. As for her parent, he definitely had opinions he'd keep to himself.

He was curious, though. "What about her grandson? Is she close to Tyler?"

"No. She's nice enough to him, but she's not the grandmotherly type."

She shrugged as if it didn't matter, but he could see that it did. That she didn't have the kind of love and support from the one person in the world who should be there for her only made him more determined to reunite her with her son.

The flash of lights shined along the side of the house into

the back as a car pulled into his driveway. "The guys are here. We'll eat, then get down to business." He stood and picked up her empty glass and his. "Want to sit here or come inside and talk to me while I finish the final dinner prep?"

"I'll come inside."

He was hoping she'd say that.

# Chapter 10

Harlow blinked at seeing all the food Grayson took out of his refrigerator. There was a tray piled high with skewered jumbo shrimp and sliced pineapples. There were asparagus spears, red potatoes, a large bowl of Greek salad and a long loaf of French bread.

"You've got quite a feast there," she said from where she sat at the kitchen island.

"Trust me, the guys will think this is just an appetizer."

"What can I do to help?"

"Dinner ready?" a male voice said before Grayson could answer.

She glanced behind her to see two men coming in through the deck's French doors. Cooper, the one she'd met, came in first, followed by a man she assumed was Liam. "Hello, Elmer," she said, smiling at him. Where Grayson was clean-shaven, Cooper had scruff on his cheeks and chin, giving him a bad-boy look. With his handsome face, light brown hair and eyes the color of dark coffee, he was a man whom women would sigh over as he walked past.

"Harlow, it's great to see you again." He gave her shoulder a friendly pat as he walked past, straight to the refrigerator. He grabbed two bottles of beer, twisted the caps off with his bare hand, then handed one to the other man, who'd stopped next to her.

"This is Liam O'Rourke," Grayson said.

Liam smiled. "Nice to finally meet you, Harlow." He glanced to where Grayson and Cooper stood side by side. "Who's Elmer?"

While Grayson explained why Cooper was Elmer, she took the opportunity to study Liam. He had dark blue eyes and jet-black hair, and like the other two men, he was tall and broad shouldered. She was surrounded by male hotness. Lucky her.

Grayson glanced at her and winked, and there was a little flutter in her stomach, as if one tiny butterfly had awoken from its long slumber and stretched its wings. Although both Cooper and Liam were as lip-licking yummy as Grayson, it was Grayson who made her stomach feel funny.

She had mixed feelings about that. The part of her that had been crushed into submission and thought she'd never be interested in a man again rejoiced that maybe Anthony hadn't permanently killed her libido. If her sole focus wasn't on getting back her son, she would definitely like to see where this attraction to Grayson could go.

"Get your fingers out of there," Grayson said, slapping Cooper's hand away from the salad bowl.

Cooper snatched an olive and popped it in his mouth as he moved next to Liam. "If you'd feed us, brother, I wouldn't have to be stealing food."

"He has a bottomless pit for a stomach," Liam said.

Cooper bumped Liam with his shoulder, Liam gave Cooper a noogie and Grayson sighed. "See what I have to put up with? They're six-year-olds walking around in big-men bodies."

She laughed. There was affection in his voice that told

her these men cared for each other. Fascinated by the dynamics of their friendship, she wondered how the three of them had come together. Grayson had been evasive when she'd asked, but maybe one day, he'd tell her their story.

Cooper grinned at her. "Run away with me, love. We'll leave these losers behind."

"Like she wants your ugly mug anywhere near her," Liam said, stepping to her side. "It's me you want to run away with, yeah?"

Grayson came around the island and bumped Liam away from her. "Clowns, the both of them." He clapped his hands. "Children, let's get dinner started."

"Aw, Dad, you're always messing with our fun," Cooper said.

As entertaining as Cooper and Liam were, she liked Grayson's steady calm, something she'd noticed about him. As everyone picked up a dish to take outside, it hit her that it had been years since she'd enjoyed an evening out with people she liked.

Their meal was delicious, the playful insults between the men flew, accompanied by much laughter, and all too soon, dinner was over, and it was time to talk. She wished she didn't have to end such an enjoyable evening talking about Anthony.

"We wanted to bring you up to date on where things stand," Grayson said. "You met Cooper, and I wanted you to meet Liam, too, because you might see both around Faberville. Liam's spending a few days at the Pressley resort, picking up some golf games with the locals."

"You'd be surprised at the gossip you can pick up on a golf course, especially in the clubhouse over a few beers after a game." Liam grinned as mischief danced in his eyes.

"Did you know the mayor's having an affair with Alderman Rice's wife?"

Harlow did not know that. "Seriously? She's so holier-than-thou. Wow, you just never know about people, do you?"

"Truth," Grayson said. "Anyway, if you see either of these clowns around town, pretend you don't know them. Cooper's looking into Dale Jenkins and his relationship to Pressley. If they've done to anyone else what they did to Miss Etta and George Pickens—"

"Oh, that reminds me. After you asked about them and then Dale Jenkins, I put the names together. George Pickens's name wasn't mentioned, but I remembered Anthony asking Dale if Etta Jankowski was going to cause them trouble. This was before we were engaged, when we had just started dating. We were at some event or another when that conversation happened."

"Do you remember Jenkins's answer?"

She shook her head, hating to disappoint Grayson. "I'm sorry, I don't. We were at a fancy gala, and I was a bit overwhelmed. I'd never been to an event where everyone was so important and beautiful. My attention was more on what was going on around me than on what I probably thought then was a boring conversation."

They'd dined outside on the deck, sitting at a round table with Grayson next to her. He put his hand on hers and squeezed. "That's okay. It's good to have it confirmed that Pressley and Jenkins were involved in stealing Miss Etta's home."

"I feel so awful about that. Do you know what happened to her?" After he told her how they'd found Miss Etta and what they were doing for her, she was blown away by these men. Because of Anthony and the kind of people he surrounded himself with, she'd forgotten there were good people in this world.

"I haven't been able to locate George Pickens yet," Cooper said. "Miss Etta said he moved away. She thinks to somewhere around Charlotte. I'm going through the tax records now, searching for anyone else they might have pulled this stunt on."

"And I'm playing golf and collecting gossip on your ex, Harlow. So far, he's not coming across as an angel from the things I'm hearing," Liam said.

Cooper mock scowled. "Why does he get to play golf, and I'm stuck in a dusty records room?"

"Because I'm prettier than you," Liam said. "You know it's true, so stop your sulking."

Cooper snorted. "I don't sulk."

"You sulked when the team ate those cookies you thought you'd hidden," Grayson said. He put his hand on her arm. "Word of warning. Never mess with Cooper's food."

"Noted." His hand on hers sent heat traveling along her arm, and she glanced up at him. His eyes were on hers, and in them was something she couldn't quite place, but it seemed important to know. For a moment she got lost in those eyes and forgot they weren't alone.

When he took his hand away, she had a sudden longing that she couldn't explain. Anthony's hands had been cruel on her, often leaving bruises on her arms from gripping her so hard. He'd enjoyed humiliating her with his words. Because of her husband, she'd gone years without wanting the touch of another man. Now she was hungry for it. And not with just any man, but this one. Grayson.

It was the worst possible timing for her girlie parts to be waking up. Maybe Anthony was right, and she was a hussy.

She slid her chair back. "I should go home." She'd go home and have a good talk with herself. Get her head straight.

Grayson put his hand on the arm of her chair. "We'll go in a few minutes. I want to hear the conversations you recorded with Pressley." He lifted his chin toward his friends. "Be gone with you."

Cooper stood. "Up, O'Rourke. We have places to go."

"We do?" Liam said.

Cooper rolled his eyes. "Dude's clueless."

"I have a clue." Liam shot her a mischievous grin. "Let's head to Faberville and see what trouble we can stir up."

"Sounds like a plan," Cooper said.

After they were gone, and she was alone with the man who was stirring up the stomach butterflies that were supposed to be dormant, she dared not look at him or those lips she'd probably dream about kissing. She got the burner phone from her purse, found the recordings she'd airdropped from her personal phone, handed it to him and then walked down the stairs of his deck, going far enough away so that she didn't hear Anthony's voice again.

She didn't need to be wanting Grayson's mouth on hers, but as she walked along the edge of the ocean, that was all she could think about.

Some minutes later, Grayson caught up with her. He slipped his hand around hers and pulled her to a stop. He looked down at her with eyes that gleamed with emotion. "I was a SEAL. I've done things in the name of my country that I never want to tell you about. I never enjoyed what I had to do." He brushed back the strands of hair that the wind was blowing across her face. "But, Harlow, I saw the photo of the bruises on your arm, and after listening to those recordings, I think I might enjoy putting a hurt on your ex. If that disturbs you, I'm sorry."

"I wouldn't be sorry," she whispered, unable to tear her gaze away from his.

"Would you be sorry if I kissed you?"

"I don't think so." Truthfully, she couldn't think at all, not with the way he was looking at her, as if nothing existed for him but her. She wanted to know how it would feel to be kissed by a kind, honorable man. One kiss couldn't possibly hurt, right?

He lowered his face until his mouth was an inch from hers. "You can tell me to stop."

She didn't, and he closed the distance until his lips were on his. It was a soft, gentle kiss at first, but as the seconds ticked by, it became more passionate. His hands found their way to her waist, pulling her closer to him, and lost in the moment, she wrapped her arms around his neck. The rational part of her brain screamed a warning that this wasn't a good idea, but…just a few seconds more, and she would have the memory of the best kiss she'd ever had. Then she'd stop, and this could never happen again.

Time got lost, and she didn't know how much elapsed between thinking she needed to stop and when he lifted his head. It could have been hours for all she knew. He took a step back, taking the heat of his body with him. Even though it was a warm night, she was chilled without the warmth of his skin against hers.

He gave her one of his soft smiles. "I won't apologize and say I'm sorry because it would be a lie. I can't bring myself to regret that kiss. But I know you're thinking it can't happen again, so it won't." His smile grew. "Unless you ask me to kiss you." He took her hand. "Come on. Let's get you home."

She wished he wasn't a mind reader and would kiss her again without her asking. Because she wouldn't allow herself to ask.

# *Chapter 11*

Grayson hadn't planned to kiss her, but he hadn't lied. He didn't regret it. How could he? She'd tasted sweet, like the berries and spice from the wine she'd been drinking. And her lips had been soft and warm against his. She'd stilled when their mouths touched, but then when she'd responded... Well, it had taken all his discipline not to scoop her up in his arms and take her to his bedroom.

She'd been silent on the ride back to her apartment, and he'd left her to her thoughts because he had his own rumbling around in his head. The most vocal one was, when could he kiss her again? He'd told her she'd have to ask, and he'd hold to that, but he wished he hadn't said it. No, it was the right decision, even if it was the last thing he wanted to do.

Harlow Pressley had buried her sexuality because of a man who had mentally and physically abused her. She might deny he physically abused her, but those bruises on her arms said otherwise, and he didn't doubt Pressley had left bruises on her skin throughout their marriage. Now she was emerging from the safety of her cocoon, and he had the honor of witnessing the first tentative steps of what promised to be a rare and beautiful butterfly.

He inwardly rolled his eyes. *Getting a bit fancy there, dude.* Yeah, but it was true.

"What if Anthony's there when we arrive?" she said.

They were only a few minutes from her apartment complex. "He won't be. Liam's there, and he would've called if Pressley was hanging around." Before he'd walked down to the beach to join her, he'd called Liam and told him to go to her place and make sure Pressley or his spy wasn't around. Liam would stay until he saw that Harlow was safely in her apartment, locked up for the night.

"If he does show up, what should I say when he asks where I was, because he will."

He glanced at her. "You say it's none of his business."

"That will just make him angry."

Although she was taking those tentative steps in finding herself again, she was still cowered by the man, and that made Grayson mad. Not at her, but at Pressley. "You left your regular phone at home, right?" When she nodded, he said, "Then if you feel you have to give him an answer, tell him you were home and didn't feel like talking to him tonight."

"Since my car is still parked there, that should work."

"Have you thought of getting a restraining order against him?"

"If I did that, he'd never let me see Tyler."

He wasn't letting her see her son now, so what difference did it make? But Grayson got her reluctance to stir the pot. "I think you should demand to see your boy, even if Pressley insists on being there when you do." The Phoenix Three team could set up surveillance for the meet to make sure she stayed safe. Pressley would never know they were there.

"I've begged him to let me spend time with Tyler, but he says I can only see him if I go back."

He wanted to wrap her in his arms and give her everything she wished for. "Instead of begging, demand to see him. Threaten to cause trouble if he doesn't agree."

"What kind of trouble could I cause? Everything is to his benefit, and everyone is on his side."

Grayson pulled to a stop behind her car. "Is there anything about him you know that would embarrass him? You said he has a mistress. Use that. Threaten to tell anyone who'll listen if he doesn't agree to give you time with your son."

She gazed out the window. "I know worse than that."

He tilted his head, her voice so soft—almost a whisper—that he strained to hear her. "Such as?"

"It's…" A shudder traveled through her. "It's bad."

"Harlow, look at me." He waited for her to face to him. "If I'm going to help you, you need to tell me everything you know about him."

"I was waiting until I was sure I could trust you."

"But you still don't?" That hurt. Yet, she hadn't known him long, and if this secret was the reason for the fear in her eyes, he couldn't make it personal.

"I think I do. I want to."

They needed to have a serious talk, and she needed to spill Pressley's secrets. All of them. He reached over and squeezed her hand. "Go inside. I'll come to you shortly, and we'll talk."

She stared down at the hand he had over hers, then she nodded as she opened her door and slid out without looking at him. Why was that disappointing? He watched until the door closed behind her, then he moved the car to an empty space.

Liam jogged out of the shadows and joined him. "Nice

car. You should let me borrow it, impress my new golfing buddies."

"Sure. Come pick it up tomorrow. No one was hanging around when you got here?"

"All clear. I didn't want to say anything in front of Harlow, but Pressley has a longtime mistress. Heard that one over lunch at the club."

"She knows. She thinks along with his regular mistress that he's had numerous affairs. See if you can get some names."

"I'm on it."

"There's something she wants to tell me about him that according to her is really bad. I'm going to move the car to a visitor's space and slip up to her apartment to talk to her."

"Want me to stick around, make sure Pressley doesn't come back?"

"No, nothing you can do even if he does."

"'Kay. Hope you meant it about this Jag, 'cause I'm coming to get it tomorrow."

Grayson tossed him the key. "Take it now. I'll drive your car home."

"Cool." Liam removed the key to his SUV from his key ring and handed it over. "Mine's parked a few spaces over."

"Yeah, I saw it." Grayson left Liam drooling over the Jag and went to Harlow's apartment.

She must have been standing at the door because she opened it as soon as he knocked. She'd changed into shorts and a loose top that fell off one shoulder. He tried not to drop his gaze to her long legs and bare feet, but his eyeballs apparently weren't so great at obeying. He'd never had trouble before keeping his eyes where they belonged when with a woman, but this woman was playing havoc with his mind. And his eyeballs.

She locked the door behind them. "Would you like something to drink? I have wine, water, tea, or I could make coffee."

"Coffee would be great."

He followed her to her kitchen. She twirled a pod carousel that was on the counter next to a coffee maker. "What flavor?" She shrugged. "I'm a coffee snob."

"What flavors you got there?" He scanned the labels. "Will you think less of me if I told you I've never had flavored coffee?"

She laughed, a sound he found himself wanting to hear more of. "No, I won't think less of you. Here, try the hazelnut. That's a good one to start with." She put the pod in the machine and pressed a button, then selected one for herself. "I think I'll have this one."

"Chocolate raspberry lava?" he said, reading the label. He gave an exaggerated shudder, making her grin. "That's just wrong."

"Don't knock it till you try it," she said, playfully nudging him with her elbow.

Her eyes were bright and filled with amusement. She took a sip of her coffee, humming a noise that he was sure she didn't intend to sound sexy but was. "Try it," she said, holding out the cup. "It's so good."

Although he had no desire to try chocolate raspberry coffee, he took the cup from her. He could see from her expression that she wanted him to like it. He didn't like the thought of disappointing her, so he was glad that it wasn't as awful as he'd expected. "Okay, not bad, but a little too sweet for me." He handed the cup back, then picked up his own and tried it. "This is more to my liking. Actually, it's pretty good."

She smiled, her eyes crinkling at the corners. "I thought you'd like the hazelnut."

Thrown off-balance from feeling a strange sense of connection to this woman he barely knew, he just nodded. He couldn't explain it, but he was drawn to her. Maybe it was the way she laughed, or the way she loved weird coffee. Maybe it was something else entirely.

"Come," she said. "I'll show you my favorite place to drink coffee."

She led him through the living room and out to a balcony. Two chairs were in the small space, and he frowned, wondering if she'd ever brought a date out here. Had she even had a date since leaving her ex? Although, based on the way she dressed and how timid she'd been when he'd first met her, there was no way she'd dated since leaving Pressley.

Something eased inside him... He didn't do jealousy, so that hadn't been the cause of the tightness in his chest. It was probably just that he worried about some douchebag taking advantage of her.

After they were seated, he took in the view and imagined that like the beach was his, this was her happy place. The lake shimmered under the three-quarter moon, and white ribbons of light danced over the water's surface. It wasn't his ocean, but it was peaceful here.

"Where are Homer and Marge?" he asked. He needed to know what secrets she held, but he wasn't in a hurry to spoil this moment. He'd like to know a more about her.

"I've never seen them at night, so I imagine they're sleeping."

He sipped on the hazelnut coffee, which was growing on him. What could he ask her that didn't seem like prying? He settled on, "If you could only live on one food for the rest of your life, what would it be?" It was the kind of question someone on his team would ask when they were on a mission and bored while hunkered down, waiting for orders to move.

His team had been the best. He'd put them up against anyone and anything. *What-if* questions had become a game between them, and the more outrageous the question and the answer, the better. There'd been that one time when the question was, if you could only keep one extremity, which one would it be? Sometimes they got morbid, because who knew, you might be the one blown to bits the next day, so they embraced black humor to diffuse tension and stress.

Stetson—a.k.a. Tex—had said in his Texan twang, "My hand, 'cause I sure ain't gonna wanna use my foot to rub one out." They'd always been able to count on Tex for laughs when they needed them the most.

"Lobster drenched in butter. What about you?"

It took a second to remember what they'd been talking about. "Depends on the season. When I was sitting under a blistering sun with seventy pounds or more of gear on my body and sweating buckets, I'd imagine eating a big bowl of salted caramel ice cream. In the winter when temperatures would drop to zero-butt freezing, I'd try to convince my brain that my MRE was really a piping hot bowl of spicy chili. I could seriously live on ice cream and chili."

"What's an MRE?"

"Meals ready to eat." He shuddered. "Nasty stuff."

"What was it like being a SEAL?"

"It was some of the best days of my life and some of the worst." He glanced over at her and smiled. "I miss it and I don't."

"That's an interesting answer."

"I'm an interesting guy." He grinned to let her know he

was teasing. He'd intended to get to know her, but she was turning the questions on him. Maybe that meant she wanted to get to know him, too. But it was getting late, and they still needed to talk about the secret she knew.

As much as he didn't want to spoil the enjoyment of the night and talking to her, it was time to get down to business. "Tell me about this bad secret."

# *Chapter 12*

Harlow had been enjoying herself so much that she'd forgotten the reason Grayson was here. However bad he thought the secret was, it was worse than he could possibly imagine. Just thinking of what she knew sent fear snaking down her spine.

If Anthony ever learned that she'd found out, much less told someone else, they'd never find her body. She'd withheld telling Grayson, wanting to be sure she trusted him first. Did she, though? Maybe it would be a mistake to tell him. She was mostly confident that he could get enough on Anthony to get her boy back without the risk of telling Grayson what she knew.

"Harlow?"

"Ah… It's nothing important." Unless you considered a secret that could send Anthony to prison important.

"I think it is." He pulled his chair around to face her. "Whatever it is, it's making you nervous and, I think, scared. What are you afraid of?"

"Really, it's nothing." He was too good at reading her.

"Is it something that will help us get you custody of your son?"

Was it ever. "I just…" She didn't know how to explain her fear without telling him the reason for it.

"Do you trust me?"

"I want to."

"Would it help if I told you a secret about me? Something no one else knows. If I trusted you with that, would you be able to put your faith in me?"

"Maybe." What could he tell her that could possibly equal what she knew?

"Maybe isn't good enough, Harlow. Full trust is a two-way street."

It had been a long time since she'd trusted anyone. Was she ready to give full trust to him? As she stared into his eyes, looking for answers, all she saw was his truth. The man sitting in front of her and looking back at her with patience and understanding would fight on her behalf. He would keep her safe. She believed that.

He put his hand over hers, something he seemed to like doing. "I can leave now if that's what you want."

"No." She shook her head. "That's not what I want. I want to put my faith in you." And oh, his smile when she said that. It was like the sun coming out after a storm, and apparently, his sunshine was all it took for a thousand butterflies to convene a butterfly convention in her stomach.

"Okay. Good." He lowered his gaze to the floor. "So, my secret. I'm a Swiftie."

"A what?" He'd mumbled and spoken so fast that the words ran together.

"You know, a Taylor Swift fan." He shrugged. "A big one."

"Seriously?" This big bad former SEAL was a Swiftie? And a blushing one at that. Just priceless. She tried not to laugh. She really did.

"I knew you'd laugh," he said as if offended.

"Sorry. But seriously…" She pressed her lips together to crush the mirth bubbling up again.

"Go ahead. Get it out of your system."

If she hadn't heard the amusement in his voice, she would have worried that she'd insulted him, or worse, hurt his feelings. But she had heard it, and his lips were twitching. He was trying as hard as her not to laugh.

"One thing, Harlow. You can be amused all you want, but you have to promise never to tell Liam or Cooper. Swear it."

"Why can't they know?"

"You've met those two. They'd never let me hear the end of it if they knew."

She grinned. "Although tempting, I promise not to share your Swiftieness with your friends."

He laugh-snorted. "Much appreciated."

"Well, I guess it's time for mine." Her amusement died a sudden death now that it was time to tell him. It was strange, but his confession and that he'd made her laugh eased her apprehension.

"I'm thinking it's important, so yes."

"Okay. Um… There's evidence in Anthony's safe of a murder." His mouth opened, then closed. Well, he wasn't expecting that, was he? She waited to see what he'd say. If this wasn't so serious, she would have enjoyed that she'd surprised him. But it was, and there was no enjoyment to be had.

"You better start at the beginning," he said as he leaned back in his chair.

"I overheard Anthony and his father talking one day. I was angry that Tyler's nanny wouldn't let me into his room because it wasn't my scheduled time. Like what the hell?" She glared at Grayson even though he'd had nothing to do with that edict. But he was a man, and men seemed to think they could make the rules. "Why do men think they can run roughshod over women?"

He threw up his hands, as if warding off her accusation. "You're right. Men suck."

"Well, most of them do, but maybe not you." She wasn't ready to put too much thought into that little gem. "Anyway, I marched myself downstairs to Anthony's study to have it out with him. This was two or three months before I told him I wanted a divorce, and during that time, I was angry a lot. About everything, but especially about how Anthony was punishing both me and Tyler for reasons known only to him."

"Before you throat punch me for being a man, and I totally understand why you might want to, can I just say that your ex needs to be first in line?"

"Yes, you can definitely say that."

"Splendid, and sorry for interrupting."

This was it. If she told him, she would put him in danger just for knowing what she did. "This is a secret that's unsafe for anyone who knows. Maybe it's better—"

"Harlow, believe me when I tell you I'm not afraid of Anthony Pressley. I've come up against much worse than he can ever hope to be, and I'm still breathing." He took her hand. "Tell me."

His hand was big and strong, and just the weight of it over hers made her feel safe. "I didn't realize Anthony's father was in the study with him, but when I heard Arthur's raised voice, I hesitated to go in. I've never liked Arthur. He's always treated me like I'm not good enough to have the name *Pressley*.

"Anyway, I was in the hallway, and they didn't know I was there. I turned to leave when Arthur said, 'You didn't have to kill her. There were other ways to shut her up.' Well, whoa. That got my attention. Then Anthony said, 'I didn't kill her, Delgado did.' I've never been sure exactly what Don's job is other than cleaning up Anthony's messes. Arthur told Anthony he was stupid if he thought just because Don killed her that he wouldn't be charged for murder, too, if Don got caught. Then Anthony said that wasn't going to happen because they... I assume he meant him and Don, that they dumped the body out in the ocean."

"Do you know who the woman was and why she was killed?"

"There's a blackmail letter in Anthony's safe from a Veronica Dunbar, so that's probably who. Neither Anthony nor his father mentioned a name. Veronica was one of Anthony's hookups, and I guess she learned some of his secrets and saw dollar signs."

"And no one suspects Pressley had anything to do with her missing?"

It amused her that he refused to refer to Anthony by his first name. "No. Anthony's good at keeping his affairs secret from the public, so I'm not even sure if there's anyone who knew he was seeing her. But in the letter, she was angry that he ended things with her. I wish I'd thought to take a picture of it, but I was afraid of getting caught. I should have gone to the police, but by then, I was afraid of my husband, and then there was the fact that he had the police chief in his back pocket. Now I realize I should have gone to the FBI or something, but I didn't even think of doing that. I was just trying to survive."

"So, you did read the letter?"

"Yes. Anthony kept my jewelry in his safe, only letting me have what pieces I needed when we were dressing up for an event." She shrugged. "Maybe he thought I'd sell the jewelry and run away. Which is what I planned to do. After he left the night I caught him kissing the nanny, I went to the safe to get my jewelry and when I saw the letter, I read it. I was shaking by the time I finished reading it. Anthony wasn't aware that I knew the combination, and if I took the jewelry, he'd be suspicious that I saw it. I didn't want to think about what he'd do to me, so I left the jewelry, closed the safe, grabbed Tyler and ran."

"You did the right thing. What did the letter say?"

"She didn't say exactly what she was blackmailing him with, just that she knew what he'd done and if he wanted to stay out of prison, he'd pay her a million dollars."

"We need to find out what she knew."

"I've thought about it, and it has to be something really bad. If he killed once without losing sleep, he could have done it before. There's also a gun in the safe. What if it could be tied to a murder?"

"I need to get into that safe."

"That's too dangerous. Anthony always has people around, and they're not of the nice variety."

"Don't mistake me for the nice variety either, Harlow."

Gone was the gentle, kind-eyed man she was growing to like…a lot. In that man's place was a hard-eyed warrior, and definitely not a gentle or kind one. She'd never thought a muscled-soldier type of guy would appeal to her. Apparently, she'd thought wrong. The raw power he'd kept hidden until now was… Well, swoon-worthy came to mind.

That just made her want to know more about him, especially how he, Liam and Cooper had connected. She suspected there was a story there, and she wanted to know it. Maybe with the secrets they'd shared, he would be more open to telling her.

"You said someday you'd tell me how the three of you came to start The Phoenix Three."

"I said that?"

"Yes." Well, she couldn't remember his exact words, but he'd said something along those lines.

"If you want to know, sure. The three of us were kidnapped during spring break in Fort Lauderdale and held for ransom when we were seniors in high school."

She gasped. "Dear God. But obviously, you are all okay."

"Now we are. The two men who did it are in prison, but they held us captive under deplorable conditions. At the time, Liam lived in Kansas City, and they grabbed him on the way home from school. They brought him with them to Florida where they knew I'd be for spring break. Our fathers were wealthy, so they figured they could get money from both of them."

"How did they know about boys living so far apart?"

"One of them had worked as a mechanic at my dad's Charleston dealership, and the other had worked as a line cook at Liam's father's Charleston pub. Liam's family has Irish pubs all over the world. As luck would have it, our abductors ended up in prison together, one for armed robbery and the other for a carjacking. The two started dreaming up schemes to get rich when they got out and came up with the idea of kidnapping me and Liam. Unfortunately for Cooper, he was in the wrong place at the wrong time with the wrong person…me. When they grabbed me, they took him, too."

"Your families paid the ransom?" She couldn't imagine getting a call from kidnappers that they had Tyler. She'd pay anything they asked to get him safely back, even if she had to rob a bank.

"No. The first demand was a million for each of us, which mine and Liam's families agreed to. The kidnappers thought that was too easy, so they demanded an additional million each. My dad was a former SEAL and decided he wasn't going to play games with them. He called in some favors, and a team of former SEALs found us and rescued us."

"That's an amazing story and thank God you all were rescued. I can't even imagine what it must have been like. I hope they got a long sentence."

"They did. Because of their previous records and then the kidnapping, they'll grow old behind bars."

"The kidnapping, that's why y'all started The Phoenix Three." It wasn't a question, she knew it was true. They'd gone from being victims of a terrible crime to being heroes dedicated to saving children. Not that they saw themselves as heroes, but they damn sure were.

"Yeah." He shrugged as if it was no big deal. "It was to make something good out of the worst time of our lives."

He wasn't just a survivor. He was a man who had taken his pain and turned it into something that could help others.

And she was blessed to have found him, to have him helping her.

# Chapter 13

Murder? Grayson had expected Pressley to be involved in any number of shady things, but murder hadn't been on his list. That Harlow had been married to the man, had slept in the same bed with him, had been touched by him made Grayson want to put his fist through the wall, or preferably, Pressley's face. And even though he'd been a SEAL, and he'd had to do things he couldn't and wouldn't ever talk about, he wasn't a violent man at heart. He was feeling damn violent right now, though.

What that said about his feelings where Harlow was concerned and what he wanted, he'd think about later. First order of business was getting Pressley out of her life and bringing her son home to her. After that mission was successfully completed, he'd circle back around to examining these Harlow feelings going on that he wasn't sure he wanted.

He needed a plan to get into that safe, but it was getting late and time to go. "I'm going to take off." When he stood, she did, too. She looked up at him, and their gazes locked. He didn't even think to resist the physical pull—almost a tangible thing—between them as his mouth sought hers.

His brain kicked into gear as his lips hovered over hers. "I said I wouldn't kiss you again unless you asked me to. Ask me, Harlow."

Her sea blue eyes met his. "It's not a good idea."

The disappointment was heavy, but he understood.

"But I don't care. Kiss me, Grayson. Please."

"Since you said please." The kiss was electrifying. He wrapped his arms around her, bringing her body flush against his as their lips moved in perfect harmony, as if they were meant to be doing this. He tasted her sweetness, and it was like nothing he had ever known before. It was as if every part of his soul was coming alive for the first time in years.

They broke the kiss, both gasping for air. Harlow's eyes were wide with surprise, but desire burned in their depths. "Wow," she whispered.

"Yeah, wow. I better go before I forget that's the right thing to do." He dropped his arms away, letting go of her.

"Will I see you tomorrow?"

"I'm not sure, but we'll definitely talk on the phone if not in person." The cat sitting on the other side of the sliding door caught his attention. Although the glass kept them from hearing Einstein, he could see the cat was talking a mile a minute. "I don't think Einstein's happy we shut him in and has a few choice words to say about that."

"He loves sitting out on the balcony, so yeah, he's not happy."

She opened the door, and he rushed out. From the tone of his chattering, he was cat-cursing them. Grayson squatted and said, "I'm thinking we need to wash your mouth out with soap, Einstein." The cat narrowed his eyes and let fly what Grayson was sure were more choice words. "Yep, you have a dirty mouth, buddy."

"He's never been shy about expressing his feelings," Harlow said.

Grayson stood. "I've never been cursed out by a cat before." He grinned. "I feel special."

She laughed. "Bet that wasn't on your bingo card."

"Not even close. Lock up behind me."

"I will."

He left before the temptation to kiss her again became too strong to resist. He waited to hear the click of the door lock before going to his car, except it wasn't until he couldn't find the Jag that he remembered he'd traded with Liam. Grayson had learned early on in his time on a SEAL team to trust his instincts, and instead of leaving, he moved the car to an empty space where he could see the stairs leading up to Harlow's apartment.

While he sat, keeping an eye on the apartment, he thought about Harlow and that kiss, how her lips felt against his. How soft and warm and responsive her mouth was. How he wanted to kiss her again and more. So much more.

He'd never had a long-term relationship, actually any relationship to speak of. Before he'd gone to spring break, like most teenage boys, he'd been girl crazy. After his kidnapping and before he joined the military, he'd been too traumatized to think of girls and wanting one in his life.

As for relationships, he'd seen his SEAL friends try and fail to make a go of having a girlfriend or wife. It rarely lasted. His life and that of his teammates meant that they could be and were deployed at a moment's notice, unable to even tell their significant others where they were going or for how long. Much of the time, they couldn't even call home to let their loved ones know they were still alive. He'd decided early on that he wouldn't put a woman through that kind of stress and, invariably, hurt.

Lately though…

Lately a certain woman was in his thoughts a lot. Although he'd always wanted a family someday, he'd decided when he became a SEAL that he wouldn't pursue a relationship until he was out of the military. Well, he was out now, and Harlow definitely had his attention.

A car turned into the complex and caught his attention as it slowly came toward him. It stopped behind Harlow's car for a moment, and then moved on, parking in a visitor's space. The driver got out and tossed a cigar to the ground as he walked toward Harlow's building. When he walked under the streetlight, Grayson recognized the man from the diner, Don Delgado.

Grayson slid down in his seat until his face was mostly hidden by the dash. Delgado went to the back of her car and looked around. Then he took something from his pocket, squatted and pressed the object inside the wheel well.

So, Pressley wanted to be able to track her car. The question was, why? He had a tracking app on her phone. Was he suspicious that she'd figured that out and was leaving her phone behind when she left her apartment?

Grayson was tempted to remove the tracker after Delgado left, but that would only alert Pressley to the fact that Harlow had someone watching out for her. What he needed to do was end this, and to do that, he needed to get into that safe. Deciding that nothing else was going to happen tonight, he went home.

Later, as sleep eluded him, and he stared at the turning blades of his ceiling fan, he made a list in his head of possible ways to get into Pressley's safe. He needed to talk to Harlow, learn all he could about Pressley, his house, his employees and his schedule.

When he exhausted all the possibilities he could think of, his thoughts turned to the woman herself. He finally fell asleep imagining his mouth on hers again as his hands learned her body and what she liked. That was probably why he had the most erotic dream he'd ever had with Harlow in the starring role.

# Chapter 14

Harlow chewed on her bottom lip as she listened to the ringtone. She half hoped Lena would answer and half hoped she wouldn't. It was silly to be so nervous about calling someone who used to be her best friend.

"Hello?"

She answered! Harlow squeezed her eyes shut at hearing Lena's voice for the first time in what? Four years? Oh, how she'd missed her best friend.

"Hello? Who is this?"

Right, she needed to speak. "It's Harlow."

"Harlow? It's really you?"

"Yeah. Hi. Long time, huh?" Lena had married and moved to Savannah, her husband's hometown, so there hadn't been any chance of running into her around town. That had been five years ago, and they'd kept in touch with weekly phone calls until Anthony managed to isolate her from her friends. Why had she let that happen?

"Too long. The last time I tried to call you, it said your phone was disconnected."

Because Anthony had terminated that phone's account and given her a new one with a new number. To keep peace with him, she hadn't given any of her friends that number. Never again, she vowed for what had to be the hundredth time.

"I'm sorry," she said. There was too much to explain for a phone conversation, but there was one thing she wanted Lena to know. "So, I'm divorced."

"Good. I never liked Anthony. I know he's the reason we lost touch. Damn, I've missed you, girl."

"Same. So much. I wish you weren't so far away. I'd love to have one of our girl nights." Girl nights for them had been wine, popcorn and staying up late talking and watching romantic movies.

"I have an idea. J.D. has to go to Boston next week for a few days. Why don't I come see you then?"

"Really? That would be so awesome."

"How about I get there Tuesday and stay until Thursday. J.D. comes home Friday morning and I'll need to pick him up at the airport."

"Perfect."

"I'm so excited. I can't wait to see Tyler. Gosh, he was only a few months old the last time I saw him."

"He's the cutest little boy now. You have my number. It's the one I called you on. I'll text you my address." She'd wait until Lena was here to explain about Tyler.

She disconnected and smiled. A feeling that had been missing from her life grew inside her. It was happiness. She was becoming herself again. She'd reconnected with her best friend. A sexy man, one she liked a lot, had kissed her, and she hoped he would do it again.

That happiness dulled an hour later when Grayson called to tell her that Anthony's man had placed a tracker on her car. The conversation was brief, and he made no mention of when he would see her again. She'd ended her earlier call to Lena with a tremendous surge of happiness. This time it was with disappointment.

He'd kissed her twice now, and last night's kiss was amazing, but maybe not so special for him? She replayed it in her mind, every detail, every sensation. The way his lips felt against hers, the way his hands held her so gently yet so firmly. The way he pressed his body against hers, the taste of him, the heat of him, the spicy scent of him. Never had she been kissed as if nothing else mattered but her, as if the man kissing her was consumed by her and only her.

As much as she wanted more, she needed to focus on getting her son back, and when she did, 100 percent of her time would be on Tyler. She hadn't seen him for months, didn't know what his state of mind would be. Had Anthony turned him against her? She suspected so, and her heart ached at the thought that her little boy would hate her.

Before she sank into a deep depression and crawled into bed, pulling the covers over her, and crying from the bone-deep hurt of missing her son, Harlow decided she had to get out of the apartment. Do something. Maybe she'd take a ride to the beach and walk in the sand. She'd liked strolling through the shallow water that day with Grayson. It had been calming, and she needed calm.

She changed into a new pair of white shorts and a pink T-shirt. A quick check in the mirror brought a smile to her face. She sure looked a lot different from her last walk on the beach. "Much better," she told her reflection.

Because there was a tracker on her car, she'd take her phone, let Anthony think she didn't know he was spying on her. She had a right to go wherever she wanted, and she wanted her toes in the sand and her feet in the water.

An hour later, as she drove down Ocean Boulevard in North Myrtle Beach, looking for a place to park, she passed

Grayson's home. She hadn't intentionally found her way to his house, but when she saw him walking up the stairs to his front door, she shrugged. Why not? This was the new her...or was it the old her coming back to life? Whichever it was, she was here, he was there, and there wasn't any reason to sneak around. With another shrug, she pulled into his driveway.

He turned and a smile ticked up his lips as she came to a stop. With that smile, her concern that he wouldn't welcome her vanished. She shut down the engine, and as she stepped out, he jogged back down the stairs.

"I didn't set out to land on your doorstep," she said when he stopped in front of her. The dark sunglasses hid his eyes, and the lowered bill of his ball cap shadowed his face as he looked down at her.

He reached up and removed the glasses. "Yet here you are." He gave her another heart-dropping smile before his gaze focused behind her. "You weren't followed?"

Where the devil was her brain? It had been an impulsive decision to stop at his house, a wrong one. Rattled, she backed away from him. "I wasn't thinking. I need to go." If she'd brought Anthony's attention to him, she'd never forgive herself.

"Public parking is four blocks down on your right. Go there, then walk back here along the beach."

"I should just go home."

"No, do what I said. It'll be all right."

She was furious with herself. Sure, she was aware of the trackers on her car and phone, but she'd... Well, she just hadn't thought. Her bad, but never again. She was well aware of what Anthony was capable of. She needed to be smarter than him, and from this moment on, she would be.

Grayson wrapped his fingers around her elbow. "Get in

your car and go to the public parking, and then walk this way." He opened her car door. "Go."

She went.

After she parked where Grayson had told her to, she walked up the beach to his house, and her eyes widened at the sight in front of her. Somehow, he'd timed it so that he was walking past her wearing board shorts, no shirt and with a surfboard tucked under his arm.

*Holy hotness!* Her feet tripped over themselves when her eyes locked on that naked—and so amazing—chest. "Huh…" she said. Her ability to use words had apparently taken off with the wind blowing past her.

"Keep walking," he said quietly as she neared him. Acting as if he didn't know her, he continued down to the water with his surfboard.

She kept walking.

Just how long was she supposed to walk, though? She guessed she'd passed him fifteen minutes ago. Did he really know how to surf? It had been a real effort not to turn and watch him. And dear heaven, she wanted to slide her fingers over that chest, and after testing the firmness of those muscles, she'd lick them. Never in her life had she had such a thought, and it made her giggle like a schoolgirl giddy with her first crush. And look, there was that very chest walking toward her.

How'd he do that? She glanced back, scrunching her eyebrows at seeing how far she'd traveled. It was impossible that he was ahead of her, but unless she was hallucinating, he somehow was. "How—"

"Go back to my house and go inside. It's the one with the red surfboard propped up next to the stairs." He kept going.

*Okaaaay.* This cloak-and-dagger stuff wasn't for her. Next time she had the bright idea to come to the beach, she was going to have Einstein hide her car keys. Ahead of her, Grayson broke into a jog, and as they had with the front of him, her eyes locked on his back and what a sight to behold. Even wearing clothes, it was obvious that he was built mighty fine, but wearing nothing but board shorts... Someone slap an oxygen mask over her face because he really was breath stealing.

She wanted her hands on that broad chest, the trim waist and...she fanned her face when her gaze reached his butt. *That* she wanted to see naked. She wanted those long legs wrapped around hers while his body covered hers. She just bet that Grayson Montana knew how to make a woman's body sing, and she wanted her body to sing if only just once.

What if she let herself have one time with him? She had faith that he would find a way to bring her little boy back to her, but until then, what if...

The *what-ifs* bounced around in her head as she walked back down the beach. She was a single woman and hadn't been with another man but Anthony since meeting him. She'd never cheated on him, not even during the last few years of their marriage when she'd been so miserable. Why shouldn't she enjoy the company of a man if that was what she wanted? As soon as she had her boy back, he would be her sole focus for who knew how long.

It could be years before she felt she could bring another man into her and Tyler's life. It all depended on the damage Anthony had done to their son. The time from now until he came home would be her only chance to have a little something for herself.

A thought nagged at her, though. Would that mean she was using Grayson for her own personal pleasure? Would that be a selfish thing to do on her part? How would he react if she was up-front with him, if she told him what she wanted? She'd be clear that as soon as she was reunited with Tyler that the affair would be over. She snorted. In only a few minutes, she'd gone from considering just one night with him to maybe having a short affair.

When he reached his house, instead of going inside, he veered off to the water. She didn't let herself watch him slip away. She didn't think anyone was following her, but if so, she didn't want to tip them off that she had any interest in him.

"Who are you, and what have you done with Harlow?" she murmured, chuckling. It wasn't that long ago that she'd been hiding inside her ugly dresses and tight buns. Now her hair was blowing in the breeze, and she was wearing shorts as she dug her bare toes in the sand while considering having a fling with a man who made her heart flutter. It was wonderful. She jogged up the stairs and went in Grayson's house.

He came in a minute later. "Back in a sec."

She blinked as the man starring in her brand-new fantasies walked past without stopping, still wearing nothing but board shorts. If he was going to put on a shirt, she wished he wouldn't. She'd really like some more chest-looking time. Although, she'd probably embarrass herself by drooling, or God forbid, actually licking him, so a shirt was probably a good idea.

When he returned, he was dressed in soft, well-worn jeans and a dark blue T-shirt not tucked in. He was barefoot, and why was that just downright sexy? Jeez, was she so sex-starved that she was now adding a man's feet to her fantasies?

"You okay?" he said.

"Huh?" Heat burned her cheeks as she dragged her gaze

from his feet to his face. "I mean, sorry? What did you say?"

Amusement along with an awareness of where her mind was filled his eyes. He leaned a hip against the island, his gaze never leaving hers. "Not that I'm not happy to see you, but is there a reason for this surprise visit?" When she hesitated, he said, "I mean it, Harlow, you're welcome here anytime, but is everything okay? Has something happened?"

"No. I just got antsy this morning and had to get out of my apartment, and a walk on the beach sounded like a good idea. I didn't mean to come to your house." She shrugged as she gave him a smile.

He smiled back. "Well, it's a nice surprise. As far as I could tell, you weren't followed."

"Oh, good. I wasn't thinking when I came here, but that won't happen again."

"I hope you mean that you'll think next time, not that you'll never come here again. I like having you here."

*Oh, silly heart, stop that fluttering thing you're doing.* "I have to ask. How in the world did you get ahead of me on the beach?"

"I swam."

"No way."

"Way." He smirked. "You forget I was a SEAL. Swimming's kind of our thing. One of our many things."

"Many things?"

His gaze raked over her as he stepped closer, his eyes locking on hers. "Do you really want to know?"

They weren't talking about his SEAL skills anymore, and a delicious shiver trailed down her spine. "I think so. Yes."

He leaned in, his lips brushing against her ear. "I'm good at a lot of things," he whispered before trailing kisses down her neck. When he reached her collarbone, he took his mouth away and stepped back. "I need a hard yes, Harlow. When you can give me that and not just a *think so*, I'll be more than eager to show you what those things are."

She wanted to snatch his mouth back. While she'd walked back to his house, she'd decided she wanted a fling, and she wanted it with him. It seemed he was open to something happening between them, and she appreciated that he wasn't willing to take advantage of her. That gave her even more assurance that she could be honest with him.

"What's going through that pretty head of yours?" He tapped her forehead.

"I…" She was so out of practice with telling a man what she wanted. She should have practiced what she wanted to say, written it down even.

As if understanding, he took her hand. "Come with me."

He led her up the stairs, through his bedroom and out to a balcony. "No one down on the beach can see us up here," he said as he put his hand on the back of a cushiony chair. "Sit here." There were two chairs, two small rattan ottomans in front of them, a table between them and off to the side a minifridge. "Water, beer or wine? That's all I have up here."

"It's barely lunchtime, but a beer at the beach sounds perfect."

He grinned. "My kind of woman." He took out two bottles. "You probably prefer a light beer, but all I have up here are dark ones." He handed her one of the bottles. "This is a craft beer, a porter with notes of chocolate and coffee. I think you might like it."

"Thanks." He was right, the few times she drank a beer,

she preferred something light, but she was on an adventure, so why not try something new?

"To new beginnings." He clinked his bottle against hers.

She smiled, liking that toast. "Oh, that's pretty good," she said after taking a tentative sip of the dark beer. She took another drink. "I can really taste a little chocolate and coffee." She eyed the label, wanting to know what to buy because she was going to get herself some.

Look at her, sitting on a balcony at the beach in her shorts with the hottest man she'd ever known, drinking a dark beer for the first time and thinking about having a fling with him. If anyone had told her a month ago this would be her life, she would've thought they'd lost their mind.

For a few minutes, they drank their beers in comfortable silence, and as seconds passed, a soothing tranquility settled over her. The waves weren't big enough for surfers, but there were windsurfers gliding by on their boards and hang gliders towed by boats were floating by under their colorful parachutes. Below them, a laughing woman was watching a man unsuccessfully try to get his dragon kite in the air.

She darted a glance at Grayson to find that he was watching her. When he caught her looking at him, one side of his mouth quirked up in a lazy half smile. Then his gaze left hers and traveled along her body in a slow perusal, and everywhere his eyes landed goose bumps rose as if they had a direct connection to those amber brown eyes that she thought she might be able to stare into for eternity.

*Get a grip, girl.* She hated that inner voice. Maybe she didn't want to get a grip. Maybe she wanted him looking at her as if he'd like to devour her.

"You ready to tell me what's going on in that head of

yours?" he said, his voice husky as if he already knew what her answer would be.

Okay, then, this was the new her, right? He asked, so she was going to put it out there. "I want to have sex with you."

# Chapter 15

Grayson managed to swallow his beer without choking. He'd suspected something like that was going on in Harlow's mind. He just hadn't expected her to say it so bluntly, but he liked that she had.

"But I have a condition," she said before he could think how to respond. "That is, if you're interested."

Oh, he was. "And that would be?" Pink tinged her cheeks, and he wanted to tell her that she was adorable, but he doubted she'd appreciate his noticing she was embarrassed. They needed to talk about her ex so he could learn everything about the man, but that could wait. She'd put sex on the table, and that was far more interesting.

"It has to be a short-term fling. As soon as I have my son back, it ends."

"I can live with that." He was pretty sure he could, but something told him this might be a woman he'd have a hard time giving up.

"He'll have to be my sole focus when that happens, so I can't—"

"I get it, Harlow. Of course, Tyler is what's important. But I have a condition, too."

"What would that be?"

He grinned. This was going to be fun. He set his empty

bottle on the table, then patted his leg. "That you come over here, sit on my lap and kiss me."

"Now?" she squeaked.

"Yes, right now." They weren't going to have sex tonight. Her question had come out of the blue, and he couldn't be certain she'd actually thought it through. Before they took it that far, he needed her to be sure she wouldn't regret it. He sure wouldn't, but he didn't want any remorse on her part on his conscience.

That didn't mean they couldn't fool around a little with the added benefit of easing her into being intimate with him. She stared at him as if she was trying to read his mind. Or maybe she was having second thoughts. He hoped not.

With the speed of a sloth, she rose, took a tentative step toward him and stopped.

"You don't have to do this," he said. "You can walk away right now, and we'll still be friends."

"I want to," she whispered.

He held out his hand. "Then come to me." When she placed her hand in his, his damn heart thumped in his chest. That was a first. He'd never in his life had such a strong reaction to a woman. Yeah, it was going to be hard to walk away when she decided it was time.

Something to think about later, but for now, he pulled her onto his lap. Even though she'd been the one to start this, she was as skittish as a feral kitten. "Hey, look at me," he said when she stared at the floor. He put his finger under her chin and lifted her face. "You're in control here. You have all the power. You can just sit here, and we'll talk if that's what you want."

"I want to kiss you."

"Then do it. My mouth is yours." She'd been so bold when she'd propositioned him, but now his kitten had lost some of her confidence. He wanted ten minutes alone in a room with Pressley for mentally beating this beautiful woman down until she took to hiding herself. He decided right then that he was going to do everything in his power to give that back to her. He'd help her find that woman again.

Her gaze dipped to his lips, and he breathed in her scent as she leaned closer. Did her skin taste like vanilla? He'd like to know. "Are you going to kiss me or not?"

"Yes."

And then she did, tentatively at first, just a brush of her lips over his. Her eyes were open and staring into his as if gauging his reaction. Then she pressed her mouth harder against his as her eyes slid closed. When her hands traveled over his shoulders and then to the back of his neck, he almost growled his approval.

He tapped her leg with his fingers. "Straddle me."

"Much better," she said with a little giggle after she'd straddled him. She lowered her mouth to his again, this time with more urgency, any hesitation on her part gone. Her hands fisted his T-shirt, as if she needed the material to anchor her to him.

It was in his nature to be in control, but he'd told her she had the power, and he was curious to see how far she'd go. So, he lightly rested his hands on her hips and didn't explore her body like he wanted to.

He let her have her way with his mouth, and they made out like teenagers. He couldn't remember when he'd last spent this much time kissing a woman without the intention of taking her to bed. Not today anyway.

She made a little noise like a kitten's growl, and it was the sexiest sound he'd ever heard. A minute later, he made his own sound, a hiss when she wiggled her bottom over his lap. She had to feel how aroused he was, and when she squirmed again, he tightened his hands on her waist to still her.

"Easy there, kitten. I'm holding on to my control by a thread, but you're testing me."

"What if I want to break that thread?"

"There's nothing I want more, but not today."

She put her hands on his chest and pushed away. "I'm sorry."

"For?"

Her gaze skittered away from him. "I practically attacked you."

"I think we just did a lot of kissing, no attacks involved." He wasn't going to allow her to fade back into her shell thinking she'd done something wrong. He brushed a lock of hair away from her face. "God, you're beautiful." Especially now with her cheeks flushed, her lips swollen and damp, and with desire burning in her eyes.

"But you don't want me. That's okay."

When she tried to get off him, he clamped his hands down on her legs. "Make no mistake, Harlow. I want you." He lifted enough to press his erection against her, letting her feel the truth of that. "Just not today. I want you to take some time and be real sure this is what you want."

"I wouldn't be sitting on your lap if I wasn't sure."

"You tell me that the next time we're together, and I'll have you naked so fast you'll think I'm a magician." She might think she was sure, but he wasn't going to risk any morning-after regrets on her part.

"A magician, huh?"

"Yes, with magic hands and other parts of me." He rocked his hips again.

"When?"

"Soon." He trailed his fingers down her legs then back

up that silky skin, and a groan lodged in this throat when she shivered. He was a saint for managing to keep his hands from slipping under her T-shirt and filling them with breasts that he was sure would be a perfect fit. It was time to end this little session before that thin thread did break. "But right now…" He stood and let her feet fall to the floor. "Let's go downstairs."

As he followed her down the stairs, his gaze slid down to her long legs, legs he now knew felt like silk under his fingertips. And that perfect ass. He wanted his hands on those round globes, too. He shook his head as he squeezed his eyes closed. If he wasn't looking at her, maybe he could get his raging lust under control. And… He missed a step and stumbled down the stairs, taking her with him.

Somehow, he managed to keep them both upright as they bounced their way to the living room floor. When they came to a stop, he was wrapped around her, his front to her back. And… Damn it, their position did absolutely nothing to fix his problem as his erection was happily aligned with the crevice of her bottom.

"Well, that was fun," she said as she glanced over her shoulder at him with a grin on her face.

"Are you okay?"

"I am. Really."

*You can let go of her now, Montana.* He reluctantly dropped his arms and stepped back. "Sorry about that. I guess I tripped." More like his brain was too busy imagining how his hands would feel on her to worry about messaging his feet on the mechanics of walking down the stairs.

He put his hand on her lower back. "Come sit at the island while I fix us some lunch."

"I can help."

"Thanks, but I got it. We'll talk while I make us a grilled

cheese sandwich." He wanted to take care of her, to feed her, to make her laugh, to show her that not every man was like her ex. "What would you like to drink?" He pulled a stool away from the island for her.

She slid onto the seat. "Water's fine."

"Told you we timed it just right," Cooper said, as he and Liam walked in from the deck and saw Grayson at the stove.

Grayson pointed a spatula at them. "I do have a front door that comes with a doorbell."

"Where's the fun in that?" Cooper glanced at Harlow and winked. "You'd never guess it, but he loves us."

"True that." Liam settled on the stool next to her.

Grayson sighed as he gathered up more bread and cheeses. "You both only love me because I feed you."

"Also true," Liam said. "Not our fault you're so good at it."

"Is there a reason y'all are here besides to eat my food?"

Cooper nodded. "Yup."

"Okay, but let's eat first, then we'll talk." He didn't want to ruin Harlow's lunch. When he glanced at her, she softly smiled. He smiled back.

"Oh, boy," Liam muttered. He and Cooper shared a look.

Yeah, *oh, boy* was right. He was falling for her, and his two best friends saw it clear as day.

## Chapter 16

Harlow decided that a heavy make-out session seriously enhanced the appetite. Either that or Grayson's grilled cheese sandwiches were so good that she couldn't resist a second one when he offered. He'd made them on sourdough bread, and inside were three different gourmet cheeses, crisp bacon and a sliced tomato. She never would have thought to put a tomato on a grilled cheese sandwich, but right then and there, she decided that was the only way she was going to eat them from now on.

She nibbled on the kettle chips he'd added to the plates while the guys ate their third sandwich. "Where are you people putting that?" Liam still sat next to her, and Grayson and Cooper were on the other side of the island, standing up to eat.

"Growing boy here," Cooper said, patting his stomach.

She loved the banter and all-in-fun insults they slung at each other. It was obvious that there was love and respect among them. She envied their friendship. She'd had close friends once, and seeing these guys together made her regret even more that she'd allowed Anthony to cut her off from her friends.

Cooper pulled the bread apart on the last half of his sandwich and eyed the cheese. "What do you call cheese that isn't yours?"

Grayson groaned. "Not the dad jokes. I beg you."

"Nacho cheese," Liam said.

Cooper poked his arm. "Hey, stop horning in on my punch lines. Just for that, I get to tell another one."

Her gaze slid to Grayson, who rolled his eyes, but she caught the twitch of his lips as he tried to hide his amusement.

"What do you call two ducks and a cow? Quackers and milk," Cooper said without giving anyone time to answer.

She laughed.

Grayson reached across the counter and tapped her hand. "Don't encourage him."

"Sorry. Couldn't help it."

Cooper winked at her. "At least someone around here appreciates me."

While they joked around, Grayson stacked the dishwasher and cleaned the counters. "Time to talk," he said as he leaned back against the sink. His eyes met hers. "I need to ask you some things about Pressley."

Must they? She sighed. "Okay."

"Can you give me a list of the people who work for him, what their jobs are, who the ones closest to him are, what his typical day is like and the layout of his house? The most important information is who comes and goes in his house and when."

"That's a lot, and it might take me a day or two. Also, I don't know what's changed since I left."

"No problem. Just be as thorough as you can. You said you know the combination to his safe?"

"Yes, unless he's changed it."

"Let's hope not. Include that and any other information you think would be helpful."

"What's your plan to get in the safe? If it's going to be dangerous for you, I… I don't want you to do it. I'll think of some other way to get Tyler back." She didn't know how, but she couldn't live with something happening to him—to any of them—on her conscience.

"You let us worry about that, okay?"

Liam leaned toward her, bumping his arm against hers. "We're like ninjas. Sneaky, invisible and badass. No need to be worrying about us."

But she would.

*Why today?* Harlow groaned. As much as she wished otherwise, that was Anthony's car in her space when she arrived home. She'd had a wonderful morning with Grayson, and she resented that her ex was going to ruin the rest of her day. What she wanted to do was sit out on her balcony and think about kissing Grayson, how her lips felt against his, how every nerve in her body had hummed in pleasure.

He'd told her to think about what she wanted before they went any further. She didn't need to think about it, she wanted more, but that he needed her to be sure only proved how honorable he was.

Unlike the man leaning against his car as she approached. Anthony couldn't care less about her feelings. The man she had at one time thought handsome until she'd seen the ugliness inside him watched her like a predator stalking its prey. And that was what she'd always been to him. Prey to be devoured until she forgot who she was.

But she was remembering.

"You've been gone all morning," he said as if she'd committed a crime. His gaze traveled over her, pausing on her bare legs, and his lips thinned.

She stopped on the sidewalk, keeping her distance from him. "What's it to you?"

"I was going to let you spend time with Tyler, but that window has closed."

*Liar!* There was no way he was going to let her see her boy. "I'm so tired of your games, Anthony." She took a step closer and let him see her hate for him in her eyes. "I'm done playing them."

A smirk played over his lips. "I don't think so." He moved until there were only a few inches between them, then he gripped her chin, his fingers squeezing so hard that tears stung her eyes. "I own you, Harlow. Don't ever forget that. I can do with you as I please."

With that said, he returned to his car. At the door, he gave her a grin so sinister that chills snaked down her spine. "And I do please."

It took every ounce of her strength to remain standing, not to sink down on legs that felt like over cooked noodles.

He backed out of her parking space, then the car stopped and he rolled down the window. "I don't know where you've been all morning dressed like that, but if I find out you're cheating on me, whoever he is, they'll never find his body. You can believe me on that."

*Oh, God.* Somehow, she managed to stay upright until his car disappeared from sight. The moment she couldn't see it anymore, her legs decided they were done pretending to be brave. He'd said to believe him, and she did. She had to fire Grayson and The Phoenix Three.

Until she'd met Grayson, kissed him, wanted more with him, nothing had mattered but getting her son back. But she knew him now, and she couldn't be the reason he got hurt or worse. Anthony had a tracker on her car and phone.

What if he knew she'd spent the morning with Grayson? They'd been careful. When she'd left, he'd sent Liam via the road to where she'd parked, to keep an eye out for anyone watching her. Cooper had walked ahead of her along the beach until she'd reached the parking lot. If any of Anthony's men had been around, they would have noticed.

So what if he'd tracked her to the beach? He couldn't know where she was or whom she'd been with. Her phone! As she sat on the sidewalk, it hit her that she'd forgotten to record her conversation with Anthony, his most threatening one now. If she'd gone for a spy career, she would have been fired her first day.

# Chapter 17

"She doesn't have a tail on her," Cooper said after returning from seeing Harlow off. "At least from the beach."

Grayson put his feet on the deck's railing and pushed his chair up on its back legs. "Yeah, with the tracker on her car, someone could be waiting along the road for her to head back home."

Pressley was used to her hiding in her apartment since the divorce, but the more independence she showed, the more he was trying to control her life. "We need to bring things to a close. I don't trust Pressley not to pull some kind of stunt."

Liam grabbed a handful of pretzels from the bowl that Grayson set on the table. "Wouldn't put it past him."

"I wasn't sure if you wanted Harlow to know, but I found Veronica Dunbar's mother," Cooper said.

"Good. Have you spoken to her?" He'd learned that Veronica's mother had filed a missing person report with the police, and he very much wanted to talk to her.

"No, I didn't know if you wanted to be the one to talk to her. Her name's Madeline Osorio. She lived in Portugal with her second husband until he died last year. She moved back to Fayetteville, where she's originally from and where Veronica grew up."

"Let's take a ride in the morning and go see her." It was about a two-hour drive to Fayetteville, so the trip would tie up half their day, but talking to her might be important.

"You want me to call and tell her we'd like to talk to her?" Cooper asked.

"No, we don't know what her relationship with her daughter was or what she thinks of Pressley. I don't want to give her time to come up with a story if she's not inclined to talk about Veronica. Let's plan on getting there around nine."

"Great, and I'm calling dibs on the Jag tomorrow. It's my turn to drive it."

"I was hoping Gray would forget I had it," Liam said.

"Not likely." He held up a finger. "Coop gets it for one day, and then I have to get it back to the dealership. It is for sale, you know, and I might know someone who can get you a great deal."

He'd gotten them both vehicles at his cost on what they drove now; Liam a metallic gray BMW SUV, and Cooper a black badass Ford 150. Even though Liam's father was worth millions, he'd cut Liam off and disowned him when Liam enlisted in the military instead of joining the family business.

Cooper—unlike him and Liam—grew up dirt-poor. His mother had overdosed and died when he was twelve, and his father couldn't hold down a job to save his life or keep his son and daughter fed and healthy. Even as young as he'd been, Cooper had done whatever necessary to put food on the table for his baby sister.

Personally, Grayson suspected that was the reason Cooper was always hungry even though life was good for him now. It was a learned behavior from never having enough to eat growing up.

"And give up my truck?" Cooper said. "Not gonna happen."

"The Jag was fun to drive for a day, but it's not me," Liam said. "I do have some news, too. I have three names of women who had an affair with Pressley while he was married to Harlow."

Cooper frowned. "What a sorry excuse for a man."

"And even that's too nice to say about him." The knowledge that Pressley cheated so blatantly on Harlow made Grayson see red. Pressley had those affairs and who knew how many more while having a mistress on the side for all the years he was married.

"I have a date with one of them tomorrow night, Alisha Austin," Liam said.

Grayson set the chair back down on all four legs. "Think she can give us any ammo on Pressley?"

"Maybe," Liam said. "From the gossip floating around, she's been vocal about how Pressley lied to her and strung her along, promising he was going to divorce his wife. Then when he actually was divorced, he ghosted her."

"Woman scorned," Cooper said. "She should be a good source of info."

Grayson nodded. "Hope so. The man's a piece of work." Pressley deserved what was coming to him, and to do that, he needed to get into that safe. "I have a plan."

"I have to fire you."

Grayson pulled his cell phone away from his ear and stared at the screen. He'd been happy to see Harlow's name light up but getting fired wasn't what he expected. He put the phone back to his ear. "What happened?" Because something did between the time she left his house to now.

"Anthony was waiting for me when I got home. He said

that if he found out I was cheating on him, whoever it was, they'd never find his body."

Grayson laughed.

"It's not funny. He's killed before and gotten away with it. We know that."

"Honey, your ex doesn't have a clue who has your six. You've got three highly skilled men behind you."

"I know that means you have my back, but—"

"It's more than just that. A normal person would say they have your back, meaning they'll stand up for you. When we say it, it means we'll give our life for yours." At hearing her gasp, he wanted to slap his forehead. It did mean exactly that, but he shouldn't have said it. That was what she was worried about, why she wanted to fire them.

"No, Grayson. Just no. I can't let you and your friends risk your lives."

This was a conversation they needed to have in person. "Listen, I'm about to go into a meeting. I'll call you tonight and we'll talk this out." Except it would be face-to-face.

"Come out to your balcony." Grayson disconnected the phone before Harlow could respond. The sun had disappeared over the horizon, but it was still the twilight hour. He glanced out at her lake and there were her swans gracefully gliding across the water. He liked that they'd made an appearance, that he'd gotten to see something that gave her so much enjoyment.

The sliding door opened, and she peeked her head out. "Grayson?"

He bowed. "My lady, would you care to join me on this beautiful summer eve?" As he'd hoped, that got a smile, albeit a quick little one. It was a start, and he'd take it.

"What are you doing here?" She stepped out, and Einstein scurried past her, going straight to Grayson. She glanced over the railing. "How did you get up here?"

"I think Einstein's asking the same questions." The cat was chattering up a storm. "Sit, and I'll give you both answers." He grinned. "I'm asking you to sit, not Einstein." Another little smile.

She slipped onto the chair closest to her. "Really, how did you get up here?"

"This way." He picked up the hook and rope he'd used. "Easy-peasy." Settling into the other seat, he reached next to him and grabbed the small cooler, taking out two beers. "You liked this one," he said, handing her the craft beer she'd had earlier today. Was that only today? Seemed like more than a few hours ago. He'd missed her.

"Thank you." She eyed the rope. "You really shimmed up that?"

"Yep. I didn't want to risk Pressley or any of his spies seeing me at your front door."

"I'm impressed, but you shouldn't be here."

"There's nowhere else I'd rather be. Tell me what Pressley said to you. Did you record it?"

"No, and I'm so mad at myself for forgetting to do that. It was what I told you over the phone, that if I was cheating on him, they'd never find the body."

"What else did he say?"

"That he owned me, that he could do with me as he pleased. He also claimed he was going to let me see Tyler but because I was gone all morning that window had closed. That was a lie. He has no intention of letting me see Tyler unless I go back."

"You're not going back." He fisted his hands. Five minutes in a closed room with the man was all he wanted. The threats were escalating, and Grayson feared Pressley would end up hurting her. This needed to end, and soon.

"No, I'm not, but you're still fired."

He tilted his face toward her and waited until she met his gaze. "Nope, gonna keep on having your six."

# Chapter 18

Harlow had to make him understand. Anthony was mean and as sneaky as a snake. He'd strike when least expected. She should know.

"Trust me, Harlow." He softly said as he skimmed his fingers over her cheek.

"It's not that I don't. I do. It's Anthony I don't trust. He plays dirty."

"Believe me, I can get down in the dirt with the best of them. As can Liam and Cooper."

Maybe so, but he wasn't getting just how ruthless and vengeful Anthony could be. It wasn't a risk she was willing to take. She'd just need to figure out how to get her son and disappear without leaving a trail.

"What's going through that mind of yours?"

She hoped she didn't have a guilty look on her face because she feared that he could see into her mind. That he read her every thought and knew the drastic measure she was considering.

She shrugged and tried for an innocent face. His piercing gaze made her uneasy and she feared she wasn't doing such a good job of shielding her thoughts. When she averted her gaze, he put his hand on her chin and gently turned her to meet his eyes.

"Talk to me." He let go of her chin and tapped her forehead with a finger. "You're planning something."

How could he possibly know that?

"If you're thinking your only choice is to go back to him out of some altruistic idea you need to protect me and my team, just forget it."

"No! No, I could never go back to him." Relief poured though her that he hadn't guessed her plan. What would he think if he knew what she was considering? If anyone could help her disappear, it would be him. Did she dare test the water? The trick would be to make it sound like a stray thought, not her plan B.

"I don't know. Maybe I should just disappear with Tyler. Go somewhere Anthony would never find us." Uh-oh, he didn't look happy.

He stood and braced his hands on the arms of her chair, boxing her in. "Listen to me right now. Get that idea out of your head."

"It was just a thought." She could see the warrior in him, in the determined and hard eyes, in the sharply spoken words that said she'd be a fool to challenge him.

"But not a good one." His expression softened slightly. "A life on the run with your little boy isn't the answer." He stepped back and leaned against the railing. "Do you want to spend the rest of your life looking over your shoulder? And if you're caught, which you probably will be, you'd be charged with parental kidnapping and most likely get a prison sentence. You'd lose any chance of getting custody of your son. Is that what you want?"

"No." Because she didn't plan on getting caught, but if she was…he was right, she'd lose Tyler forever. The thought of a life without her son was unbearable. She pressed her trembling lips together. Over her years with Anthony, she'd learned to hide her tears because he liked making her cry. Fed off her misery.

He held out his arms. "Come here."

The invitation to be held by gentle arms was too much to resist, and she walked into them. "I'm sorry," she said when a sob escaped. "Men hate it when women cry."

"Hush. It gives me no pleasure to see you cry because you're hurting, but sometimes it's good to just let it out. You're safe with me. You don't have to be strong right now."

The understanding he gave her, his kindness, and trusting that she was safe with him, she let her tears fall. She buried her face against his chest, and as she cried, he stroked her hair, then down her back, the touch of his hands soft and gentle. "I just miss him so much."

"I promise you, we'll bring your boy home to you." When she looked up at him, he smiled as he swiped his thumbs over her cheeks, wiping away her tears. "And, Harlow, I don't make promises I can't keep."

"Thank you. Thank you so much."

"No more talk about firing me or taking off on your own, yeah?"

"I trust you, so I'm not going anywhere." How had she gotten lucky enough to find this man to help her?

"Good. Now, why don't we go inside, and let me take care of you."

"Okay." She hoped that "taking care of her" meant what she thought it did.

Apparently not. But, as she sat in the bubble bath with a glass of wine in her hand, she decided the man did know how to treat a lady. He'd even run the bath for her. And what was he doing while she was rejuvenating in a soothing lavender-scented bath? He was in her kitchen, cooking her dinner. She let out a contented smile. She'd never been pampered like this, and as she leaned her head back against the tub, she thought of the gentle way he'd touched her as he'd wiped away her tears.

It would be so easy to fall for this man, but she couldn't allow that to happen. A fling was the most there could ever be between them until the day she had her son back, then they would go their separate ways. All she would take with her of this time were her memories of the kindest, smartest and sexist man she'd ever known. He'd already proved that he could kiss... Boy, could he ever. That had to mean that he would be a good lover.

The bathwater was getting chilly, and she pulled the plug. After drying off and slathering lotion on her arms and legs, she slipped on the denim shorts that she'd never wear outside because they were so short and a white tank top. Although she put on panties, she decided on no bra. The top was soft and thin, making it obvious she wasn't wearing one. Let him think of that what he would. Barefoot, she followed the tantalizing aroma to the kitchen.

"Whatever you're making smells delicious." His back was to her as he stirred something on the stove.

He turned and went silent as his gaze traveled over her body, down to her bare toes, then he made a slow perusal back up to her face.

She smiled, feeling both shy and desirable. Now that she was standing in front of him, she wasn't sure what to do. Should she step close to him? Touch him? Tell him she was sure she did want him?

While she hesitated, he removed the pan from the burner. With his eyes locked on hers, he took the decision out of her hands and closed the distance between them. He placed his warm palms on her cheeks. "I'm going to kiss you. If you don't want me to, tell me now."

"I want you to." He asked for permission, and she loved that about him.

"Thank you." His mouth slowly lowered to hers.

His lips were soft yet urgent as they met hers, and she surrendered to this thing that was building between them. His hands skimmed down her arms, trailing goose bumps in their wake before they wrapped around her waist, pulling her body close to his. She could feel his heat, and her body responded with a shiver of desire. She parted her lips, allowing him to deepen the kiss, and he took full advantage of the invitation, kissing her deeply.

When they finally broke apart, she was breathing hard and standing on weak legs. He held her steady, his gaze never leaving hers. "Tell me what you want."

That was easy. "You."

"Okay, then."

She yelped when he scooped her up. "Wasn't expecting that," she said with a chuckle as she wrapped her arms around his neck. Lord, he smelled good.

"I like surprising you. Unless you tell me no, I'm taking you to your bedroom, where I'll have my wicked way with you."

"I like the sound of that."

As he carried her down the hallway, it surprised her that she wasn't nervous. Although she knew why. It was because of him. She nuzzled his neck, smiling against his skin when he grunted. She'd have to remember that he liked that.

When they reached her bed, he lowered her to the mattress, then sat on the edge and removed his socks and shoes. That was a good start, but she wanted his shirt off. He glanced at her and smiled, making her heart beat faster and her belly flutter.

He put his hand on her ankle. "No regrets in the morning?"

"Not a one."

"Good." He trailed his fingers up her leg, stopping at her knee.

She squirmed, wanting his hand to start moving again, and when he knowingly chuckled, she glared at him. That brought a big grin to his face. Why was he torturing her?

"Want something?" he teased.

She shrugged, pretending to be indifferent to his teasing, but his playfulness made her happy. She'd never had fun in the bedroom before, and she liked it. She could play, too. "You told me you had magic hands. Maybe you should prove it." She lifted her brows in what she hoped was a doubting expression.

"Feisty. I like it." He moved his hand up her thigh a few inches before stopping again. "I did promise you magic, didn't I?"

"You sure did, but I'm not sure you can live up to your own hype."

He laughed. "Hmm, a challenge. I better get busy."

"Busy would be good." With his humor and playfulness, he'd made her want him even more than before he brought her to her bedroom.

His hand left her leg, and she wanted to snatch it back... well, until she realized he needed it to remove his T-shirt. Her mouth dried up at the sight of his bare chest. Yes, she'd seen him without a shirt at the beach and had appreciated how cut he was, but he hadn't been in her bedroom on her bed about to make love to her. Now, staring at his chest and broad shoulders, and knowing what was about to happen, an involuntary sigh escaped. She was going to get to have her hands on that amazing body.

*Give me. Give me,* she wanted to say as she wiggled her fingers at him.

After tossing his shirt to the floor, he put his hand along the side of her head, leaned over and lowered his face to within an inch of hers. "You can't begin to know how much I wanted this," he said before brushing his lips over hers.

Electric! That was what his touch did, sent sparks of electricity through all her nerve endings. All thoughts of fun and games vanished when his tongue invaded her mouth. She wrapped her arms around his neck and pulled him closer. He kissed her until she was breathless.

He pulled away and stared down at her with an intensity that made her heart pound. "What are you doing to me?"

Before she could answer, Einstein ambled in, chattering away.

"Nope, no talking cats allowed." He picked Einstein up, deposited him in the hallway, then shut the door in his face. "Now, where were we?"

# Chapter 19

Grayson returned to the bed, to the woman who was shyly smiling at him. "You're beautiful." She really was, both inside and out.

"Thank you."

He liked that she didn't try to blow off his compliment by denying it. A week ago, she would have. He put his hand on her knee. "Do you want to be in control?"

"What do you mean?"

"You get to say how this goes, what we do here tonight." He didn't know what her sex life had been like with Pressley, but he guessed the man hadn't much cared what she wanted or liked. He was going to show her that what pleased her mattered.

"So, if I tell you to do something, you will?"

"Tonight, here in your bedroom, yes." A grin appeared on her face, and he was a little worried about the mischief in her eyes.

"Take off your jeans."

"Yes, ma'am." He stood, removed his wallet and set it on the night table. Deciding to give her a show, he slowly lowered the zipper. Just as slowly, he pushed the jeans down over his hips all while keeping his eyes locked on hers. Damn if she didn't lick her lips after he kicked his jeans aside and stood there in his boxer briefs…his very tented ones.

"Now the rest," she said, her voice now a little husky.

He'd half expected the little mouse who'd first walked into The Phoenix Three to make an appearance, that she would revert to being shy and not sure of herself and what was about to happen between them. He was happy to be wrong.

When he stood in all his naked glory, she licked her lips again as she stared at his erection. While her gaze traveled over him, he stayed silent, waiting for her next command. He couldn't remember being as hot for a woman as he was her, and his endurance was closing in on being nonexistent.

"I don't know what to do now," she said, lifting her eyes to his.

"What do you want to do?" he gritted out. She really needed to stop teasing her tongue over her bottom lip if she didn't want him to fall on her like a starving man seeing a delicious meal for the first time. *A bit dramatic there, Montana.* Maybe so, but it was her fault he felt like a barbarian wanting to ravish the beautiful woman in front of him. She hadn't even taken her clothes off yet, and he was ready to blow.

"I'm royally screwed," he muttered. He hadn't been looking for *the one*, and maybe she wasn't that, but by the way his heart was pounding against his chest, he wasn't sure of anything where she was concerned.

"Sorry. What?"

He wasn't going to repeat what he hadn't meant to say out loud, so he said instead, "Tell me what you want, Harlow."

"I want to touch you."

Every single part of him liked that idea. His feet reacted first by taking him to her. He sat on the bed near her legs. "I'm yours to touch." She happily smiled, and he wanted to say a prayer of thanks to whoever brought her to him. He was pretty sure he wanted to keep her.

She tucked her feet under her legs, leaned forward and pressed her hands against his chest. "You're harder than I thought you'd be."

He snorted. "You have no idea, kitten."

"Why do you call me that?"

"When I first met you, you reminded me of a shy kitten that was unsure of her place in the world." He wasn't about to tell her he'd actually thought of her as a shy mouse. "Then you grew into yourself, and my kitten got claws."

"Your kitten?"

He hadn't meant to claim her...yet. "Only if you want to be."

"That would mean you're my what?"

"I'll be whatever you want me to be." He could happily fall into those sea blue eyes looking at him with desire in them and never care about finding his way back. "Why do you still have clothes on?"

She laughed, and it was such a beautiful sound. "Because you haven't taken them off."

"We need to rectify that. Right now." She lifted her arms, and he pulled her top up and over her head. He blew out a breath. She didn't have a clue what she was doing to him.

Her skin was soft and warm under his fingertips as he traced the curve of her breast. He leaned in, pressing his lips to hers, and when she opened up to him, he deepened the kiss. He slid his hand down to her waist, his fingers trailing along the edge of her shorts.

With their mouths still fused together, he deftly unbuttoned her shorts and slid the zipper down. He broke away so he could remove them. "Up." She lifted enough for him to tug them down, revealing white bikini panties. "Killing me," he murmured.

"Aren't you going to take off my panties?" she said when he stretched out next to her.

"Not yet. I'm not done looking at you in them." From her soft smile, that pleased her.

He lifted onto his elbow, leaned over her and brushed his lips over hers. From there, he trailed kisses down her neck and across her collarbone. She moaned and arched her back when he twirled his tongue around a nipple. He inwardly smiled when she clutched his hair, urging him on. He moved to her other breast, and while he lavished attention on that one, he slid his hand down her stomach to her sex.

Even though he was dying to be inside her, he locked his need down. Her pleasure came first. He eased his hand under her panties and a finger inside her. The scent of her arousal was in the air, and he inhaled her essence deep into his lungs. Sweetest smell in the world.

He'd barely touched her wet heat when her body tensed, and he knew she was on the edge of falling. "Let go," he whispered, then took her mouth again as a shudder tsunamied through her body. She was so damn responsive.

"Grayson! Oh God," she said through gasps to catch her breath.

When her eyes—amazement in them—latched onto his, he wanted to promise her that he'd dedicate his life to hearing her rasp those words every night for the rest of her life. He wanted her in his life. He wanted to sleep next to her every night. He craved her in ways he'd never craved anyone before. He hadn't been looking to fall in love. Wasn't sure that was where he was headed, but he'd never felt this way before.

He stayed with her until early morning, once making love to her hard and fast, later making love to her slow and easy. Slept for a few hours with his body curled around hers. Made love again. Wondered if he really was falling in love with her. Decided to think about it later.

In the early morning, he slipped out of her bed, and after dressing, he cleaned up the kitchen from the dinner they didn't eat. He left a note on the counter in front of the coffeepot, and while it was still dark, he left the way he'd arrived.

# Chapter 20

Harlow opened her eyes and smiled as she turned toward Grayson…who wasn't there. Her smile dropped when she slid her hand over the sheets where he should be. Cold. When had he left? As soon as she fell asleep? Had he gotten what he wanted and then been anxious to leave?

*That's what happens when you spread your legs like a slut,* Anthony's voice said in her head. She slapped her hands over her face. "Shut up, Anthony!" Gah, now she was screaming at an imaginary voice.

Angry at herself for the doubts tumbling around in her head, she headed straight for the coffeepot to get some caffeine in her. She'd think better after a cup of coffee…or six. A piece of paper was propped up against the coffee maker. She picked it up and read it.

> Good morning, kitten. I'm going to think about you
> all day. I'll call you tonight.
> XO
> Gray

Wow! Just wow. She fanned her face as she read his note for the second time. She grinned. Then she laughed. He hadn't bolted in the middle of the night with no intention of seeing her again after getting what he wanted as Anthony's voice would have her believe.

Even though she hadn't gotten much sleep thanks to Grayson—she wasn't complaining, not at all—after reading his note, she made plans for her day with a light heart and a smile on her face.

She had her assignment from Grayson to do, which she would do this afternoon. First, she needed to prepare for Lena's visit. A trip to the grocery store was necessary, so she wrote out a menu for the meals on the days her friend would be here.

Halfway to the store, she thought about what she'd wear when Lena visited. She hadn't bought much on her recent shopping trip. Just a sundress, some shorts, a pair of jeans and a few T-shirts. She wanted some nice things to wear while Lena was here, and on a spur-of-the-moment impulse, she turned the car for the mall.

Two hours later, and with several shopping bags hanging from her arms, she walked by Victoria's Secret. With new clothes, panties and bras, she returned to her car. That had been fun, and she had some pretty new clothes and underwear she wouldn't be embarrassed for Grayson to see… and soon, she hoped. The next stop was the grocery store.

Back home, she put the groceries away, then took her new clothes to her bedroom. How long had it been since she'd bought something really pretty? It was such a good feeling to even want to shop again for pretty clothes.

"No, Einstein, no cat hairs on the panties." She picked him up from the bed and set him on the floor.

"Merghp," he said in his annoyed you're-no-fun voice. He twitched his tail and strutted out of the bedroom.

"Be that way," she said to his retreating back. If she got a chance to wear the panties for Grayson, she did not want him getting cat hair in his mouth. Should said mouth end up there. She shook her head, amused with herself.

Only one thing kept her from being truly happy, and that was not having her son. But that was finally going to happen. Grayson had promised he would get Tyler back for her. She didn't know how he planned to achieve that, but he'd given her a task, so she put her new clothes away and got to it.

It took most of the afternoon to complete the list of things in her assignment. When she was done, she emailed everything to Grayson. She'd started on a new website for The Phoenix Three, and she wanted to get back to it, but her brain needed a break. Spending the afternoon recreating Anthony's life was not fun. She poured a half glass of wine and took it out to her balcony. Apparently forgiven by Einstein, he followed her out.

"Look. There's Homer and Marge." The swans were lazily floating along. She sipped her wine and let the peacefulness of the swans and the lake and Einstein's chatter clear her mind.

Refreshed and ready to get back to work, she herded Einstein back inside. She had just logged on to the new website she was building for the guys when her doorbell rang. Was Grayson here? Her heart bounced in anticipation as she set her laptop aside. Einstein loved doorbells because it meant someone was on the other side who might give him attention, and he beat her to the door.

She put her eye to the peephole, and when she saw who was on the other side, she stilled. If she stayed quiet, maybe Anthony would go away. She wanted to bang her head on the door. Why couldn't he leave her alone?

"I know you're there, Harlow. Look out again."

No, she wasn't going to let him order her around, and she wasn't going to open the door to him.

"Mama."

She squeezed her eyes closed. Tyler wasn't out there. This was just another of Anthony's cruel tricks. But, God, it hurt to hear her son's voice, even if it was only a recording. Her arms ached to hold him and inhale his little-boy scent. She couldn't remember what he smelled like, and that seemed like such a minor thing, but it wasn't. A mother should know her child's scent.

"Look," Anthony said again. "You'll want to see who's here."

She didn't believe him, but what if he had brought Tyler to see her? She put her eye to the peephole again, and her breath caught in her throat. "Tyler," she whispered. His nanny was holding him, the same one Anthony had kissed in front of her. Elation at seeing her son outweighed the rage that the woman was still in Tyler's life every day when she wasn't.

Only a slab of wood separated her from her boy, and she fumbled with the locks. Once the door was finally open, she stepped into the hallway to get to her son. But he wasn't there. "Where is he?"

Before she could run to the elevator, Anthony grabbed her arm and pulled her into her apartment, slamming the door behind them. She stumbled as he dragged her into the living room. "Let go of me," she screamed. He was scaring her. She tried to pull away, but his fingers were wrapped around her arm like a vise.

"When you calm down, I'll tell you how it's going to be."

"You're hurting me. The police will arrest you for domestic abuse when they see the bruises on my arm."

He laughed. "You should know by now that will never happen."

"Because you pay off the police." Not a good idea to bait him, but the words had slipped out before she could think better of it.

His eyes turned cold. "You don't want to be spreading that rumor around, doll. It won't be good for your health."

"Where is my son?" she demanded, her voice shaking with fear and anger. He'd just threatened her life, and once again, she wasn't recording him.

"*Our* son. If you want to see him, come home where you belong."

He let go of her, and she backed up until she hit the entry wall. "Why, Anthony? Why do you have to be so cruel? You don't love me, so why are you so insistent that I come back?"

"Honestly?"

"Yes, for once in your life, tell me the truth."

"I don't love you. Never have. Father chose you for me because you were beautiful and compliant. He wants me to run for political office and you were good for my image."

"This is all about your image?" His father chose her? What a gullible fool she'd been. It shouldn't hurt by now that he'd never loved her because she hated him. But she had loved him for a brief time, and hearing that he had never returned the feeling—not even in the beginning when he'd made her believe that she was the love of his life—hurt.

"More than ever. I'm going to run for mayor, and I need you by my side." He grinned. "Think of the power we'll have. You will come home, Harlow, and you will stand by my side and smile as I announce I'm running. You will attend dinners and lunches and tell everyone you talk to what a wonderful mayor you know I'll be. People like you and will listen to you."

"You've got to be kidding. Step into the current century, Anthony. Men can no longer press their will on a woman." And Anthony with that kind of power was frightening.

"No can do. Father wants you home. I want you back where you belong, so that's what's going to happen."

"You both can go to hell." Anger was taking over her good sense. She knew better than to talk to him like that.

He pushed his body hard against hers, pinning her to the wall. "You have one week, Harlow. In seven days, if you aren't back, I'll drag you there myself." He slammed his mouth over hers.

Bile rose in her throat when he forced his tongue into her mouth. When she gagged, he laughed, enjoying her reaction. He bit her bottom lip hard, and she tasted blood. "Stop it." She put her hands on his chest and tried to push him away.

"We're just getting started, doll. I was going to wait until you came home to take what's mine, but what the hell. Why wait?" He glanced around, his gaze stopping on the hallway. "Let's take this to the bedroom."

She dug her feet into the floor and screamed, praying that a neighbor would hear and call the police. Einstein raced out from under the sofa where he'd been hiding, howling in a way she'd never heard from him before. He jumped on Anthony's leg and dug his claws in.

Anthony yelped and let go of her, and she raced toward the door. She glanced over her shoulder to see Anthony pull Einstein off him and throw him against the wall. She almost went back to get him, but he got his feet under him and took off for the bedroom.

*Okay. Okay.* Einstein was safe and she needed to get the hell out of here because Anthony was stalking toward her with murder in his eyes. Her hand was on the doorknob when she was jerked back by her ponytail.

"Bitch," he snarled. "You're lucky I don't kill you right now."

She clawed at his hand as she screamed again. *Please, God, let someone hear me.* As if her prayer was answered, someone banged on the door.

Anthony slapped his hand over her mouth. "One word, and I'll break your neck."

The knocking came again. "Harlow? Hey, it's your neighbor. I heard you scream. Are you okay?"

Her relief that someone had heard her was so great that her legs buckled. Anthony let go of her hair, and with her body shaking, she folded up on herself right there on the floor.

"One word, Harlow. Just one word from you and you'll never see Tyler again. I'll make sure of it." He walked past her, opened the door. "Everything is fine here."

*Liar!* She lifted her gaze to her neighbor, intending to tell him the truth, but the man staring back at her, giving a slight shake of his head, wasn't her neighbor or the police. He was Grayson's friend Cooper.

# Chapter 21

"What's that smile for?"

Grayson glanced at Cooper. "Was I smiling?" He probably was since he'd been thinking of Harlow. Had she found his note yet? He hadn't wanted to leave her this morning, but this trip to talk to Veronica's mother was important.

"Have you made contact with Pressley's driver?" he asked to change the subject. He wasn't ready to share where he'd spent the night.

"He plays racquetball a few mornings a week at the club. I'm going in the morning and try to get a game with him. Start feeling him out." Cooper turned the Jag onto Mrs. Osorio's street. "You sure about this plan?"

"It's the best one I can come up with to get close to Pressley. It depends on the driver." He was working on a plan B should Pressley's driver have scruples. They came to a stop, and Grayson opened the door. "Let's see what the lady has to say."

Madeline Osorio was an attractive woman, and even at nine in the morning and not expecting visitors, she was dressed as if she'd expected company. Grayson estimated her to be in her early fifties, and even though it didn't appear that she had a lot of money based on the sparse furnishings in her small apartment, she was stylishly dressed in a blue silk blouse and black pants. Her brown hair with blond highlights was cut short, and her makeup was flawless.

When she'd answered their knock at the door, as soon as they explained that they were looking into the disappearance of her daughter on behalf of a client, she'd invited them in. She seemed to welcome their company even though they were strangers, and she'd insisted on serving them coffee.

Although Mrs. Osorio had reported Veronica missing, she had never been found. Even though Grayson assumed Veronica had been killed and dumped in the ocean based on what Harlow had overheard and what she'd seen in Pressley's safe, he wouldn't tell her mother that. Not without definite proof.

Grayson took a sip of coffee, then set it on the coffee table. "Mrs. Osorio—"

"Madeline, please. Do you know where my daughter is?"

"No, ma'am, but we're searching for her and hope you can give us some insight into her life before she went missing."

"Why are you searching for her?"

On their drive here, he and Cooper had discussed possible questions Mrs. Osorio might ask, and that had been one of them. They couldn't tell her about Harlow. For one thing, there was client privilege, but even if Harlow gave them permission to do so, he wouldn't. He didn't want her name floating around as a connection to Veronica.

"Her name came up in another investigation, but I'm sorry, I can't tell you the reason at this time. What I do want you to know is that we're very interested in finding your daughter. Look at it this way. You're getting a skilled team of investigators at no cost to you."

Tears welled in her eyes. "I tried to find her, even hired

a private investigator. About all he was good for was emptying out my small savings account. It was his opinion that she didn't want to be found. As if my girl would just disappear like that knowing what it would do to me. I told him she wouldn't do such a thing, but he thought he knew better."

"We're very sorry to hear that," Cooper said. "Would you be willing to give us his contact information?"

"Yes. And you can tell him that he won't get any references from me."

Grayson smiled. "We'd be happy to pass on that message." Along with a few choice words about taking a client's life savings and not delivering any results. "Did Veronica seem excited or depressed or different in some way before she went missing?"

"Honestly, I'm not sure. I was still living in Portugal at the time. My husband had recently died, and I was both grieving and trying to tie things up so I could move back here. Veronica was going to come and help me, and we were going to fly home together. She never showed up and stopped answering my calls. I knew something was wrong then."

"But not before that?"

"Ever since she's been missing, I've tried to recall anything that might give me a clue. My husband's family owned the house we lived in, along with resorts in Lisbon and Braga, and they're rich. Benedito loved me, and we were happy together, but his family never welcomed me because I'm American. They'd wanted him to marry a nice Portuguese girl. When he died, they were glad to see me leave. I'm telling you this because at the time, I was dealing with so much that it was hard to see past losing my beloved husband and my home. If only I'd paid more attention to Veronica."

He was disappointed that she wasn't going to be much help.

"She did buy the tickets for our flight home, and when I told her she didn't have to do that, that I had a little money saved, she said she had a big payday coming. Veronica was a Realtor, and I assumed she was expecting a good commission on something she'd sold."

They needed to talk to Veronica's employer to verify that. He doubted that was what Veronica was referring to. Based on the timeline, it fit with her expecting to get blackmail money from Pressley.

Cooper turned one of his I'm-your-friend smiles on Madeline. "Who did your daughter work for?"

They already knew that, but Cooper was easing her toward the more difficult questions. Grayson sat back and let Cooper charm the woman. He tuned them out for a few minutes while he thought about their next steps. The plan he'd decided on would be risky, but it was the best one he could think of to get close to Pressley.

"Was she seeing anyone?" Cooper asked.

The question caught his attention, and he turned back to the conversation.

Madeline nodded. "She was, but she never told me his name. She did say he was married but was getting a divorce. That was maybe four or five months before she went missing. I didn't like that she was seeing a man who was still married, even if he was getting a divorce, and I told her so. She didn't want to hear it."

It had to be Pressley she was referring to.

"In her diary, she refers to him as A."

"Diary?" Could they be so lucky as to have it all spelled

out in Veronica's own words? Maybe this wasn't a wasted trip after all.

"Yes. I had to sell her condo after she disappeared. I couldn't make the mortgage payments, and instead of letting the bank take it, I sold it. I didn't spend any of the money from the sale," she was quick to assure them. "It's all in a bank account waiting for her, and I put all her things except for the diary in storage."

He didn't like that she felt guilty for being forced to do something she didn't want to. "You did the right thing, Madeline. Veronica's lucky to have you looking out for her. Do you still have her diary?" He wanted his hands on it.

"Yes. Do you want to read it?"

Did he ever. "Do you have it here?"

"Yes, I'll get it."

When she disappeared down the hallway, he gave Cooper a thumbs-up. "We may have hit pay dirt."

"Let's hope."

"See if you can use that Cooper charm of yours to get her to let us borrow the diary."

Cooper grinned. "I'm on it."

Madeline returned a few minutes later, holding a dark red leather-bound journal. She sat back down and trailed her hand over the book, caressing it. She lifted her gaze to Grayson. "I'm going to let you read it in the hope that there's something in here that will help you find her."

Had she even considered that Veronica might no longer be of this earth? He took the journal when she handed it to him. He opened it and fanned the pages. It was filled in almost to the last page. It would take a while to read it all.

"Madeline," Cooper said, his voice gentle. "We're going to do everything possible to get you answers, and I hope you're right, that something in there will lead us in the right direction. Would you allow us to borrow it? You have our word that we'll return it to you. I'll give you my personal cell phone number, and you can call me at any time if you have questions, or even if you just need to talk."

"That's very kind of you." She shifted her gaze to the journal. "A part of me wants to not let it out of my sight. If she comes home before you return it, she'll be furious that I let you read it." Tears filled her eyes. "I'm trying not to let myself think it, but I'm not sure she's ever going to come back to me. I'm going to trust you boys and let you take it."

Cooper stood. "I think you need a hug. Come here." She didn't hesitate, and Cooper wrapped his arms around her. "Thank you for trusting us." He stepped back. "We'll have it back to you in a few days, I promise."

Only Cooper could walk into a stranger's house and have her accepting a comfort hug within an hour. After a few more questions, and after promising to keep Madeline informed as to what they learned, they took their leave.

"I hate that she hopes her daughter is alive and that we'll find her when it's likely that Veronica's dead," Cooper said as they drove away.

"I don't like it either." He needed to get in that safe. Then hopefully, Madeline would get closure. Although he'd read the diary from beginning to end when he got home, while Cooper drove them back to Myrtle Beach, Grayson skimmed through it.

The first half seemed to be Veronica writing about normal days, nothing about Pressley. She wrote about some dates she had with various men, nothing unusual for a young, single woman. If she was intimate with any of them, she didn't share that in her diary.

Around six months before she disappeared, things got interesting. "Listen to this. 'I met a man tonight at Corks and Cocktails, and there was an instant connection. We clicked in a way that's never happened with me before. A told me he wants to see me but that he's in the middle of a nasty divorce. He said his wife's a bitch and out to take everything he has so we have to keep our relationship a secret until the divorce is final.'"

"No doubt in my mind, A is for Anthony," Cooper said.

"Has to be." He skipped farther ahead. It burned that Pressley painted a false picture of Harlow. He read the page he'd stopped on. "Get this. Harlow and Veronica met."

"That had to be awkward."

"Not for Harlow. She didn't know who Veronica was." He read the page to Cooper. "'I met A's wife tonight at the Annual Christmas Ball. I saw her come in with A when they arrived, and she wasn't at all what I expected. She was dressed like some kind of cult member with her old-fashioned clothes, her hair in a bun and no makeup. Weird. Not at all the kind of woman A would choose.'"

"Why would she dress like that?"

"That's right, you never saw her when she first came to us for help. She was hiding herself, but that's neither here nor there right now. There's more. 'We found ourselves in the ladies' room at the same time. Of course, she didn't know who I was. She was really nice and kind of shy. She asked me if I was enjoying myself, and I wondered what she'd think if she knew A had arranged for me to get an invite to the ball. The plan for later was that he'd send her home with his driver, and he'd come home with me. For the first time since meeting A, I felt a little guilty. And what about her supposedly being a bitch? I just didn't see it.'"

Cooper shook his head. "The man's a real piece of work."

"Yes, he is. And he's going to get his due." He skimmed ahead some more, stopping when he came to a passage of

Veronica writing about having sex with Pressley. Grayson closed the book. He wasn't ready for that. Besides, he wanted to start from the beginning and read it through.

"You going to tell Harlow about the diary and what's in it?"

"I don't know." Did she need to hear the sordid details of her ex-husband's affair? Would she even want to?

They were a few miles from Grayson's house when Cooper's phone dinged. He darted a glance at the screen. "That's a man in Charlotte I have looking for George Pickens." He handed Grayson the phone. "Put it on speaker."

Grayson did, then held up the phone toward Cooper.

"Mike," Cooper said, "I'm with my partner Grayson Montana and you're on speaker. You got something for us on Pickens?"

"Yeah, and it's not what you're going to want to hear. He was killed three years ago."

"Damn," Grayson said. "The police know who did it?"

"No, the case has gone cold. He was shot at close range, and the police have the bullet, but no leads. They haven't been able to find anyone who held a grudge, and it doesn't appear to be a robbery as nothing was taken from his home. Not that he apparently had much to take."

Grayson would bet his beach home that he knew who killed a defenseless elderly man...or more like had him killed. He doubted Pressley did any of the dirty work himself.

*I'm coming for you, Anthony Pressley.*

Grayson set Veronica's diary on the kitchen island when he got home. Thinking he was going to need a stiff drink while he read it, he decided to check his emails and messages first. There were a few from his dealerships' general managers, and he dealt with those easily enough. Fortunately, his father had had good people in place, and Grayson rarely had to do much more than agree with the solutions they'd already come up with to any problems.

He deleted a few spam emails, then came to one from Harlow. When he saw what it was, he was impressed with how detailed it was. Everything he'd asked for was there: Pressley's normal routine, a list of the people close to him—including things she knew about them—a detailed layout of his house and the code to the safe. He'd call her tonight to thank her for doing such a great job.

Once the emails and messages were dealt with, he intended to get the diary and start on it, but the ocean caught his attention, and he veered to the glass doors. The waves were up today, and since it was too early to start drinking—which he intended to do when reading the journal—he went surfing instead.

Two hours later, he returned to the house, showered, then poured a half glass of whiskey. He'd only read a few pages when his phone alerted. The video from the Ring camera appeared on the screen, and his blood froze. Harlow opened her door and Pressley stood there. She said something as she tried to get around him. He grabbed her arm, pulling her into the apartment, slamming the door behind them. As he dragged her by the arm, they disappeared from view.

Why would she open the door to him? What had she said, and why had she tried to see around Pressley? They should have installed a camera that also recorded sound. Grayson called Cooper.

"I need you to go to Harlow ASAP. Pressley just pushed his way into her apartment."

"I'm on the way."

"How long?"

"Five minutes. Who should I be?"

Good question. "Play it by ear. I'm leaving now, but it'll take a good hour to get there." He would've sent Liam, too, but it was possible Pressley had seen him around the country club.

"I'll stay with her until you arrive."

Why in God's name had she opened the door to Pressley?

# Chapter 22

Oh, God. Anthony was going to rape her. Would have if not for Cooper showing up. Cooper held his hand out and she took it, letting him pull her up from the floor. She didn't resist when he tucked her next to him. Even though she was safe now, her body wouldn't stop trembling. The only thing keeping her on her feet was the support of his arm around her waist.

"You need to go," Cooper said to Anthony.

Anthony glared at him. "My wife and I were having a little disagreement that doesn't concern you."

"Sounded like more than a little one to me." Cooper lifted his brows as he glanced at her. "Didn't know you were married."

"I'm not." She willed her body to calm down, not to show Anthony how badly he'd unnerved her. She didn't want to, but she forced her eyes to meet his. "Unless you want me to call the police, you need to leave." She should call the police anyway, but what good would it do? Nothing would come of it other than making Anthony angrier.

"You need to listen to the lady and go," Cooper said.

"And you need to mind your own damn business. You don't want to be on my bad side."

Cooper laughed. "You're funny, dude."

Then at the blink of an eye, Cooper morphed into a man she would be afraid of if she didn't know him and know he was here for her.

His eyes went cold and deadly as he leaned toward Anthony. "I'm done with messing with you." He put his hand behind Anthony's neck, did something that brought a gurgling sound out of him and marched her ex out the door.

As soon as Anthony was in the hallway, Cooper closed and locked the door. "There." He grinned. "Took the trash out."

"Thank you." But now that Anthony was gone, how close she came to being raped hit her. She tried to hide her shaking hands, but apparently, Cooper was observant.

"Hey, you're safe now. You're lip's bleeding. What did he do to you?"

She shook her head. "I want Grayson." She could tell him what had almost happened.

"He's on the way. Why don't you sit. I'll stay until he gets here."

"Okay." She managed to walk to the sofa without deciding the floor was a good place to land. Again. "Thank you, Cooper. How did you know to come here?"

"Grayson called. He saw it on the Ring camera."

"I forgot about that. Well, thank you for putting that in. If you hadn't…" She couldn't go there. She'd never thought Anthony would physically hurt her, not the way he almost had. That he'd used their son to get her to open the door was despicable. She had to get Tyler away from him.

"Can I make you a cup of tea? Maybe you'd like something stronger?"

"Tea would be lovely. I can make it."

"I got it."

"Just fill a cup with water and stick it in the microwave

for two minutes. Tea bags are in the cabinet to the left of the sink. A chamomile would be nice."

His phone rang as he headed for the kitchen. He pulled it out of a pocket, looked at the screen, then returned to her. "It's Grayson. Why don't you talk to him while I make your tea."

She took the phone. "Grayson?"

"Hey. Are you okay?"

"Yes…no, not really. Cooper said you're on the way here?"

"I'm a half hour out. Pressley's gone?"

"Yes, thanks to Cooper. I…" She didn't know what she wanted to say. Only that she needed him.

"We'll talk when I get there."

"Okay." Just hearing his voice calmed her, and she didn't want to hang up. But she was being silly. Anthony was gone, and nothing had happened. Other than her ex-husband scaring her to death. Cooper brought her the cup of tea, and she handed him back his phone.

"Your lip's still bleeding." He held out a wet paper towel. "Gray's going to go ballistic if he sees blood on you."

Was it wrong to like the idea of Grayson going ballistic on her behalf? She took the wadded-up paper towel and put it on her lip. It was cold from the water and soothed the stinging from Anthony's bite.

Einstein peeked around the corner from the hallway. For once, he was silent. "Come here, sweet boy. The bad man's gone." Was he hurt? He studied Cooper for a moment and apparently decided he wasn't a bad man and ran to her.

"Last time I saw him, he was talking my ear off." Cooper settled in the chair across from her.

"He's confused. He's never met a bad man before." She

ran her hands over him, checking for any swelling. "Maybe I should take him to the vet."

"Did something happen to him?"

"He tried to be a hero and attacked Anthony. Anthony threw him against the wall."

"Just another reason your ex needs to be taught a lesson."

"One of many." Einstein hadn't flinched or made a sound when she'd pressed her fingers against him, and she hoped that meant he was okay. He made a tiny chirping noise, then curled up on her lap and went to sleep.

"Gray told me that you're designing us a new website. We need one. I slapped up something, but it's not great."

"It's not bad, but I can do better." It seemed as if he understood she needed a break from thinking about Anthony and what had almost happened. "Want to see what I have so far?"

"I'll wait until you're finished and be impressed all at once."

"Give me a few days, and I'll have it ready for you guys to see." There was something really sweet about Cooper, and she wondered if he had a wife or girlfriend. He wasn't wearing a wedding ring, but that didn't necessarily mean anything. He was going to be a great husband or boyfriend to some lucky woman.

A ding sounded from Cooper's watch, and he glanced at it. "Your man is here, so I'll take myself off."

"Thank you for—"

"No thanks necessary." He shook a finger at her. "No more opening your door to that scuzzbag."

"Good word for him."

"I have more, but they're not as nice as that one."

She chuckled, surprised that she could find something amusing after what had almost happened.

After looking through the peephole, Cooper opened the door. He and Grayson talked for a minute, their voices too low to hear. As he spoke with Cooper, his gaze slid to her, and he winked. And whoa, her stomach had more butterflies fluttering their wings than she had room for. Like thousands. Millions maybe.

She didn't know what to do with the happiness his being here gave her. Was it a good thing or not? But she needed to remember that being with him was only a temporary thing. That meant she had to guard her heart. Keep it tucked away where it wouldn't be vulnerable. Her time with Grayson was simply something she was selfishly taking for herself while she had the freedom to do so.

Cooper gave her a smile, and then left.

The door closed behind Cooper, and silence fell between her and Grayson as they stared at each other. Cooper must have told him what little he knew about Anthony being here. There was fury in Grayson's eyes, and if she were the enemy, she'd be looking for an escape exit because the man standing in her foyer looked lethal.

She should be afraid of a man who by all appearances would be deadly to anyone who got in his way, but she wasn't. Not at all. This man would offer his body to protect hers, and as cliché as it sounded, she knew in her heart that he would take a bullet for her. That truth hit her with a force that took her breath away. There had never been anyone in her life—including her mother, who'd often neglected the needs of her daughter to march for her latest cause—who made her feel as safe and secure as he did.

"Hey," he said as he came to her, his gaze never wavering from hers as the eyes that only seconds ago had been hard and filled with rage changed, the hardness in them turning soft, the cold in them turning warm.

She lifted Einstein and set him on the floor. She didn't want anything between her and Grayson. Of course, Einstein found his voice and let her know his feelings about being dumped, but whatever.

"Hi," she whispered when he stopped in front of her. When he dropped to a knee, she gasped. "Uh…" *He's not about to propose, silly girl.* Right, she wasn't going to have to refuse an offer of marriage. She was still unsettled by what had almost happened before Grayson arrived, and obviously, her brain wasn't working so great.

"Uh," she said again, proving that she really was a silly girl when Grayson was on a knee in front of her because out of nowhere, an image of him actually proposing flashed through her mind. That wasn't what unsettled her, it was hearing herself say yes that flustered her.

A grin lit his face. "Einstein steal your words?"

He had no clue.

# Chapter 23

Grayson's grin turned to a scowl when he saw the drop of blood on her mouth. He touched his finger to her swollen lip. "Did he do this?" She nodded, and he fiercely regretted that the man wasn't still here when he'd arrived. Although, it was probably for the best because he'd likely be in handcuffs and on his way to jail.

"He bit me," she said, her voice trembling.

Not wanting to scare her with his rage, he took a deep breath to calm down. "Why did you open the door to him?" That question had been bugging him. He moved to sit next to her and wrapped his hand around hers. "Start from the beginning and tell me everything."

"I had no intention of opening the door, but then I heard Tyler's voice, and when I looked through the peephole, there was my boy. Then I was angry that the woman I'd caught kissing Anthony was holding him. I didn't even think about it. Tyler was on the other side, and I had to get to him. But by the time I got the door opened, Tyler was gone. It was just Anthony in the hallway."

The bastard had used their son to trick her. What kind of man used his child like that?

"He wants me back because he's going to run for mayor, and I'm good for his image."

"Going to be hard for him to run for mayor from prison." The goal of this mission had started as a simple one. Help her get her son back. That goal had changed. Now he intended to see Pressley behind bars.

"All he had to do was agree to a reasonable custody arrangement, and I would have been happy."

"But he didn't, although in the end, he's going to wish he had. What happened after he got inside?" When she got to the part where Pressley was dragging her to her bedroom, intending to rape her, he shot up, unable to remain still. What if they hadn't installed the Ring camera? What if Cooper hadn't been close enough to arrive in time to stop Pressley's assault?

"Grayson?"

He stopped his pacing and faced her. "What?" After hearing her story, he wouldn't have cared if he'd landed in jail if it meant teaching that man a lesson for biting her, for throwing Einstein against the wall, and he could barely bring himself to think about her almost being raped.

"I'm okay."

Well, he wasn't. Not even close. He'd been on missions that had gone south in the worst of ways, and he'd kept his calm. He'd been shot at so many times he'd lost count, and he'd kept his calm. He'd sweated off pounds in desert temperatures that threatened to give him heatstroke, and he'd kept his calm. He'd barely avoided dying from hypothermia when the thermometer dropped below zero and his SEAL team was hunkered down in the middle of nowhere, and he'd kept his calm.

Yet, standing here in her living room where no one was shooting at him and there was no chance of the weather killing him, he was not calm. But he had to be…for her. He took a deep breath and crushed the rage burning inside him.

The plan was going to be set in motion this week if Cooper could get Pressley's driver onboard, and Grayson was counting on that happening. He returned to the sofa. Once he stepped into the role of driver, it would be risky for him to be seen coming or going to her apartment. He could have the rest of the day and tonight with her before he became Richie Kaplan, first cousin to Pressley's driver.

"Come here." He sat back and lifted her over his lap. The soft smile she gave him as she straddled his legs stirred something deep inside him.

She trailed her fingers over his cheek. "I've never seen you with scruff before. It's kind of sexy."

"Maybe I'll keep it, then." He preferred to be clean-shaven, but he was growing the beard to help disguise his face since Pressley's man had seen him.

"Can you stay awhile? Maybe take this to my bedroom?"

"Are you sure…after what just happened?" She was just attacked, her lip was cut, and the last thing he wanted was to take her to a place she wasn't ready for.

"I need you to hold me. I feel safe with you." She pressed her forehead against his. "Please."

There she went, taking another piece of his heart. He stood with her legs wrapped around his hips and carried her to the bedroom.

Einstein, chattering away like a magpie, was close on his heels, and Grayson kicked the door closed before he could follow them in. *Sorry, buddy, but you're not invited to this party.*

"Kitten, wake up." He chuckled when she buried her face in her pillow. They'd talked late into the night, shared childhood stories and played twenty questions. She'd had her first kiss at fifteen, her favorite color was yellow because it was cheerful, her favorite food was cheese and her dream was to take Tyler on a safari when he was older.

He'd answered the same questions, and she now knew more about him than any woman he'd ever been with. He couldn't explain why she was different or why the chemistry between them was off the charts. But the reason didn't matter.

In the early morning hours, they'd made love. Every minute spent with her, every touch, every word shared between them only reinforced the growing feeling that she could be *the one*. He hadn't been looking for her but now that he'd found her, he wanted to keep her.

He'd never been so motivated to successfully complete a mission, but he'd never had a reward as great as Harlow waiting at the finish line.

"Harlow." He leaned down and kissed her. "I need you to wake up."

"Hmm?" She blinked sleepy eyes at him. "What time is it?"

"Early. I need to go, but I want to talk to you a minute."

She pushed up and leaned back against the headboard, keeping the sheet pulled up over her chest. He wanted nothing more than to pull the sheet down and worship her body all day long.

Her gaze slid over him. "Why are you dressed?"

"Because I have to go." He'd considered not telling her what he had planned, but he didn't want any secrets between them. And she had a right to know. "Unless it's an emergency, I can't see you again until we have the proof of what Pressley did and he's in handcuffs."

"Oh. Okay. I guess you'll be too busy?"

The disappointment in her eyes twisted him up inside. "I'll never be too busy for you. What I'm going to tell you,

you can't repeat to anyone, not even Einstein because that boy can't keep a secret to save his life."

She chuckled, which was his goal. "True, but tell them what?"

"I'm going undercover, and we can't have your ex find out that there's any connection between us."

"Undercover? Like going to work for Anthony?"

"Yes."

"That's too dangerous, Grayson. If Anthony even suspects you of spying on him…" She shuddered.

"Hey, I'll be fine. I just need to know you're safe until this is over. Cooper and Liam will be watching over you, and you have their numbers. No matter how minor, if anything happens, you call one of them. Promise you will."

"I can't call you?"

"No. I can't take the chance of Pressley getting a hold of my personal phone, so I won't have it on me. I'll be using a burner that will be set up to look like my personal phone."

"This is all so—"

"James Bondish?"

"I was going for *scary*. Don't ask me not to worry about you, because that I can't promise."

"Everything's going to be fine." He glanced out the window. The sky was turning gray, and the sun would be up soon. "I need to go."

"Please, be careful."

"I always am. Come here." He held out his arms. "I need a kiss to hold me over until I see you again." She leaned toward him, and he cradled her cheeks with his hands and lowered his mouth to hers, careful to gently kiss her because of her sore lip. She sighed against his mouth, and he was tempted to crawl back into bed with her, but he had a long list of things to do to put the operation in motion.

When he finally broke away, they were both breathing hard. He smiled as he brushed his thumb over her bottom lip, damp from their kiss. "I love this look on you. Your sultry eyes and flushed cheeks."

"Sultry, huh?"

"Oh, yeah." He gave her a quick kiss before standing. "Take care, kitten."

"Bye." She waved her fingers at him.

He forced a smile he didn't feel as he walked away from her. In the back of his mind lived a fear that once this was over and her son returned to her, she wouldn't want him back in her life. But from this point on, he had to stay focused on the mission, so he slammed a door on that fear.

Outside her apartment, he blended into the shadows. He'd texted Liam when getting dressed, telling him to come and scout the parking lot to make sure Pressley or one of his minions wasn't hanging around. That he had to be so secretive at seeing her chafed. She was a single woman, entitled to have him spend the night with her if that was what she wanted.

Liam texted back as Grayson stepped outside. All clear.

He typed another message. Meet me at that diner outside of town. Mel's?

Yep. See ya there.

Next, he texted Cooper to meet them at the diner. Liam was already seated at a booth in the back when Grayson arrived. "Cooper will be here in a few."

"I guess we're getting close to go time?"

"Hopefully this week. It all depends on Pressley's driver and if he's bribable."

"Since he works for a man like Pressley, I'd say it's a good chance he is."

"Let's hope." Plan B was to break into Pressley's house, but he wasn't keen on doing that. It was too risky.

The server, a woman who looked to be in her sixties, came to their table. "Morning, boys. I'm Ria. What can I get y'all?"

"There's one more joining us in a few," Grayson said. "We'll start with coffee and order when our friend arrives."

"You got it, sugar." She left them with menus and returned a minute later with a coffeepot.

Cooper arrived as Ria was filling the cups, and he slid into the booth next to Liam. He flashed her a smile. "Morning..." His gaze landed on her name tag. "Ria. How are you this fine day?"

Ria seemed startled for a moment, then an ear-to-ear smile appeared. "Much better now that you handsome boys showed up."

She probably didn't get asked often how she was, and not for the first time, Grayson was amused by how Cooper could draw out a smile from anyone...man, woman or child.

"Y'all ready to order?" she said once their coffee cups were filled.

After they ordered and were alone, Grayson said, "Considering what Pressley pulled yesterday and what he would have done if you—" he glanced at Cooper "—hadn't arrived in time to stop him, it's go time. You need to get his driver onboard."

"I did a deep dive into him, and he's got a sick wife and some big medical bills. Not that I wish anyone to be sick, but that should work in our favor," Cooper said. "How much are we going to offer him to disappear for a week or so?"

"Whatever it takes." And he meant that literally. He'd

pay however much it took to make sure Harlow was safe. "Let's start with a hundred thou, see if he bites."

Cooper's eyes widened as he sat back in the booth. "I doubt it will take that much. I was thinking ten or twenty thousand."

"I don't want to get in a drawn-out negotiation over his price. If he accepts the offer, he'll feel more indebted than he would the lesser amount. Less likely to betray us. Besides, he's going to be out of a job when we take down Pressley, and with a sick wife, I'd feel better if he had some money in the bank." He'd barely notice the trifling dent in his bank account.

"And if the hundred's not enough?"

"Everyone has a price. Find out what his is and agree to it."

Ria returned with plates stacked up her arms, and as she sorted them out, Cooper chatted with her. By the time they each had the right breakfast, he'd learned that Ria's husband was a long-haul truck driver, and that they had seven grown children and fifteen grandchildren.

Liam laughed as he bumped Cooper's shoulder after Ria left. "Man, you can charm the birds out of the trees. I need to take lessons. That skill could come in handy with the ladies."

"Like you have a problem charming ladies," Grayson said. "You do that Irish accent, and a woman goes all soft and buttery." It was true. Liam didn't normally speak with an accent, but he had a perfect one that Grayson had witnessed him do on more than one occasion. Women loved it.

"Buttery?" Liam rolled his eyes. "I don't even know what that means."

Cooper pointed his fork at Liam. "It means when you go all Irish on a woman, she melts into a puddle at your feet."

"Aye, sure, 'tis a grand gift, it is."

Ria walked up with a coffeepot just as Liam spoke, and her gaze locked on him. "Sugar, I'll leave my husband if you promise to talk like that to me."

Liam winked at her. "Well, now, Ria, luv, ye know I can't go breakin' up a happy home. But I'll be happy to bless yer ears with me Irish charm anytime ye fancy."

"Buttery," Cooper muttered.

Grayson chuckled as he scooped up a forkful of hash browns. After Ria snapped out of her Liam trance and refilled their coffee cups, she left to refresh another customer's coffee. "I have things to do today, so let's get back to business. Coop, I'm counting on you to get Pressley's driver onboard. I want to take his place ASAP."

"I'll do my best."

"Also, can you pay a visit to Veronica's real estate office sometime today? See if there's anything to learn? Specifically, I'd like to know if anyone there knew she was seeing Pressley."

"Can do."

"Want to know about my date with Alisha Austin?" Liam said.

"She have anything useful to say about Pressley?"

"Nothing big, but she didn't hesitate to badmouth him. He told her he loved her and made her all kinds of promises. By the time his divorce was final, he'd lost interest in her and moved on to his next conquest. She did find out later that he was seeing Veronica at the same time as her. She's really pissed about that."

"Can't say I blame her." Grayson pushed his empty plate aside. "Anything else?"

"Only that when she heard Veronica was missing, she immediately thought that Pressley had something to do with that. She told me about several times he got physical with her. Nothing serious, just yelled at her or grabbed her arm when she displeased him, and once, he pushed her."

"Basically, she confirmed what we already know." He grabbed the bill Ria left on the table, glanced at it, then pulled a hundred-dollar bill out of his wallet. "Tell Ria we don't need change," he said, sliding it across the table. "I've got a PI to see this morning." The man wasn't going to enjoy his visit.

# *Chapter 24*

Harlow slept a few more hours after Grayson left. When she did drag herself out of bed, she padded to the kitchen for a much-needed cup of coffee. As soon as he realized where she was going, Einstein spoke to her in his I'm-dying-of-hunger-here-so-feed-me-right-now voice.

"Patience, buddy." She felt off this morning. Tired from being up half the night making love with Grayson, yes, but that wasn't it. She kept hearing Tyler say "Mama" in her mind. It was the only word she'd heard him speak since she moved out of Anthony's house, and her heart was breaking. "I miss him so much," she told Einstein.

Tears burned her eyes. No, she wasn't going to fall apart. She had work to do, and she had to get ready for Lena's visit. She didn't want to spoil her time with Lena by being depressed, so she needed to find her cheer.

Although she did have work she needed to accomplish today, she decided to plan the meals for when Lena was here. Meal planning and cooking was something she enjoyed. Anthony had a chef, so she'd never been allowed in the kitchen, and now, she only cooked for herself. Not much fun in that.

Since Lena and she had been friends forever, Harlow knew what she liked and didn't like. It didn't take long to plan a menu, and after dressing, she grabbed her purse and car keys. Her mood was improving, thankfully. As she reached to open the door, she stilled. What if Anthony was out there? She stuck her eye to the peephole. He wasn't in the hallway. Okay, it was safe. But what if he was in the parking lot? She fished in her purse for her phone and set it ready to record.

She wouldn't at all have been surprised to see Anthony waiting to accost her, but she was surprised when she reached the sidewalk to see his father walking toward her. She almost turned around and raced back to the safety of her apartment. Arthur had always intimidated her, and he was the last person in the world she wanted to see. But no, she wasn't going to give him the satisfaction of cowering. Keeping her gaze on her car, she hit Record on the phone.

When she attempted to walk past him, he stepped in front of her, forcing her to stop. There had been a time when he had as much control over her as Anthony, but that time was no more.

"I have nothing to say to you, Arthur. Good day." She moved to her left to walk around him.

He blocked her again. "Well, I have much to say to you. Why don't we go up to your apartment so we can talk?"

"No." Like hell she'd invite him into her home.

"Fine, we'll just have our chat here for the world to see."

She laughed, which by the thinning of his lips he didn't appreciate. "The world is not watching you and I, so get over yourself. Again, good day." And again, he kept her from walking around him.

"It's time for you to do your duty as a wife and mother, Harlow. You need to return home. Anthony needs you."

"Wow, one would think you and your son are living in the Middle Ages where men wrongfully had the power to tell women what to do." She leaned her face close to his. "Well, screw you. I'm never returning to your son and that house of misery. And I'm not ever going to stand by Anthony's side and smile and talk about what a great mayor he'll make. Like I could even say that with a straight face."

"You will if you ever want to see that kid again." He smirked. "I can make your life miserable, dear, but I'd prefer to see you back where you belong. You know I don't have much patience, so don't take too long to decide." He marched back to his car.

*That kid?* That kid was his grandson, but like Anthony, Arthur had no use for Tyler…at least until he was old enough to be useful. Arthur's threat had the opposite effect than what he'd intended. All he'd done was fuel her determination to get the Pressley men out of her and Tyler's life.

She dropped the phone into her purse, and refusing to let Arthur spoil her day, she headed to the grocery store where she'd have fun buying the meals she'd planned. She hadn't entertained since she'd moved into her apartment, and she was excited. Yes, she was.

The rest of her day was productive, and later that night, as she mindlessly flipped through TV channels from the comfort of her bed, her thoughts turned to Grayson. She wanted to tell him about Arthur showing up, and she should probably tell him Lena was coming for a visit. Something she'd forgotten to do last night. He'd said he wouldn't have his personal phone with him. She could leave a message, though.

She called on the burner, and as expected, the call went to his voice mail. After leaving a message, asking him to call if he got a chance, she returned to channel surfing. A while later, she startled when the burner phone chimed.

"Hello," she said, expecting it to be Cooper or Liam.

"Sorry I missed your call. I was in the shower."

Oh, it was Grayson. And he was in the shower? Her mind visualized his hair damp, drops of water lazily making their way down his chest and him wearing nothing but a towel around his waist. Wow! That was a pretty picture.

"Harlow?"

"Hmm?"

"I asked if you're okay."

"You did? I mean, I'm fine. Well, except for Arthur showing up. That's why I called. I thought you should know about that."

"What did he want?"

Boy, his voice had just gone hard and cold. "To tell me I needed go back to Anthony or else. I'll send you the recording."

"Do that now."

"Hold on a sec." She managed to send it to him without disconnecting their call. "On the way to you."

"Your turn to hold on while I listen to it."

"Okay." While she waited, she imagined him using that commanding voice on her in the bedroom, and she fanned her face. He wasn't even in the same room with her, and he was heating things up.

"He definitely threatened you," he said, coming back on the line. "I want you to be very careful. If that happens again, you can't call me after tonight, but do call Liam or Cooper."

"I didn't mean to bother you. I just thought you'd want to know about Arthur."

"Definitely, and you're never a bother. I didn't tell you this morning, but last night was special. I want you to know that."

"It was special for me, too."

"As soon as this is over, I'd like to take you out on a date."

"We'll see." It hurt to think about never seeing him again, but it had to be. Tyler had to be her sole focus.

"Oh, we'll definitely see. Be careful and aware of your surroundings, okay?"

"I will. Oh, and before you go, I also wanted to tell you that a girlfriend is coming for a visit."

"Are you sure that's a good idea right now?"

"Yes, I haven't seen her for a long time because Anthony isolated me from all my friends. I'm excited to finally be able to see her again, Grayson, and she knows what's going on. She's only going to be here for two days, and we're not leaving the apartment."

"Just be careful, okay?"

"I will. I promise. That goes for you, too."

He'd sounded confident that their date would happen, and she wished he was right. He wasn't, though, and sadness washed over her. Was she going to walk away from the best man she'd ever met?

Tyler needed her, but what about her own happiness?

# Chapter 25

Grayson ended his conference call with Liam and Cooper. He'd called them first thing the next morning to tell them about Arthur threatening Harlow and to keep a close eye on her while he was undercover. The good news, Pressley's driver hadn't hesitated to take the money Cooper had offered. Turned out he hated Pressley and would've quit if his wife hadn't been sick, and he needed the job.

Tomorrow morning, Benny Kaplan would introduce Grayson as his cousin to Pressley. The success of the mission depended on Pressley accepting Grayson as a temporary stand-in for Benny.

Because Don Delgado, Pressley's man, had seen him with Harlow at the diner, a change in appearance was in order. To prepare for that, he'd been growing the beard from the time he'd come up with the plan to get close to Pressley. But that wasn't enough, so after getting off the phone with his teammates, he went to the bathroom.

"Here goes nothing," he said to his reflection, taking a moment to appreciate having hair. It only took a few minutes to shave his head, and he was pleased with how much different he looked as a bald man with a beard. He picked up the black-rimmed eyeglasses with clear glass for lenses and slipped them on. "Perfect." Delgado would never recognize him as the man with Harlow.

He removed the glasses and slid them back into the case. After one more glance in the mirror at the man he didn't recognize anymore, he went shopping. His clothes were more expensive than what a stand-in driver in need of a job would wear, so a shopping trip was necessary. Goodwill was his store of choice for what he needed. An hour later, he was back home with pants and button-down shirts that were in surprisingly good condition but were obviously not new or expensive. Tonight, he'd move into the pay-by-the-week apartment Liam had found with the promise that it wasn't a roach-infested dive.

That done, he opened the weapons safe in his closet. Two guns, three sets of comms and his favorite knife went into a canvas tote. He grabbed the envelope that had a burner phone and his fake ID and added them to the tote. The laptop he'd set up to have a history of porn and sports programs viewed went in the bag. If Pressley got nosy and sent someone to snoop in the apartment Grayson was renting, all they'd find was a single guy who liked to watch porn and sports. He took his weapons bag and a small suitcase downstairs and set them next to the door.

His stomach growled with hunger, so he made a sandwich, grabbed a beer and Veronica's diary, taking everything out to the deck. While he ate his lunch, he watched the people enjoying a beautiful day at the beach. The waves weren't up, or he'd be out there on his surfboard. His thoughts turned to his visit to Madeline Osorio's PI yesterday. He'd gone there before returning home from his night with Harlow.

Monty Hightower had no business being a PI. Young and inexperienced, a wannabe cop who'd failed both the physical and the written exam, so he decided that being a PI would be fun. When Grayson asked to see his license, he first claimed he didn't have it on him. Since Grayson already knew he didn't have one, he gave Hightower a choice. Return Mrs. Osorio's money or Grayson would report him for practicing without a license. Hightower was sweating by the time Grayson finished with him, and he promised he would refund the money. Grayson was going to report him anyway as soon as Madeline had her money back. It had been a satisfying visit.

Finished with his lunch, he opened Veronica's diary. He'd planned to read it yesterday, but then Pressley had attacked Harlow, and she'd needed him... Fine, he'd admit it, he'd needed to go to her. He started reading from the beginning. It wasn't until the last thirty or so pages that Pressley entered the picture. For most of those entries, Veronica gushed over him. He was so handsome. He was so generous. He was a stud in bed. He was a long list of perfect in her mind. They were going to have a future together as soon as he divorced his wife. Then the tone changed.

At first, it was subtle. He canceled a date. He said he'd call her, then didn't. He came over one night but was irritable. He snapped at her for no reason. And so on. His shine was fading in her eyes. It reached a point where Veronica grew suspicious, doubting anything he said to her. Then she overheard a damning conversation. Grayson reread the passage.

*I overheard a conversation between Anthony and Don Delgado. We were at Anthony's house, the first time I've been there. His wife finally moved out, so he brought me home with him. All I could think was that someday soon I'd get to live here. My God, his house is awesome. I could so see myself as the hostess for the parties we'd have.*

*Then Don arrived and he and Anthony went to Anthony's office. What is it they say? Curiosity killed the cat? They'd both seemed tense, so curious me eased down the hall. The door wasn't fully closed, and I could hear them talking.*

*I think Anthony stole some people's homes. Don told Anthony he didn't have to worry about Pickens, whoever that is. The other one's name is Etta something. Apparently, she's been complaining for a few years now to anyone who'd listen that the tax office cheated her out of her home. Don's afraid she's going to find someone who'll believe her, and he wants to scare her into shutting up, but Anthony said no one listens to a crazy old woman.*

*Anthony has to be behind this, otherwise why would Don be worried and talking to Anthony about it? I don't know. Maybe my imagination's working overtime. Anthony wouldn't steal someone home, would he?*

"Yes, he would," Grayson said. It was good evidence that both Pickens's and Miss Etta's names were included in the journal. The next few entries were back to her talking about Pressley and how much she loved him and looked forward to a future with him. She'd apparently decided that it was her imagination and had dismissed what she'd overheard. A few weeks passed, and he skimmed over the pages detailing their dates and sex life. Then…

*Anthony broke up with me tonight. Who does he think he is? He made promises, told me he loved me, said we'd be married as soon as his divorce was final. If he thinks I'll go away quietly, he's in for a surprise.*

If only she had gone away quietly, she wouldn't be missing, and a stranger wouldn't be reading her diary. There was a five-day gap between that entry and the next one.

*Anthony refuses to see me, and I'm so angry. He used me then threw me away. Well, that doesn't work for me.*

*I wrote him a letter telling him I knew what he'd done to
that poor Etta woman and the Pickens man, and unless he
wanted me to tell the police, he'd pay me a million dollars.
He owes me that for being a lying, cheating bastard. Yeah,
I found out he cheated on me and he needs to pay.*

Grayson took a break from reading for a few minutes and
let the view of the ocean and the sound of the waves hitting
shore ease his mind from thoughts of a woman scorned who
he was 99 percent sure was dead. So foolish to think that a
man like Pressley would just shrug and hand over a million
dollars. He shook his head as he picked up the diary again.
The next entry skipped ahead by three days.

*Anthony called. He said he'd pay me half what I asked
for, and I could take it or leave it. He wanted to make sure
that I understood I'd never get another cent out of him. I
could push for the full million, but honestly, I just want to
be done with him. Even if he wanted me back now, I'm not
interested. I'm so over him.*

*I'm meeting him at midnight behind the bowling alley.
I asked him why he couldn't just mail me a check, and he
laughed. "Are you really that stupid?" he said. "You think
I'll agree to having a paper trail that I paid you off?"*

*Guess he has a point. The thing is, Anthony scares me
now. His voice was so mean and cold, not that of the Anthony who'd wooed me into his bed. There's a voice in my
head saying I shouldn't go. That it's a very bad idea. But I
want my money, so I'm going. I'll just be alert and careful.*

That was it, her last entry. Grayson closed the journal.
Foolish, foolish woman. He called Cooper.

"Yo," Cooper said on answering.

"Did you go by Veronica's real estate office?"

"Just left there and was about to call you. Veronica
wasn't working on a big deal before she disappeared. No

one there really knows anything about why she went missing. One woman who was apparently a work friend said that Veronica had a secret boyfriend, and she thinks they ran away together. I asked her why she thinks that, and she said because Veronica had told her the boyfriend was married but his wife wouldn't give him a divorce, so they went to Canada."

"Canada?"

"Yeah, I asked that, too, and she said that was where she'd go if she ever ran away. Basically, not much help. None of them have entertained the thought that Veronica's dead."

"I didn't expect they'd know much, but it was worth a try. I finished reading Veronica's diary. She did try to blackmail him. He told her to meet him behind the bowling alley at midnight and he'd give her the money."

"And she didn't think that was a bad idea?"

"She did think it was but went anyway. I need you to see if there are any cameras in that area." He gave Cooper the date recorded in the diary of the meet. "I'm guessing Pressley would make sure there weren't any when he picked the location, but maybe we'll get lucky."

"We can hope, but most companies don't save their recordings that long. Anything else?"

"Not right now. I'm about to head to Faberville."

"What if that dude who saw you at the diner recognizes you?"

"Stand by a sec." He jogged inside, put on the fake eyeglasses, took a selfie and sent it to Cooper.

"Who's that?"

Grayson laughed. "You don't recognize him?"

"Should I? Wait, is that you?"

"Yep."

"I would've walked right by you on the street."

"That was the goal. I'm heading to the dealership shortly to pick up a used car. We still on tonight?" Cooper was bringing Pressley's driver by to go over the plan.

"We'll be at your new digs around nine."

"Great. See you then."

The apartment was better than Grayson expected. It was small and had the barest of furniture: a worn leather sofa, a small dining table with two chairs and a full-size bed. He was going to miss his king, and he should have thought to bring his pillow. The two on the bed weren't going to cut it. And sheets. He was not going to sleep on a bare mattress.

He dropped the bag with his clothes and toiletries on the bed, then slid the bag with his weapons deep underneath. A trip to find sheets and decent pillows was in order. Also, he'd swing by the grocery store… Was there a coffee maker in the kitchen? He checked, and no, there wasn't. Nor were there any dishes or silverware. And he needed a towel. If he left now, he'd have time to get the things he needed and be back before his meeting at nine.

Although he was tempted to stop by Harlow's and show her his new appearance, it wasn't a good idea. If he went to her apartment, he'd want to stay.

# Chapter 26

Harlow needed to make one more trip to the grocery store before Lena arrived tomorrow, but she didn't want to risk another confrontation with Anthony or Arthur when she was alone, so she called for an Uber. It was a relief that neither Anthony nor Arthur was waiting to accost her.

She wouldn't be long and asked the driver to wait. Since she didn't need to get much, she grabbed a small cart. Fruit, tomatoes and romaine lettuce were first on her list, so she steered the cart to the produce department. Fresh bread was next, and she added a loaf of French and one of sourdough to the cart. Last was the makings for sundaes. She'd already bought the ice cream but thought it would be fun to make sundaes.

As she pushed the cart around the corner to the chocolate syrup aisle, she collided with another cart. "Oh, I'm sorry. I wasn't loo…" She blinked at the man standing in front of her. He was Grayson but he wasn't Grayson. The man's head was shaved, and he wore glasses, but she'd know those eyes and that body anywhere. "Gra—"

He shook his head. "No problem, pretty lady. I wasn't watching where I was going either." He pushed the cart around hers, and as he passed by her, he winked.

It took every bit of her control not to turn around and

stare at him. Two aisles later, they passed each other again, and all she wanted to do was stand there and let her eyes soak up this new bad-boy-looking Grayson. There was an edge to him now that sent a delicious shiver down her spine. Lust pure and simple sent heat spiraling through her. As if he could read her mind, one side of his mouth quirked up, and she felt her cheeks blushing.

"I'll come to you late tonight," he whispered without looking at her. "Now go."

Flustered, she snatched the closest thing to her and dropped it in her cart. As she headed for the chocolate syrup, she glanced down and saw that she'd grabbed a package of birthday cake sparklers. She laughed. Well, she was feeling rather sparkly after seeing the new Grayson. When she reached the front of the store to check out, Grayson was gone.

Back home, she put her groceries away while having a chat with Einstein. "Yes, I bought you something, so cool your jets for a sec." She always brought him a treat or a toy when she shopped. He knew where she'd been because of the groceries she was putting away, and he didn't appreciate not getting it immediately.

Tonight, she'd chosen a fuzzy ball. He loved batting those all over the apartment, but they kept disappearing after he played with them for a day or two. When she eventually moved, she'd probably find his secret stash of toys behind her dresser. She found the ball and as soon as he saw it, he chirped and made circles around her legs.

"Ready?" She laughed when he ran toward the living room, prepared to catch the ball he knew she was going to throw. "Catch." She threw the ball across the room, and he leaped into the air, his body twisting effortlessly to snatch it midflight. A triumphant meow echoed through the apart-

ment, making her smile. As she knew he would, he pranced
back to her and dropped the ball at her feet. He stared up
at her and told her to throw it again.

Was it weird that she could talk cat? Did that mean she
was bilingual? She was being silly, but that was what happened when one had no one to talk to but a cat. Although, he
was an intelligent and talkative feline. She played toss the
ball for a while until he tired of the game and disappeared
with his new toy, the ball probably never to be seen again.

Not sure what time Grayson would make an appearance,
she showered, shaved and lotioned up. She wasn't going to
assume that he'd stay or that they'd make love, so she put
on shorts and a T-shirt instead of something sexy.

After she finished designing the website for The Phoenix
Three, and she'd caught up with her other work, she poured
a glass of wine. She took that and her Kindle to the sofa.

After rereading the same page for five minutes, she gave
up and set her Kindle on the coffee table. Turned out it was
impossible to concentrate on a book when one's mind was
filled with the sexy man who could appear at any moment.
Would he enter through the front door, or would he shimmy
up a rope again like a ninja and just magically appear?

She sipped on her wine while she thought about Grayson and how much she'd changed since meeting him. In all
the best ways. Would those changes have happened if she
hadn't met him? She'd like to believe she'd eventually get
her act together and find herself again.

It just happened faster after meeting Grayson. It started
with that one little change in her clothes, wearing the black
pants and white blouse the second time she saw him. How
she'd looked in the mirror and cringed, wondering what he
must have thought of her at their first meeting.

For being the catalyst in speeding up her need to find

herself again, she'd always be grateful to him. For making her feel like a desirable woman again, she'd forever hold a piece of him in her heart. For returning her son to her when that happened, she'd be indebted to him for the rest of her life.

If she let herself, she could fall in love with him. But she just couldn't allow that to happen. Her little man would need all of her when he came back to her.

"And that's that." No falling in love, no wishing for a future with Grayson, no daydreaming of what could be.

Einstein raced into the living room and jumped on her lap. "Meeeeeow!"

"Where's your ball?"

In the middle of his discourse that it was none of her business where his ball was, there was a soft tap on her door. Einstein cut off his conversation in the middle of a sentence and raced for the door.

She followed close behind and put her eye to the peephole to make sure it was Grayson. It was, and she let him in. His appearance still surprised her, and she stared at him. Just wow! Put him in leathers and on a Harley, and he would be an antihero right out of a romance book. She liked both versions of him. A lot.

"Hey." He wrapped his hand around her neck and brought her mouth to his.

*Oh.* Not the greeting she expected as soon as he walked inside. Not that she was complaining. Time seemed to stand still as he took possession of her mouth, his kiss so demanding and consuming that it ignited a fire inside her.

When he took his mouth away from hers, he rested his forehead against hers. "As much as I want to, I can't stay."

Lord, the man could kiss. "You want a beer or something?" She'd bought a six-pack of the beer she'd seen him drink at his house, and what did that say about her that she was stocking his preferred beer? Nothing. It said nothing. Her heart was in the condition she'd willed it and was not falling for him.

"No, I really need to go. I shouldn't be here at all. As much as I wish otherwise. But I just needed to see you for a few minutes, to get a kiss for good luck. I made sure no one was watching your place before I came up, and Liam's keeping watch to make sure it stays that way while I'm up here." He brushed his fingers over her cheek. "I'm sorry I was rude to you in the grocery store."

"You weren't rude. And honestly, I'm glad I got to see this new you. Pretty hot if you want my opinion."

"Yeah?" He grinned as he slid his hand over his head. "Feels strange. Tomorrow, Pressley's driver is going to tell your ex that he has to go away for a short while and that his cousin…that would be me, is going to step in while he's gone. I really won't be able to come to you again."

She shook her head. "Grayson, that's too dangerous."

"I love that you're worried about me, but I know what I'm doing. I need to get in that safe, and getting close to Pressley is the best way. I don't want you to worry, okay?"

"That's like telling the sun not to rise tomorrow."

"Okay, worry a little but not too much. How's that?"

"I'll try. My friend will be here tomorrow for two days, and I guess she'll help keep my mind off worrying about you."

"I'm glad you'll have someone with you, but again, please be careful. I'll try to call you every few days. If you don't hear from me, don't fear. If…and it's a big *if*, something does happen, Liam or Cooper will be in touch with you."

"Please stay safe."

"Always. Now for that good-luck kiss." He cradled her face with his hands and pressed his lips gently against hers. When he stepped back, he said, "I'll be looking forward to doing that again soon. You stay safe, too. Don't let either of the Pressley men catch you alone."

"I'll be careful."

Einstein rubbed against his legs, demanding attention.

"What's that?" Grayson said, bending over to scratch Einstein's ears. "She won't give you any tuna?"

Einstein gave a lengthy answer.

"Well, I wouldn't put up with that if I were you." He chuckled as he glanced up at her and winked. "You need to be nicer to my buddy here."

"Don't believe a word he says. He's a little liar. He gets plenty of tuna." She loved that Grayson had a great sense of fun. Anthony would have never talked to her cat. Actually, he would have never allowed her to have a cat.

Einstein raced down the hall, and before Grayson could leave, her cat returned with his ball and dropped it at Grayson's feet.

"He wants to play fetch with you."

"Does he think he's a dog?" He picked up the ball and threw it, then laughed when Einstein returned with it, dropping it at his feet. "I guess he does." He threw the ball a few more times before giving her one last kiss. With one last lingering look, he walked out the door, closing it behind him.

She leaned her forehead against the door as a sense of unease crept over her. No, she had to have faith in him. He was trained to deal with men more dangerous than Anthony could ever hope to be, and he had Liam and Cooper watching out for him.

"Maughp," Einstein said as he stared at the door.

"I didn't want him to go, either," she said. "He promised that he's going to be okay. We're going to believe that."

# Chapter 27

"Just be yourself and remember that you're telling the truth," Grayson told Benny Kaplan. He'd suggested last night when they'd talked that Benny get an appointment at the Mayo Clinic for his wife. Benny had called them this morning and was given a consultation appointment in five weeks. It wouldn't be a lie that he was taking his wife to the clinic, it just wasn't this week.

"I got this, boss."

Benny had started calling him boss as soon as Cooper had introduced them. The man wasn't anything like what Grayson had expected. He'd visualized someone who was a lesser version of Anthony Pressley, a little arrogant and sleazy, but he was nothing like that. Probably in his forties, he was thin and on the short side with dark brown hair cut short and a craggy face. The feature that Grayson found the most interesting was his kind brown eyes. There was sadness in them, though, and Grayson attributed that to his worry over his wife. Grayson hadn't expected to like the man, but he did.

"Do you like working for Pressley?" he asked as Benny pulled to a stop in the circular driveway of a house in a gated neighborhood of million-dollar homes. Houses that exuded a sense of opulence and grandeur.

"I'll be honest, boss. I thought I'd won the lottery when I first landed this job. Mr. Pressley pays me good money. It wasn't until I'd worked for him a while that I realized he was really paying me to keep my mouth shut. Lately though, I feel like I'm dancing on the edge of a knife. Like if I make one wrong move, I won't like the consequences. Things are getting weird with these people. I'd quit, but I need the money more than ever now."

He couldn't tell Benny that there wasn't going to be a job waiting for him to return to. He'd have to help the man find something else. When this was over, he'd tell the FBI that they needed to talk to Benny. He was probably a font of information on the family.

As much as Grayson would love to interrogate him now, he didn't want Benny to start asking questions. The offer of a hundred thousand to let Grayson take his place for a week came with a don't-ask-why rule. If Benny's wife hadn't been sick, he wasn't sure the man would have jumped on the offer. Benny seemed to have integrity, another reason Grayson liked him.

"I called Mr. Pressley's secretary this morning and told her I needed a few minutes of his time, so he's expecting me." Benny pushed the doorbell.

"Come in, Benny," a voice said through the Ring camera.

Grayson followed Benny down a hallway, their shoes clicking on the brilliantly white marble floor. He cataloged the layout and the rooms they passed. Heavy furniture filled the living room. Gold and royal blue brocade upholstery, floor-to-ceiling thick gold drapes and a baby grand piano all shouted "Look at me, I'm somebody important."

He'd have to ask Harlow who played. When he tried to imagine her living in this house… Well, he just couldn't.

Nothing about it was her. They came to a closed mahogany door, and Benny knocked once.

"Enter."

Grayson braced himself for his first meeting with the man he was going to destroy. He had to get this right and not give Pressley any reason to be suspicious. The walls of the study were rich mahogany like the door, and shelves lined two of the walls with leather-bound books. Most likely just for show and never read. A massive desk sat at the center, meticulously organized, as if every item had its designated place, and behind it sat Pressley.

From the photos he'd studied of the man, Grayson already knew what he'd look like. In person, though, he was… *Slick* was the word that came to mind. His black hair was combed straight back with product to keep it perfectly styled. He was clean-shaven and his almost black eyes held no trace of warmth or emotion. He exuded an air of confidence and arrogance. From Harlow, he knew this was a man used to getting what he wanted, no matter the cost.

Pressley's gaze shot past Benny to Grayson, and his eyes narrowed. "Who's this, Benny?"

Benny came to a stop in front of the desk. "My cousin, Richie Kaplan. Richie, this is Mr. Pressley."

"Sir," was all Grayson said, instinctively knowing Pressley wouldn't want niceties from him. He also avoided direct eye contact with the man, taking on a subservient persona.

"And he's here because?"

"You know my Anna's got cancer. It's bad, sir. I've been trying to get her an appointment at the Mayo Clinic. They have mighty good cancer doctors there, but they got a long wait. Well, last night, they called. A time unexpectedly opened up, but it's for tomorrow. I have to take her, Mr. Pressley. It might be her only chance." He glanced at Grayson. "Richie here, he's going to take my place for a few days while I'm gone."

"You don't think you should have asked me before you agreed to the appointment?"

What a dick. Grayson bit down on his cheek to keep from saying that out loud.

"No, Mr. Pressley, I did not. They had to have an answer right then, else they were gonna go to the next person on their wait list. I hope you can understand I have to do what's best for my Anna. I value my job, sir, and I don't want to lose it. That's why I'm making sure you won't be inconvenienced by my absence this week. Richie's reliable and knows how to keep his mouth shut."

"I'm a vault, sir," Grayson said. He wanted to present Benny with an Oscar for his performance. He was playing this perfectly.

"You have a license to carry?" Pressley asked, his cold gaze on Grayson.

"I do." When Benny had told Cooper prior to last night's meeting that Pressley required his driver to be armed, with the help of Liam—who had scary forgery skills—he'd made up a fake carry license. He had a real one, but, of course, he couldn't show Pressley that one. He took the fake one from his wallet and handed it to Pressley. He also had a fake driver's license should he be asked for that.

Pressley barely glanced at it before dropping it at the end of his desk for Grayson to pick up. He lifted his chin at Grayson. "Let me see your gun."

"It's in the car, sir. I didn't want to bring it in before you knew I carried." He shrugged. "Didn't want to make anyone nervous."

"Go get it."

"I'll go," Benny said, walking away before either of the other two men could object.

Left alone with Pressley, Grayson clasped his hands behind his back in an at-ease position and kept his gaze on the top of the desk. Not surprising, but he'd already concluded that Pressley got off on having power over those he deemed below him. He wanted to throttle the man if for no other reason than what he put Harlow through. But there were other reasons, like that he'd probably killed Veronica.

"What do you do when you're not covering for my driver? Who I just might fire anyway for assuming he can take time off without coming to me first."

"A little of this, a little of that." Let Pressley use his imagination, but the implication was that he was up to no good.

"Where you in the military?"

"I was in the Navy. Got to see the world. Some of the world sucks, some's not so bad. I have particularly fond memories of how much the ladies loved to bed a man in uniform." He inwardly cringed at even saying that, but when Pressley chuckled, Grayson knew he was in.

Benny returned and handed Grayson the holster and gun. Grayson met Pressley's gaze for the first time. "Did you want to see it?" Why else had Pressley wanted the weapon brought in?

"No, but if you're going to drive for me until Benny returns, you're to have it on you at all times."

"Not a problem, sir." He clipped the gun and holster to his belt. "When I'm on duty, I'll have it in a shoulder holster under a jacket." He wasn't going to walk around in public with a visible gun even though he had a carry permit. Made people nervous unless they also saw a badge along with the gun.

"Be here tomorrow morning at eight sharp. I have a meeting with the mayor you'll need to drive me to. Benny, give him my agenda for the week, and show him around the garage on your way out."

"Thank you for understanding, Mr. Pressley," Benny said.

Grayson gave a curt nod before following Benny out. They'd only taken a few steps when Don Delgado walked in. He glanced past Benny to Grayson, and his eyes narrowed. Grayson met the man's stare. Looked like he was about to find out if Delgado recognized him from the diner.

"Who's this?" Delgado said.

"Richie Kaplan, my cousin," Benny said. "He's covering for me this week."

"Why?"

"Don't worry about it, Don," Pressley said. "Come in and close the door. We have business to discuss."

Delgado stared hard at Grayson as he walked past. It was a twisted game he was playing with opponents who played dirty. The faster he could get into that safe, the sooner he could end this.

He and Benny had reached the living room when a little boy ran toward them. "Benny!" he yelled, his face lighting up.

Benny grinned. "Good morning, Tyler. Where are you off to?"

After glancing behind him, Tyler whispered, "I'm hiding from Ava." He eyed Grayson. "Who are you?"

Grayson squatted, bringing himself to eye level with the boy. "I'm a friend of Benny's. You can call me Richie." Tyler was a cute as a button with Harlow's unique blue eyes and blond hair, and Grayson wanted to pick him up and carry him out of this house. Take him to his mother.

"Tyler Pressley, you get your butt back here." A beautiful woman dressed as if she was on the way to a club walked down the stairs, and when she reached them, she grabbed Tyler's shoulder, jerking him to her. "Your father isn't going to be pleased when I tell him you're disobeying me."

"Please don't tell Daddy."

Grayson bit down on his cheek. No matter how much he wanted to, he couldn't interfere, and he especially couldn't pick the boy up and take him out of this damn house. The woman lifted her gaze to Grayson, and he didn't like the interest in her eyes.

"Hello. I'm Ava Crawford." She glanced at Benny. "Introduce me to your friend."

"I'm Benny's cousin," Grayson said, cutting Benny off from answering, "and we have a meeting we need to get to." He smiled down at Tyler. "See you around, little man."

"Well, Benny's cousin, don't be a stranger." She shot Grayson a sultry smile before marching Tyler away.

The woman was unquestionably beautiful with her long auburn hair, pouty lips and a smokin'-hot body, but her calculating eyes said she was trouble. She did nothing for him.

"Let's get out of here," he said, suddenly needing to breathe fresh air. This place was suffocating. He couldn't imagine what it had been like for Harlow during her years of living here.

"That woman's a piece of work, and I'd advise that you stay away from her," Benny said once they were outside. "I don't know why Mr. Pressley lets her anywhere near his son."

"I can think of a reason why." Was Ava the same nanny that Pressley had kissed in front of Harlow and Tyler? "And trust me, I plan to stay as far away from her as possible. She's trouble with a capital *T*."

After a tour of the garage and seeing the three cars he'd be driving—depending on Pressley's mood—and getting his agenda for the week, he parted company with Benny. As he drove back to his temporary home, one question took over his mind.

Should he tell Harlow he'd seen Tyler?

# Chapter 28

"He shimmied up a rope like a freaking ninja warrior. He was even dressed in all black." Harlow fanned her face as she grinned at her friend. "Makes me hot just thinking about it." They were sitting out on her balcony at sunset, enjoying a glass of wine.

"Girl," Lena said, drawing out the *r* so it sounded like there were a half dozen of them in the word. "Tell me you nailed that man."

Harlow snorted. "I forgot how unfiltered your mind is." She'd told Lena all about how it had ended with Anthony, how he was keeping her son from her and how she'd hired Grayson to bring Tyler back to her. That had included admitting that she had the hots for him...temporarily.

"Well, have you?"

She shrugged. "Maybe he was the one to nail me. Ever think of that?"

"Potato, potahto. Did you do the dirty with this hot ninja man?" Lena pressed her palms together as if in prayer. "Please say yes."

"Yes." She tried to keep a serious expression on her face, but when Lena squealed, Harlow lost it, and just like that, she found herself side-splittingly laughing with her old friend the way they used to.

"I need details. Was it good? Did he look great naked?"

"I'm not telling you—" Harlow made air quotes "—*details.* Anyway, it's just a temporary thing until I have Tyler back."

"Why?" Lena refilled their wineglasses.

"Because. I don't know what Tyler's mindset's going to be after all the time he's spent with Anthony and that Ava witch. He has to be my sole focus. I can't bring a strange man into the mix. That will be too confusing for him."

"I get what you're saying, but that doesn't mean you can't find some time for yourself. It's not healthy to ignore your own needs. Find a good babysitter and let your hot ninja recharge your battery once a week." Lena waggled her eyebrows.

Harlow shrugged. "My battery will be just fine, thank you." If she saw Grayson once a week, even if he agreed to that, it wouldn't be long before she'd want more. "We agreed this thing was a temporary fling until I have my boy again. Anyway, when this is over, Grayson will want to return to his life."

"You don't know that unless you ask."

"Oh, look. There's Marge and Homer." And perfect timing. She didn't want to talk about recharging batteries, and she especially did not want to think about never seeing Grayson again when this was over.

"Huh?"

"The swans." She pointed to the lake where they were floating by.

"You're deflecting, girlfriend."

"Guilty as charged. So, everything's great with you and J.D.?"

"Sure is. I'll drop it for now, but I have all day tomorrow to convince you that you should think about the well-being of your battery."

Harlow laughed. "Stop it. Never say the word *battery* to me again."

"Battery. Battery. Battery." Lena stuck out her tongue.

Maybe it was because they were on their second glass of wine, but they looked at each other and dissolved into giggles. "Stop. My sides hurt." It felt amazing to have her friend back.

A clunk sounded as a hook shot up from below and caught the balcony's rail.

"What was that noise?" Lena said between gasps of breath. "Whoa! Is that a hook?"

It sure was, and Harlow's heart thumped against her chest. "I think you're about to meet my ninja."

"For real?" She jumped up and peered over the railing, then glanced back at Harlow. "This is so cool."

"You don't have to whisper." Harlow joined Lena at the rail. Sure enough, Grayson was rapidly climbing the rope, hand over hand. They stepped back when he put his hand on the rail. He swung his legs over and landed in front of them.

He grinned. "Hi."

She was already giddy from the wine, and that he'd appeared when he had and the way he had, as if she and Lena had conjured him up, struck her as hilarious. She... Well, to her ears it sounded like she'd cackled.

"Sorry," she rasped, wiping the tears from her face. "We, ah, we were just talking about you." Why had she told him that?

His grin widened. "Were you, now?" He shifted his gaze to Lena. "You must be Harlow's friend. I'm Grayson."

"Sorry," Harlow said again. "I don't know where my manners went. Lena, this is Grayson Montana. Grayson, my friend Lena Nolan."

"It's a pleasure to meet you." Lena shot Harlow a mischievous look before saying, "I've heard you excel at re-charg—"

Harlow slapped her hand over Lena's mouth. "Nothing. She's heard nothing."

Amusement danced in his eyes. "I'm curious to hear what I excel at recharging."

"Batteries," Lena said.

"Oh my God," Harlow said.

"Is batteries a euphemism for something?" Grayson said.

"Who knows what she's talking about." Harlow was going to die of mortification…right after she strangled her friend.

Grayson glanced behind him before turning his attention to Harlow. "Can we take this inside? As amusing as you two are tonight, I need to talk to you."

"Sure." She followed Lena in with Grayson coming in behind her. He put his hand on her lower back, sending a delicious shiver up her spine.

"I don't know why I came in when my wine's out there." Lena gestured toward the balcony. "You know where I am if you need me."

"Sorry for interrupting your time with your friend," Grayson said after Lena closed the sliding door behind her.

"That's all right. Is everything okay?"

"Before we get to that, I need to do this." He slid his hand behind her neck and brought her to him.

She knew his kisses now, the taste of his lips, the feel of his arms wrapped around her, the heat from his body. She almost regretted knowing him. If she'd never met him, she wouldn't have to miss him the day they parted to return to their own lives. That day was near, and the knowing was bittersweet. She'd have her little boy back, but she wouldn't have Grayson.

A low hum sounded deep in his throat, and she melted against him as he deepened the kiss. But then he let go of her and stepped away. She wanted to pull him back, to steal all the moments with him she could. Their connection was intense, a magnetic force almost impossible to resist. In the end, though, she would because she had to.

He brushed his thumb over her bottom lip. "I shouldn't be here. I could have told you this over the phone, but I can't seem to stay away. And I wanted to be with you when I told you that I saw your son today."

"What? You saw Tyler? How was he? Where did you see him? Did you talk to him?"

"Hey, hey. Take a breath, sweetheart."

She pressed her hand against her pounding heart. He'd seen her boy. It wasn't fair. She was Tyler's mother. Why couldn't she see him? "Tell me everything."

"Come sit a minute." He took her hand and led her to the sofa. When they were seated, he said, "I saw him at Pressley's house. I was with Benny... You know who he is, right?" She nodded, and he continued, "We were leaving when Tyler ran up to Benny, excited to see him."

"He likes Benny. Benny's always nice to him and sometimes sneaks him a peanut butter cup."

"I like Benny, too. He seems like a good man."

"He is. Tell me the rest." She wanted every sliver of information about her son.

"Tyler ran up to us. Said he was hiding from Ava. I take it from your sour expression that you don't like her?"

"That's an understatement. Anthony hired her against my wishes. She's the one I caught kissing him in front of Tyler. Tyler never liked her."

"Can't say I blame him. Before we could talk to him, Ava showed up."

"What did she do?" Ava refused to see Tyler as a little boy who should be laughing and enjoying his childhood. She expected him to stay in his room and be quiet.

"She told him that his father wasn't going to be pleased to hear that he was disobeying her. Tyler begged her not to tell his daddy. Then she took him away."

"Oh, God." She buried her face in her hands. She should have taken him and disappeared when she'd left Anthony. Before Anthony had lied about everything and gotten full custody.

Grayson wrapped his arm around her back and tucked her next to him. "I know it's hard for you right now, but it will be over soon."

She leaned her head against his strong chest. "It is hard. I should've disappeared with him the day I left."

"That's not the answer. You'd always be looking over your shoulder, and that's no way to live. I want you to trust that I'll get your boy back for you."

"I do. I really do, but—"

"What if the worst happens and I don't make it happen?" She nodded.

"Then I'll help you and Tyler disappear."

"You'd do that for me?" Who was this man that he'd break the law for her?

"As a last resort, but it's not going to come to that." He put his finger under her chin and lifted her face. "Trust me, Harlow."

She hadn't had someone in her life she could trust since... Actually, had she ever?

# Chapter 29

Dressed in black pants, a white button-down and a blazer to hide his shoulder holster and gun, Grayson stood outside the black Mercedes sedan the next morning, waiting for Pressley to appear. He'd had a text from Pressley's secretary earlier that the Mercedes was Pressley's choice today. The other two cars were a black BMW XM and a black Range Rover. None of Grayson's dealerships sold Range Rovers, and he was hoping that would be the car of choice. He'd love to drive one.

When Pressley appeared, Grayson opened the back door. "Good morning, sir." Pressley ignored him as he slid into the car. "Rude," Grayson muttered after he closed the door.

As soon as they were on the way to the mayor's office, Pressley got on the phone. "Hey, babe. Something came up. I'm not going to make it to lunch." He listened, then, "I know. I was looking forward to eating…you." He chuckled. "Let's make it dinner instead. I'll be real hungry by then if you get my drift." Another chuckle.

Grayson inwardly rolled his eyes. Pressley sure thought he was clever with his innuendos. They arrived at town hall, where the mayor's office was located, and Grayson parked in a space close to the entrance.

Pressley waited for him to exit the car and open the back door. "Be here when I get back."

"Yes, sir." Like he'd go for a joyride or something.

Pressley's meeting lasted an hour, and their next stop turned out to be the police station. Again, Grayson was ordered to be here when Pressley returned. He was inside for twenty minutes, and from the station, they went to the tax office.

On arriving there, Pressley made a call. "Come outside."

A few minutes later a man Grayson recognized from photos he'd obtained as Dale Jenkins—who he suspected had been involved in stealing Jankowski's and Pickens's homes—came out.

"Wait for me outside," Pressley said.

"Yes, sir." He got out as Jenkins slid into the back with Pressley. He wanted to kick himself for not bugging the car. He'd remedy that tomorrow. The two men talked for ten minutes, then Jenkins exited the car and walked past Grayson without looking at him. Jenkins's expression was sour. Had he been ordered to steal someone else's home?

Grayson returned to the car, and Pressley directed him to go back home. When they arrived, he said, "Go to the kitchen and tell Anders to make you a sandwich. I won't need you again until five."

Grayson had no idea who Anders was, but he was all for getting the chance to talk to members of Pressley's household. Turned out Anders was the chef, a good one Grayson decided after he was seated at the biggest kitchen island he'd ever seen and eating a sub and homemade chips.

"Best meatball sub I've ever had," he said. Once he'd introduced himself as Benny's cousin and Pressley's temporary driver, Anders had treated him like an old friend. Grayson estimated him to be in his late sixties, and best of all, he liked to talk.

"My Italian mama, God rest her soul, taught me how to

make the world's best meatballs. Mr. Pressley dines out a lot, and when he does eat in, he likes fancy food. I make the meatballs for the boy. He loves them."

"The boy?" Gray said, letting Anders believe he didn't know who Tyler was.

"Mr. Pressley's son. It's not good that his mama isn't here. A boy needs his mama."

"How old is he?"

"Five."

"A five-year-old definitely needs his mother. Where is she?"

Anders took Grayson's empty plate. "She—" He shook his head. "It's not our business, and I talk too much."

"How long have you worked for Mr. Pressley?" He looked around the kitchen. "Seems like a great place to work."

"Three years, and it's a fine kitchen."

*But do you like cooking for Pressley, and what secrets do you know?* He wouldn't push for more now. Hopefully, Anders would get talkative again over the next few days.

"Anders!" Tyler ran into the kitchen. "I'm hungry."

"Good, because I have your lunch ready for you, young Mr. Pressley. Climb up on that stool." Anders placed a plate with two meatballs, a slice of buttered bread and apple wedges in front of Tyler.

"Oh, boy," Tyler said, clapping his hands. "Did you know this is my favorite lunch?"

Anders smiled. "I sure did."

"Did you have meatballs, too?" Tyler asked, looking at Grayson with his mother's sea blue eyes.

"Sure did. They were my favorite lunch, too."

"I forgot your name."

"Richie."

"Oh, I remember you said that." He turned his attention

to his lunch and scarfed down one meatball. "Will you play with me after I finish my lunch, Richie?"

"Don't talk with your mouth full," Anders said. "You know better."

Tyler let out a big sigh. "But Daddy's not here now."

"Doesn't matter. It's a bad habit to have, and if you do it now, you'll forget and do it in front of your father."

There was kindness in Anders's voice when speaking to Tyler. He was trying to help the boy stay out of trouble.

"Daddy gets mad if I talk with food in my mouth." Tyler lifted those big blue eyes to Grayson. "He takes my dinner away and makes me go to bed hungry."

Grayson exchanged a glance with Anders. The boy was five years old, for God's sake. Teaching him good manners was one thing, but sending him to bed hungry? Wrong on so many levels. Grayson didn't doubt there were even more serious ways Pressley was failing as a father. Like hiring the woman who walked into the kitchen as Tyler's nanny.

Ava's eyes widened and a smile appeared when she saw Grayson. "Well, hello, Benny's cousin."

Grayson dipped his chin in reply. He didn't want to be anywhere near the woman, but maybe he could learn something if he stayed.

She moved next to him. "You going to tell me your name?"

"His name's Richie," Tyler said.

Without sparing a glance the boy's way, she said, "I wasn't talking to you."

Anders removed a plate that appeared to hold a salad from the refrigerator, carrying it and a glass of water with a lemon to a small table. "Tina, your lunch."

There was no warmth in his voice as there had been for Tyler. Another of Pressley's employees that Grayson decided he liked.

"I think I'll have my lunch at the counter today. Keep Richie company." She put her hand on Tyler's arm. "Go take your nap."

"But I haven't—"

"Don't talk back to me, Tyler Pressley. Do as I say if you don't want me to tell your father."

Was tattling to his father a constant threat she used on the boy? Grayson wanted to throttle her.

"He hasn't had his cookies yet," Anders said.

Tina shrugged. "He can take them to his room."

The air was tense between Anders and Ava, and Anders opened his mouth, then closed it. He turned his back on her, got a small baggie and put four cookies in it.

"I get four?" Tyler said when Anders gave him the cookies.

Anders smiled. "It's a special day."

"Now go," Ava said irritably.

Grayson waited until Tyler turned the corner and was out of sight before saying, "Gonna hit the restroom. I'll be right back." He caught up with the boy. "Tyler."

Tyler's eyes lit up. "Are you coming to play with me?"

"I wish I could." He squatted. "Maybe another day I can. I just wanted to tell you that I think you're a smart and interesting boy. If you want, I'd like us to be friends."

"Really?"

Grayson nodded.

"I don't have any friends. You can be my first."

Did he not go to preschool where he would meet children his age? "I'd be honored to be your first friend."

"My mommy used to be my friend, but Daddy said she left because she doesn't love us anymore. Why doesn't she love me? I'd be a good boy if she came back."

He hated Pressley more with each new revelation from

both Harlow and her son. "You know what? I don't believe that for a minute. I think your mommy loves you very much, and I promise you, it's not your fault she's not here."

"Do you know my mommy?"

"No, but if I ever see her, I'll tell her how much you miss her." He hated lying to this lonely child with the sad eyes. "You better go on up to your room so you don't get in trouble."

"Can I tell you a secret?"

"You sure can."

He leaned close to Grayson. "I don't like Ava," he whispered. "She's mean to me."

What the hell to say to that? He couldn't risk agreeing and having Tyler repeat that, but he couldn't not say something. "Can you keep a secret, too?"

Tyler nodded.

"You have to promise not to tell anyone, not even your father."

"Okay."

He was taking a big risk, but his gut said Tyler could keep secrets, and he had to give the boy something to believe in. "I think you're going to see your mommy again real soon, but it's really important that stays our secret."

"When?"

"I can't tell you exactly when, just know right here in your heart—" he tapped Tyler's chest "—that she loves you and you'll see her again."

"I love her, too."

"She knows that, my little man. Now, go on before you get in trouble."

"Okay."

Grayson returned to the kitchen with the hope that he'd given Tyler something to hold on to. This was a conversation he wouldn't tell Harlow about because it would break her heart to know that her son thought she had left because she didn't love him.

Tina was on the barstool that Tyler had been sitting on, and when he retook his seat, she gave him a sultry smile. "You don't look like a Richie."

"What do I look like?"

She shifted to face him, and her gaze traveled over him. "Like a Maverick...or maybe Cruz. No, Ryker. Yeah, Richie just doesn't do it for me, so I'm going to call you Ryker. That's close enough to Richie."

The woman was ridiculous. Standing off to the side, out of her line of sight, Anders rolled his eyes. Grayson wanted to roll his, too. "That's an interesting name, but it's not mine."

"Consider it your nickname. Everyone has one of those."

"Is that so? What's yours?"

"Why don't you give me one?"

He made a show of checking her out. "I think I'll call you Trouble."

Anders snorted.

There was nothing to be learned here, at least not today, and he'd had enough of Miss Trouble. "Thanks for lunch, Anders. It was good."

"You're not leaving already?" she said...pouted.

"Things to do, places to go." Fresh air to breathe. Why was it whenever he was in this house, he felt like he was breathing toxic fumes?

# Chapter 30

Harlow's time with Lena went by too fast. "I don't want you to go." She hugged her friend.

"Promise you're not going to disappear on me again."

"Never. I promise. Text me when you get home so I know you arrived safely."

"I will." Lena hugged her again.

"Tell J.D. I said hi."

"You should come tell him yourself. He'd love to see you."

"I'd love a trip to Atlanta. As soon as I have Tyler back, okay?"

"That will be soon, Harlow. I just know your man's going to come through for you."

Harlow chuckled. "He's not my man."

"So you say. I better get on the road. Love you, girl."

"Love you, too."

Harlow closed the door, locked it, then leaned back against it. Alone again. The apartment was too quiet. Even Einstein was silent. Probably because he'd worn out his voice the past two days nonstop chattering to Lena, telling her his life story.

She walked to where he was curled up on the sofa napping. "Well, boyo, it's just you and me again." He twitched his tail, but otherwise ignored her.

There was work to do, but she just didn't feel like it. Having Lena here for two days had been what she'd needed, but now, the emptiness of the apartment was unbearable. The walls were closing in on her, and she needed to get out for a while. Grabbing her keys, she headed out the door and down the stairs.

Without thinking of where she was going, she ended up at the dog park a few blocks from home. She came here on her walks sometimes, always thinking how much Tyler would enjoy watching the dogs play with each other. A tiny Yorkie was busy bossing around a German shepherd and a beagle. She smiled as she watched them.

Soon, she would be able to bring Tyler here. She'd be able to watch his face as he laughed at the dogs' antics. She'd be a mother again. "Soon, baby," she whispered.

A warm summer breeze brushed across her cheeks, and she closed her eyes, lifting her face to the sun. The short walk, the fresh air and the sunshine had been the medicine she'd needed. Work she'd ignored during Lena's visit was waiting for her, and she was ready to get to it.

As she pushed away from the fence, movement behind her caught her eye, and she grinned at seeing her downstairs neighbor jogging up to her. "Hi, Ronnie." Ronnie was a nurse practitioner at a pediatrician's office by day and a drummer in an alternative rock band by night. Quite a juxtaposition was Ronnie. For his day job, he wore his hair in a man bun, and when he drummed, he let it fall loose. She'd seen him leaving for a gig wearing black eyeliner and his fingernails painted black.

He slung his arm around her. "Hey, neighbor. Haven't seen you in a while."

"That's because you're never home."

"When are you going to go out with me?"

She laughed. He asked her that every time he saw her. "And try to compete with all your groupies? Besides, I'd feel like a cougar if I dated you." He was only three years younger than her, but her life and his were so far apart that it felt more like a decade.

He growled like a big cat. "I like cougars."

They both knew they'd never date, but she liked him. He made her laugh. "You going or coming?"

"Coming. I don't have a gig tonight. Want to order a pizza?"

"Sure." He was a sometime friend, and occasionally, they'd order pizza and watch a movie.

As they approached their building, she groaned at seeing the black Mercedes parked behind her car. "You better head on to your apartment."

"Is that the ex?"

"Yep." Although Ronnie didn't know the full story, he knew she had an ex that showed up sometimes. "It would be best if you walked away from me."

"I don't think so." He kept his arm around her shoulders. "What kind of man would I be if I didn't make sure a lady was safe?"

"You don't underst—" Her breath caught in her throat when Grayson stepped out of the car. His gaze locked on her before shifting to Ronnie and the arm he had around her. "He's…" She'd almost explained that Ronnie was just a friend, but she wasn't supposed to know Grayson. It was a good thing she'd seen his new appearance, otherwise she might have given them away with her reaction.

Grayson opened the back door for Anthony to step out, and she recognized that expression on his face. It was the same look of possessiveness and anger that she had seen far too many times before.

Tension bristled between the three men. Why was this her life? "What do you want, Anthony?"

"I want to know who the hell he is."

"Not that it's any of your business, but he's a friend." She darted a glance at Grayson. He stood straight with his hands behind his back, his expression blank. She'd never seen him look so cold and remote before.

"A friend?" Anthony took an aggressive step toward Ronnie. "I don't tolerate men sniffing around my wife."

"Then it's a good thing I'm not your wife, isn't it? Why are you here?" She really wished Ronnie would leave and not put himself in Anthony's sights. No good could come of it. There would be no talking sense into Anthony, and she needed to remove Ronnie from the situation before it got ugly. "Let's go inside," she said to Ronnie.

"Good idea."

It would have been a great idea if Anthony hadn't grabbed her arm as they tried to walk around him. She attempted to pull it free, but he tightened his grip. "Let go of me."

Grayson made a sound, a low growl, and panic welled inside her. He was about to step in, and she had to do something. If he outed himself trying to protect her, she'd lose her chance of getting Tyler back.

The trick with Anthony was to let him think he'd won, and although she'd promised herself when she left that she'd never cower before him again, it was the only thing she could think of doing. He was glaring at Ronnie, and she chanced the moment when his gaze wasn't on her to try to send a message to Grayson. She gave a slight shake of her head and prayed that he got the message and that he understood the plea in her eyes not to interfere. His lips thinned in frustration, but he dipped his chin.

She folded in on herself, letting her arm go limp. "I'm

sorry, Anthony," she said in the spineless voice she'd hoped never to hear again. A voice and words she hated because they brought back memories she'd tried so hard to put behind her.

His grip on her arm loosened ever so slightly. "Get in the car." When she hesitated, he tightened his fingers around her arm again. "Just to talk privately, Harlow."

"Okay, but just to talk." God, she hated that meek voice. The last thing she wanted was to be closed up in a vehicle with him. If it wasn't for Grayson, Anthony would have to physically put her in the car. But Grayson was here, and he wouldn't let Anthony hurt her or take her away, so she obeyed.

"Hey now," Ronnie said as she was sliding onto the back seat. "You don't have to listen to him."

"I'm all right. Please, go home."

When he moved toward her, Grayson stepped in front of him. "Do as the lady says."

"This isn't right." Ronnie's gaze sought hers. "Do you want me to call the police?"

"No. Really, everything's okay. I promise." *Just please leave.*

Grayson used his bigger body to herd Ronnie away. "This isn't your problem," she heard him quietly say to Ronnie. "Go home before you make it worse."

She startled when Anthony got into the car and closed the door. She scooted to the other side until she was hugging the door. Her gaze was drawn back to Grayson and Ronnie. Grayson was walking him toward the building, and she wondered what he was saying to Ronnie.

"Who is he?" Anthony said.

She needed to be careful and not let him see her pay

Grayson any attention. "Just a kid, a neighbor. He's no one and nothing to me, all right?"

"He had his hand on you."

"Why do I have to keep reminding you that we're divorced? That you have no right to tell me what I can do and not do."

"Divorce be damned. You're my wife. It's time to stop this foolishness and come home."

"You don't love me, so why do you care?"

"What's love got to do with it?"

She burst into laughter. "You didn't just say that, *Tina*." He grinned and for a second, she saw the man she'd fallen in love with. Then that man was gone, replaced by the one she'd grown to hate.

His eyes turned hard and cold. "Your week is almost up. You now have three days to pack up your things and close up your apartment."

"Or?"

"Or I do it for you. Actually, don't bother packing anything. Everything you need is at home where you belong. I'm announcing my candidacy for mayor at a dinner two weeks from Saturday, and you will be by my side."

"Screw you." She opened the door, got out and slammed it behind her. When she rounded the front of the car, he was standing outside.

"Three days, Harlow," he called after her.

Why couldn't he leave her alone? Why couldn't they co-parent their beautiful boy, do what was best for him? Tears burned her eyes, and she forced herself to walk past Grayson, but couldn't resist looking at him when he took a step toward her. His eyes held hers for a brief moment. In them, she saw understanding and a promise. She wanted to believe, but Anthony had put doubts in her head. He always won, and she was so very afraid he would again.

# Chapter 31

Grayson unclenched his fists. Standing outside the car, helpless to intervene while Harlow was inside with Pressley, went against everything he believed in. He was wired to protect; it was in his DNA. Especially for those he cared about, and he very much cared for Harlow.

That it appeared to be happening with the woman who'd appeared in The Phoenix Three's office that first day, afraid of her own shadow, was the biggest surprise of all. Even though he'd been lucky enough to witness the emergence of a beautiful butterfly from that brown cocoon she'd cloaked herself in, he was afraid he wasn't going to be able to keep her.

She'd set an expiration on their time together. They would be over the day he brought her son back to her, she'd said. Even if he lost her the day he put Tyler in her arms, he'd keep his promise. He'd put her happiness ahead of his. That very thought hit him right in his heart. Was that love?

His attention stayed on the two people in the car as the question rumbled around in his mind. He narrowed his eyes. Did she just laugh? Sure looked like it, and that was an unpleasant surprise. She wouldn't go back to him, would she?

*For her son, she would sacrifice her happiness,* a nasty

voice whispered in his mind. But wait. There was anger in her expression as she said something to him. She got out of the car, slammed the door behind her and strode past him. For a second her eyes sought his, and in them he saw fear and hurt. He came close to blowing his cover by taking a step toward her. When he realized what he was doing, he stilled and let her pass.

He returned to the car. "Where to, sir?" They'd been heading home when Pressley had received a phone call from Delgado that Harlow was out for a walk. That had resulted in a detour to her apartment.

"Home."

Pressley tended to make phone calls when being chauffeured around town. Some were quite interesting. Like the one to the police chief. Jefferson Proctor had been the chief for twenty-four years, and from the rumors Liam had picked up at the country club, he wasn't well liked by his officers. There were also whisperings that he could be bought.

Harlow believed Pressley had the police chief in his back pocket and based on two of Pressley's phone conversations with the chief Grayson had overheard, that was a fact. Pressley was insisting Proctor make life miserable for someone. Unfortunately, he never said the man's name. Just, "Put the heat on him so hard that he decides there are better places to live than Faberville."

It was interesting that Pressley was comfortable having the conversations where Grayson could overhear. Grayson thought that over and concluded that Pressley was arrogant enough to believe his minions wouldn't dare go against him.

"I didn't like the way she looked at you," Pressley said.

"Pardon, sir?"

"My wife, I didn't like how she looked at you."

*Hell.* "I didn't notice. Actually, I don't think she looked at me at all." *And she's not your wife.*

"She better hope you're right."

Grayson gritted his teeth and managed to keep his mouth shut.

"I'm driving myself today," Pressley said the next morning.

Grayson fell into an at-ease position. "All right. Is there something you'd like me to do instead?"

Today's agenda was a meeting with the planning commission, followed by lunch with the mayor and one of the aldermen. Why didn't Pressley want him driving? Was Pressley suspicious? A part of him wanted to pump a fist in the air and say, "Right on!" Because frankly, he hated driving the man around. The part that had to absolutely ensure his mission was successful was worried.

"Yes, I need you to drive my son to his doctor. He was up sick all night. Ava will accompany you."

"Of course. Does he have an appointment time?"

"Dr. Patel will see him as soon as he arrives at her office. Take the Mercedes. You'll find Tyler's car seat in the garage."

"I've seen it there. Do you want me to move the BMW out of the garage for you?"

"Yes, park it near the front door. Ava will be down with Tyler in a few minutes."

"All right." He'd put the bug in the Mercedes this morning, and he needed to move it to the BMW. After relocating the bug to the BMW, he parked it and left the keys in it for Pressley. Then he installed the car seat in the Mercedes and moved it to the front of the house.

A few minutes later, Ava came down the steps with Tyler

lagging behind her. One look at the boy, and it was apparent he didn't feel well. Since she didn't seem to care, Grayson went to him. He kneeled in front of the boy.

"I hear you're not doing so good, bud."

"My tummy's sick. I threwed up all night."

Grayson smiled at *threwed*. The kid was cute. "Well, let's get you to the doctor."

Tyler glanced over Grayson's shoulder. "Ava's mad at me," he whispered. "She said I'm gross."

*Bitch.* "Well, I don't think you're gross. It's not your fault you're sick, and we're going to get you to feeling better." He took the boy's hand and led him to the car.

Ava was already seated in the front passenger seat, so Grayson got Tyler buckled in the car seat. When he was secure, Grayson touched his hand to Tyler's forehead, finding it hot. Once they were on the road, Grayson glanced at Tyler through the rearview mirror. The little boy was huddled in his car seat, looking miserable.

Ava glanced back at Tyler and wrinkled her nose. "He barfs in the car, I'm getting out. He's gross."

"I'm sorry, Ava," Tyler said.

Grayson hated the meekness in Tyler's voice. He spied a coffee shop and turned into the parking lot. When he stopped, he scowled at Ava. "Get out."

She gaped at him. "What?"

"Go inside have a coffee, call your friends, do whatever. We'll pick you up after he sees the doctor." And if she called Tyler gross one more time, he might forget he was supposed to pick her up.

"I can't do that."

"Why not?"

"Anthony won't like it."

"You gonna tell him? Because I'm not."

"The kid will."

"I won't," Tyler said.

"See. No one's telling, now get out."

"If he tattles, he won't like—"

"Out."

She huffed as she opened the door, and when she closed it behind her, Tyler giggled. Grayson turned and winked. "You doing okay, bud?"

He nodded. "I like you."

"I like you, too, kiddo." He wasn't happy that he'd done that in front of Tyler, but he'd had enough of Ava making the boy feel bad. Besides, she was useless as a caretaker... nanny. Whatever she was supposed to be. He didn't remind Tyler not to tell his father that Ava didn't go with them to the doctor. The boy could keep a secret.

"He has a mild case of the flu," Grayson told Ava when he returned to the coffee shop and picked her up.

"Then he can stay away from me."

"Isn't it your job to take care of him?" What the boy needed was his mother. As tempting as it was to drive straight to Harlow's apartment and turn Tyler over to her, he didn't have a choice but to continue on to Pressley's house.

"I don't do sick people, especially sick kids who barf all over the place."

Disgusted with her, he ignored her the rest of the way back to the house. When they arrived, she exited the car and went inside, leaving him to get Tyler in. He got Tyler out of the car seat and carried him inside. The boy laid his head on Grayson's shoulder and sighed. A sense of protectiveness he'd never felt before welled inside him.

"You hungry?" It was lunchtime, and the kid should try to keep something down.

"No. I'll barf it up, and Ava will get mad at me."

"I won't let her get mad at you. How about we see if Anders has some chicken noodle soup. That always made me feel better when I was sick."

"Really? Did you barf?"

He chuckled. "Sometimes." He walked into the kitchen. "Anders, you have any chicken noodle soup? A can of Campbell's, maybe? Our boy here could use a little something in his stomach that he can keep down."

"Canned soup?" Anders huffed, giving Grayson a disgusted look. "No, I do not." He then smiled at Tyler, who still rested his head on Grayson's shoulder. "But I did make some chicken noodle soup this morning after I heard you were sick."

"I'm not hungry," Tyler muttered.

"Maybe not, but I promise you, my soup will help you feel better. Let's just try a little, okay?"

Between him and Anders, they got Tyler to eat a half bowl along with a few saltine crackers and some ginger ale Anders had gone to the store and bought after hearing Tyler was sick.

"You're a good man," Grayson said to Anders as he picked up Tyler to take him to his room.

"Back at you, Richie."

Grayson hated that name, hated that he was lying to the people here he liked. As for the ones he didn't like, he had no qualms about deceiving them.

Ava had done a disappearing act, so he took Tyler to his room, removed his shoes and his pants. Leaving him wearing a T-shirt, his underwear and socks, he got Tyler tucked into bed.

"Will you read to me?"

"Sure." He picked a random book from the bookshelf and settled in a chair near the bed. Tyler fell asleep a few pages in, and Grayson wasn't sure what to do. Ava hadn't made an appearance, and he hesitated to leave Tyler alone should he get sick again. Since Pressley didn't need him, Grayson stayed to watch over the boy.

That was how Pressley found him.

"Where's Ava?"

"Not sure."

Pressley stepped into the room and glanced at his son. "What did the doctor say?"

"He has a mild case of the flu, but he'll be okay."

"The flu?" He stepped back to the doorway. "Is he contagious?"

*You're his damn father. You shouldn't care if he is.* "Maybe for a day or two. He'd love it if you came to see him when he wakes up."

"Find Ava and tell her to keep an eye on him. Be here tomorrow at nine." He left without another glance at his sick son.

Ava was nowhere to be found, so Grayson returned to Tyler's room. He closed the door, and while the boy slept, Grayson opened the app on his phone that had recorded any conversations Pressley had in his car today.

He'd only made two calls, both to women. "Hi, beautiful. It's Anthony," he said on the first call.

"I was hoping to hear from you," she said, her voice whispery.

"Yeah? I've been thinking about you. The chamber's dinner party was boring until you walked in. You stole my breath, darling, and I knew I had to meet you."

"Well, you did. Would you like to come over tomorrow night?"

"Tonight would be better because I'm a desperate man." Pressley chuckled. "I blame you for that."

"Then you'll be even more desperate by tomorrow night. The anticipation will be delicious."

"Cruel, baby. Just cruel. But I'm yours to torture. Text me your address."

"I will. Be here at seven. I'll have a little dinner ready for you, then we'll play."

"See you then. And babe, dinner is great, but what I really want to taste is you."

"If you're lucky." She giggled, then disconnected.

Grayson wanted to take a page from Tyler and barf. Pressley was divorced, so there wasn't any reason he couldn't see other women. Except there was… He wanted Harlow back. If he was so determined to win his ex-wife back, he shouldn't be having these kinds of conversations with other women.

The next call was to another woman. "Hey, babe. What are you doing?"

"I'm getting a pedicure right now. Then I'm going to the mall to do a little shopping. Thought I'd pick up a sexy little negligee to wear when you come over tomorrow night."

"Ah, darling, you're getting me hard just thinking about you wearing a sexy piece of lace. Makes me want to blow off my meeting tomorrow night, but I can't. That's why I'm calling."

"No, Anthony, you promised we'd have a romantic evening."

"I know, babe, but this meeting's too important. Let's reschedule for Thursday night."

The woman sighed. "Fine, but if you cancel again…"

"You'll what, Mia?" Pressley said with a clear warning in his voice.

"Nothing. I'll see you Thursday."

"Good girl."

"You're a pig, Pressley," Grayson muttered when they disconnected. Mia was Pressley's longtime mistress. Then there was Ava. He probably called them all babe so he wouldn't mix up their names.

It was time to end this, and with Pressley out with the new woman in his life, tomorrow night would be the perfect time to get into the safe.

## Chapter 32

Harlow was at loose ends. She was caught up with her work, the book she was trying to read wasn't holding her interest and she hadn't seen or heard from Grayson since he'd made a surprise appearance when Lena was here.

Was he making any progress on finding the evidence against Anthony? Had he seen her son again? How long was it going to take before she had Tyler in her arms? He'd said she couldn't call him, so she'd have to wait to hear from him.

"He said I could call Cooper or Liam if I needed to," she told Einstein.

Einstein meowed a long response.

"So, you think that's a good idea, too?" Einstein was never wrong. Since she was more familiar with Cooper, she called him.

"Harlow," he answered. "Everything okay?"

No. Everything would only be okay when she had her son back. "Pretty much. I'm sorry to bother you, but I haven't talked to Grayson in a few days. I just need to know that things are going as planned."

"First, you'll never bother me. As for things going as planned, yes, they are. I feel confident enough to say that it will be over soon, and you'll have your boy back."

It sounded like he knew something. "Thank you. I needed to hear that. I also need to know that Grayson will be safe. Anthony isn't to be trusted."

"He knows that, but you can trust Gray."

"I do, but I still worry that something will go wrong."

"Liam and I have his back. It's going to be over soon."

"Okay. Thanks for talking me down."

"Anytime. You're important to Gray, so you're important to us."

That meant a lot to her. After talking to him, she made a cup of tea, settled down with her book and Einstein purring on her lap. A few hours later she was lost in the story when her burner phone buzzed with an unknown caller. Only Grayson and the guys had this number, so she answered. She didn't know whether to fear that something had gone wrong or to be excited that it was over.

"Hello."

"I hear you're worried about me."

Grayson! Her heart did cartwheels. "I am, but Cooper promised that he and Liam have your back, so I'm a little less worried."

"I like that you are. Makes me feel special."

He was more special than she wanted him to be, but that was something to think about another day. "Anthony doesn't suspect anything?" Her ex-husband had a sixth sense for anything that might be a threat to him.

"No. He's seeing a new woman tomorrow night and will be gone for hours. I'm going to get into the safe while he's out of the house."

"And then what happens?" It seemed too good to be true that it could be over in a day or two.

"I talked to an FBI agent friend earlier tonight. That's one reason I wanted to talk to you. He wants me to take a picture of Veronica's letter and anything else in the safe that might be incriminating, but to leave everything there."

"Why?"

"Chain of command. If I take anything away, we can't prove it was in Pressley's possession. The agent, Sean Danvers, is going to call you shortly. He'll ask you to meet with him first thing in the morning so he can take a statement from you. Tell him everything you know. Between that and the photos I'll get tomorrow night, he can get a warrant to search Pressley's house."

"What about Tyler? I don't want him in the house when it's raided. What if Anthony decides he's not going down without a fight?

"I'll be there when it goes down and will get him out of the house."

"And bring him to me?"

"Yes."

It was what she wanted to hear, and she was elated. She crushed the nagging fear that something was going to go wrong.

Early the next morning, Harlow met Sean Danvers at a coffee shop in Freemont, a nearby town. Liam had picked her up so that she wouldn't have to drive her car since it had a tracker on it. When they arrived, he parked in the shop's lot and stayed in the car to keep an eye out.

The agent had told her to look for a blond man wearing a light green button-down. She saw him right away at a table in the back, two coffee cups on the table.

When she slid into the seat across from him, he pushed one of the cups to her. "Good morning, Harlow. Just to confirm, I'm Sean."

"I'll admit I'm a little nervous, Mr. Danvers. I've never talked to an FBI agent before."

"Just Sean." He smiled. "We don't bite…well, except for bad guys."

"Good to know." He'd settled her nerves with a little humor, and she liked him. "I thought FBI agents always wore dark suits and mirrored sunglasses." She guessed he was in his midforties. The little bit of gray in his hair gave him a distinguished look, and he had kind eyes.

"That's only in the movies. We do wear suits if we're appearing in court or something like that, otherwise we can dress as we wish as long as we're presentable."

"Grayson said you're a friend of his."

"We go back a ways to when we were both in the Navy. He told me about your ex-husband and what all he's involved in, including two possible murders, but I'd like to hear it from you. What all you know."

Two murders? "I'm not sure where to start."

"Does the name George Pickens mean anything to you?"

"Grayson mentioned that name. He had his home stolen, too, right?"

"Yes, and he was killed."

"I didn't know." She felt physically sick hearing the news.

"We'll get him, Harlow, and he'll go to prison for a very long time, if not for life. Start at the beginning. From when you met your ex-husband. Especially the things that you saw or overheard that made you uncomfortable or suspicious." He set his phone face up on the table. "Do you mind if I record our conversation?"

"I'm agreeable to anything that will help me get my son back."

"Along with seeing justice done for the people he's wronged, that's our goal."

She talked for a little over an hour and when she finished, he asked a few questions. After she answered them, he stopped recording and put his phone in his pocket.

"With what you've told me and the photos Grayson's going to get, we won't have any problem getting a search warrant. Grayson said you're worried about your son being in the house when we serve the warrant. I've told him that we won't stop him from leaving with Tyler and taking him to you."

"Words don't convey my gratitude, but thank you." Soon, she'd hold her little boy in her arms again, and she was so very grateful. To him. To Cooper and Liam. And most of all, to Grayson.

"We live to put bad guys away." He grinned. "So thank you for bringing us one."

It was her pleasure. Truly.

# *Chapter 33*

It was happening tonight, and Harlow hadn't been able to concentrate on work all day. She'd tried if for no other reason than to keep her mind from thinking of all the things that could go wrong.

*Stop thinking the worst.* Grayson would be safe. All he would be doing was taking pictures while Anthony was gone. In and out in a few minutes, Anthony none the wiser. She didn't know how long it would take the FBI to get a search warrant after they got the evidence, but it had to be a matter of only a few days before she'd have her boy back.

Would he be happy to see her? That was a worry she'd tried to ignore, but now that the time was near, the fear that Anthony had turned him against her refused to be silent. She didn't doubt for a minute that Anthony would have told Tyler she was to blame for the divorce and her absence from their son's life.

Tyler would probably hate her at first, and it would take time and much understanding on her part for him to trust her again. Would he remember the bedtime stories, the times they played with his robots together, talked about when dinosaurs roamed the earth? It would take patience and love to rebuild their bond, and all her time and focus had to be for him.

What she needed was a cup of chamomile tea to settle her nerves. As she heated water, she glanced at the microwave clock. Was Grayson at this very minute breaking into Anthony's safe? She should have asked him to call her when it was done so she wouldn't spend all night worrying.

After dropping a tea bag in the heated water, she took her cup to the living room. As soon as she sat on the sofa, Einstein jumped in her lap. He purred, as if he knew she needed comfort.

"You're the cure for anxiety," she said as she combed her fingers through his soft fur. "I should rent you out. I'd make a fortune."

He purred louder, apparently agreeing.

When someone banged on her door, she startled, spilling hot tea on her fingers. "Ow. That hurt."

Einstein raced to the door. She put her eye to the peephole and gasped at seeing Ava holding Tyler.

Her fingers fumbled with the lock as she tried to open the door so she could get to her son. *It's a trick.* She didn't want to listen to that voice in her head, but this was exactly what Anthony had done the last time. She dropped her hand from the lock and pressed her forehead to the door.

She wasn't going to fall for another of Anthony's tricks. Even if she opened the door, Ava would disappear with Tyler like before, and it would be Anthony standing there. She hated him with a passion for using their son in his cruel games. "Just a few more days," she whispered. She just had to be strong a little longer, and then all this would be over.

"Harlow, please," Ava yelled. "I'm scared. Anthony's in a rage. I've never seen him like this. You have to open the door before he finds us here."

Fear and desperation filled her voice, but could Harlow

trust her? She'd never actually seen Anthony lay a hand on anyone, but he did have a fearsome temper.

"Please. He hit Tyler, and then he tried to hit me when I pulled Tyler away from him. You have to let us in."

He struck Tyler? Rage filled her. She put my eye to the peephole again. Her little boy was crying. Her mother's instinct took over, and she could only think of getting to her son. She opened the door.

"Thank God," Ava said as she rushed past.

Harlow pushed the door to close it, but it bounced against a shiny black Ferragamo dress shoe. Her heart dropped to her stomach. She knew that shoe.

"No," she screamed as she fought to keep Anthony out. Even though she put all her weight against the door to keep it from opening enough for him to enter, he was stronger.

"Mommy!" Tyler cried as his arms reached for her.

The door was pushed so hard that she stumbled, then tripped over Einstein and landed on her knees. Einstein yowled, and deciding he wanted no part of whatever was happening, he disappeared down the hallway.

The only thing that registered in her mind was Tyler's cries, and she pushed up to her feet. Ava didn't fight handing him to her, which was smart of her. Harlow was in mama bear mode, and nothing and no one was going to keep her from her son.

Tyler latched onto her like a spider monkey, and her heart rejoiced that he hadn't forgotten her. "Hey, baby. Mommy missed you so much." It was amazing to have him in her arms again. She inhaled his little-boy smell, her tears freely flowing down her cheeks.

"Leave, Ava," Anthony said.

Harlow backed up until her knees touched the sofa. He wasn't taking Tyler away from her again. As Ava walked past her, she smirked. Apprehension slithered through Harlow. What was Anthony up to?

She'd been so focused on Tyler that she hadn't noticed Don Delgado standing by the door, staring at her with mean eyes. Her apprehension turned to stark fear. She'd known Don for years and had always been afraid of him. Too terrified to speak, she held Tyler close as she waited to learn why they'd invaded her home.

"You're shaking." Anthony smirked, enjoying her fear. "Sit."

She wanted to refuse, but her trembling legs weren't going to hold her up much longer. As if sensing her fear, Tyler burrowed into her as she sank to the sofa.

"It's okay, baby. Mama has you," she whispered. Not that she could protect him against these two men, but she would die trying.

Anthony stared down at her. "Who is he?"

"Who is who?" But she knew.

"Don't play games with me, sweetheart. I'm not in the mood. Who. Is. He?"

"I don't know who you're talking about." Damn that tremor in her voice. He wanted her afraid of him, and she was.

"Last chance."

She pressed her lips together, refusing to speak.

"Take the boy." He stepped aside, making room for Don to approach her.

"No, please." She tightened her arms around Tyler, but he was snatched away from her.

"Tell me who he is, Harlow, if you don't want to watch Don break one of the boy's fingers."

Her stomach lurched. "You wouldn't. He's your son."

Anthony shrugged. "He's a means to an end."

Who was this man she'd married? She'd learned to hate

him for his verbal and emotional abuse, but she'd never dreamed that he would hurt his own son. She looked into his eyes, praying that she'd see that this was some kind of sick joke, but all she saw was a soulless man.

"Mommy." Tyler was sobbing and reaching for her.

She stood, intending to get to him. Anthony pushed her back down. "If you don't answer the question, Don will break his finger. If you continue to refuse, he'll break another, and another until you tell me what I want to know."

Oh, God. "You wouldn't."

"You really want to try me, wife?" He nodded at Don. "Start with his pinky."

When Don grabbed Tyler's hand, Harlow swallowed the bile rising in her throat. She couldn't let these bastards torture her son. Grayson would understand and forgive her. She had to believe that.

"His name's Grayson."

"Grayson who?"

"I don't know. He never told me his last name. Said it was better that I didn't know." She hoped she was somehow giving Grayson a bit of protection by not giving his last name. "Please, give me Tyler." He was still crying for her, and it was breaking her heart.

"Not yet. You have more questions to answer. Why is he pretending to be Benny's cousin?"

There wasn't anything she could tell him that would make sense or be believable other than the truth. "I hired him to help me get custody of Tyler." It was killing her to betray the best man she'd ever known, but what choice did she have?

"By spying on me?"

She shrugged. "I was desperate."

"If you wanted to be with Tyler, all you had to do was come home."

No, she couldn't bear the thought of living in that house again.

"There's more," Don said. "She's hiding something."

Anthony tilted his head as he studied her. "He's right. What else? What does he expect to find?"

She pressed her lips together, refusing to answer.

"Very well." Anthony nodded at Don. "Break it."

"Stop!" *Please forgive me, Grayson.* "Give me Tyler, and I'll tell you."

"Give her the boy," Anthony said.

She hugged her little boy when he was back in her arms. "He… Grayson's going to get the letter that's in your safe. The blackmail Veronica wrote you." *He's going to prove that you killed her.*

"How do you know about that?"

"I saw it." He was getting angry, and that made him unpredictable.

"When is he breaking into my safe?"

He grabbed her chin, squeezing so hard that tears stung her eyes when she didn't answer.

"When, Harlow."

"Tonight," she whispered.

He grabbed her arm and jerked her up so hard that she almost dropped Tyler. "You're hurting me."

"You're coming with me."

"Please, no. I've told you everything. Just leave." *And don't take Tyler with you.* "How could you even think to hurt your son?"

"You truly are naive, wife. I would have never hurt him. I just had to make you believe I would."

"You're a bastard, and I'm not your wife."

"Keep telling yourself that."

# Chapter 34

"Testing. Testing." Liam had left earlier in the afternoon on a new case, so it was just Cooper at his six. It was going to be a quick in and out, so no problem.

"Copy," Cooper said, verifying their comms were working. He was parked at the end of the street where he could see if Pressley unexpectedly returned.

Grayson had unlocked a window in a never-used bedroom at the back of the house earlier in the day. Clothed in all black, he made a stop in the garage, collected the keys to the three vehicles to keep Pressley from possibly escaping, and then he slipped though the dark to the window. "Still unlocked," he quietly said after sliding it up.

"It spooks me when things go too easy," Cooper responded.

"Shut your mouth. You'll jinx us."

Cooper chuckled. "Just saying."

"Going in." He pulled himself up and rolled through the window, landing quietly on his feet. "I'm in and going silent." He checked that his gun was still tucked safely in the back of his waistband. He also had one in an ankle holster and a knife strapped to his belt. Not that he needed to be armed to the teeth for this little caper, but once a SEAL, always a SEAL, and a SEAL came prepared for the unexpected. No exceptions.

On silent feet, he moved through the house. Pressley's home office was on the second floor, and as he made his way up the stairs, he was careful to avoid the steps he'd previously memorized that creaked.

The office door was closed, and he eased it open. The room was dark, which he'd expected. He stepped inside and closed the door behind him. As he reached for the light switch, the hair on the back of his neck stood on end.

*Danger. Danger. Danger.*

He'd heard that warning voice on many of his missions, and he always paid it heed. With his finger on the switch, he hesitated long enough to whisper "FUBAR," knowing that would alert Cooper. Then he turned on the lights.

It was only because he'd been trained for years that he didn't react at seeing Pressley standing in front of his office chair, a gun in his hand. The chair was turned away, but Grayson didn't need to see who was sitting in it, hidden from him, to know it was Harlow.

He felt her, sensed her, smelled her fear.

Pressley was a dead man. He just didn't know it yet. There was no sense in trying to come up with a reason he was sneaking into the man's study late at night, so he stood at attention and waited for Pressley to make the first move.

"You got nothing to say?" Pressley said. "Like about why you're here?"

Grayson shrugged. "Why bother? You won't believe whatever excuse I try to come up with." He let his gaze shift to the back of the chair. "Let her go, and I might let you live."

"Her? This who you mean?" Pressley put his hand on the top of the chair and spun it around.

"Affirmative. And the boy." Grayson was surprised his voice sounded normal. Rage like he'd never known turned his vision red at seeing Harlow and Tyler with duct tape over their mouths. She had her arms around Tyler as he slept against her chest. The boy's cheeks were red and tear-stained. "And you call yourself a father," he disdainfully said.

"Careful, *Grayson*. You don't want to push me."

Oh, but he did. Pressley would soon learn he had picked the wrong person to mess with. But first, "How do you know my name?" He was truly curious.

"Interesting that. Ava insisted you couldn't be a Richie, and Delgado didn't trust you. I decided to have a little chat with my wife. She was more than happy to give you up."

Harlow shook her head. Even without her denial, he would have known she hadn't been *happy* to. She'd been forced to. Just another reason Pressley wasn't going to see tomorrow. And damn Ava and her fixation on his name.

He locked eyes with Harlow and winked, sending a message to Harlow that she and her son were going to be okay. He'd make sure of it. So far, Pressley was keeping the gun down by his side. The moment that changed, it would be time to act. But Grayson intended for this to end before Pressley decided it would be a good idea to point his weapon at anyone.

"I'm making my way inside," Cooper said over the comms.

Grayson stepped farther into the room. "What do you want?" he asked Pressley.

"A long list of things." Pressley chuckled. "But from you? Nothing, because you won't be around much longer to be a threat."

"Actually, I—" The air behind him changed, alerting him that someone was sneaking up on him. The stink of cigars wafted to him. Delgado was about to find out he wasn't as clever as he thought.

What most people didn't realize, if you were going to

use a gun against someone, never come within striking distance. A trained warrior could disarm you before you could blink. He had no doubt Delgado had a weapon, and he could see in his mind how this was going to play out. So, he waited.

"Let Harlow and Tyler go, and I won't hurt you too badly."

Pressley laughed as his gaze settled behind Grayson. *Fool.* "Don't say I didn't warn you." The moment he felt the barrel of Delgado's gun touch his back, he spun, grabbed the man's wrist and twisted it, causing him to lose his grip on the weapon, while at the same time, he swept his leg behind Delgado's knees, sending him to the floor with a heavy thud. Delgado grabbed Grayson's leg, attempting to bring him down. Anticipating his move, Grayson twisted his body, extricating his leg from Delgado's grasp.

Grayson snatched up the gun, then put his foot on Delgado's chest and pressed down. "You move, you die."

"I'm coming in," Cooper said. "Don't shoot me."

"Copy." When Cooper stepped next to him, Grayson handed him Delgado's gun. "He's all yours." He leveled his gaze on Pressley, and his blood turned to ice. During the minute it took to remove Delgado as a threat, Pressley had dragged Harlow and Tyler out of the chair. He dared to hold a gun to her head. He was a dead man, all right.

"You really don't want to do that, Mr. Pressley."

"How about if I just shoot you?" He swung the gun from Harlow to Grayson.

Grayson shrugged. "You could, but you shoot me, my friend here will shoot you. Let them go." Thankfully, Tyler was still sleeping through this, but Harlow's eyes were wide with fear, and that just didn't work for Grayson.

"I think it's time to make our exit." Pressley put the

gun to her head again and moved behind her, using her as a shield. "Pick up my briefcase, wife."

Grayson was getting really tired of the man calling her *wife*. Pressley knew if he pulled that trigger, he was a dead man, so Grayson wasn't worried...yet. But leaving with Harlow and Tyler as hostages? Not happening.

"You try to follow me, and I'll shoot her." He poked Harlow in her head with the gun. "Get the briefcase."

She gently lowered Tyler to the chair, then ripped the duct tape from her mouth, wincing as she did. "I can't carry a briefcase and hold Tyler at the same time."

"Figure out a way," Pressley said.

"Unless you want to carry him, Tyler's staying here." She locked eyes with Grayson. *Take care of my son,* her eyes said.

He smiled. *You know I will.* She was both brave and smart. He'd already noted that the safe was open, and no way was Pressley leaving the briefcase behind.

"Get the damn briefcase," Pressley snarled.

As soon as she picked up the briefcase, Pressley pulled her back to a door behind them.

"Stay with her son," Grayson said after they were gone. "Call Sean, tell him what's going on." He went out the door he'd come in. It was a faster route to the garage than the way Pressley was going.

He was counting on Pressley being smart enough to not do something stupid, like hurting Harlow before he could get away. After that, though? All bets were off. Grayson had no intention of letting the man leave with her.

Tyler was safe now, so he only had one more person to rescue, and rescue her he would. He ran to the garage. The trick would be to herd Pressley to one of the cars. The Mercedes, he decided. It was the one Pressley drove the most, and there was more room in the back for Grayson to hide. He kept the keys to the Beemer and the Range Rover and returned the Mercedes's key to the hook.

The SEAL's motto ran through his mind as he crouched down behind the driver's seat. *The only easy day was yesterday.* "Ain't that the truth," he muttered.

Not more than a minute later, the side door to the garage banged open.

"I'm not going anywhere with you," Harlow said.

"Get in the damn car, Harlow, or I'll shoot you right here," Pressley roared as he jerked the driver's side door open.

"No."

Grayson needed her to get in the car, too, for his plan to work.

"Fine, we'll stay here, and when your hero comes to rescue you, I'll shoot him and then you."

"I hate you," she said as she got in and climbed over the console.

Pressley slid into the driver's seat. "It didn't have to be this way." He pushed the garage door opener, and when it was up, he backed out.

"No, it didn't," she said. "But unfortunately, you turned out to be a lousy husband. A total jerk, actually."

"Careful," Pressley growled. "You don't want to push me."

*No, but I do.* He would make his move—ending this while the car was still going slow and before they got out on the highway—as soon as Pressley drove the car forward. He put his hands on the floorboard, ready to push up and attack.

# *Chapter 35*

"**I** gave you everything," Anthony said as he backed out of the garage.

Harlow snorted, which earned her a glare. She had a plan. It was a surprise that Anthony had allowed her to leave Tyler behind, but not having to escape with Tyler was going to make it easier.

The gun was on the seat between Anthony's legs, which made her nervous, but she was counting on getting out of the car and running for the house where Grayson and Cooper were before Anthony could react. She really didn't want to get shot. As soon as the car was even with the house, she'd jump out.

She resisted putting her hand on the door handle and giving away her intention before it was time to go. The element of surprise would be the only advantage she had. Just a few more feet. Her heart thumped hard in her chest and her muscles bunched up in her legs in preparation to leap out.

*Now!*

She reached for the handle, and at the moment she touched it, an apparition dressed in all black rose up from the back seat. She screamed.

The apparition wrapped his left arm around Anthony's neck and with his right hand, he put a gun to Anthony's head. "Stop the car."

Grayson had come for her! Her relief and joy at seeing him turned to horror when Anthony gunned the engine. They shot toward the street like a bullet train out of control. If a car was coming, they would be T-boned. Someone would die. Innocent people could die, something she couldn't live with on her conscience.

Before she could think it was a bad idea, she dived for Anthony's gun, got it in her hand and shot his foot. The bang reverberated in her ears, along with Anthony's scream of pain, both sounds startling her so much that she dropped the gun on the floor.

Grayson lunged forward, somehow pushing his big body into the front seat and on top of Anthony. He slammed on the brakes, bringing them to a body-jerking stop just feet from the street.

Silence. Blessed silence. She sucked air into her lungs as her heart pounded and adrenaline coursed through her veins.

Grayson glanced over at her and winked.

A giggle bubbled up. That was it? A wink? He wasn't even breathing hard. The giggle erupted into uncontrollable laughter. When Anthony's moans of pain joined her laughter, she really lost it.

"I shot his foot," she gasped.

Grayson grinned. "That you did."

"And you're sitting on him."

His grin widened. "That I am."

Anthony's howls mixed with sirens.

"Calvary's a little late," Grayson said.

It was the dry tone of his voice as he still sat on Anthony that set her off again. It was a day of fear, of bravery from Grayson and Cooper…and yeah, from her. She was rather proud of herself, but it was a day she never wanted to repeat.

\* \* \*

The police and the FBI were gone, taking Anthony, his gun and briefcase filled with the evidence of his crimes with them. Don Delgado was carted off in a separate FBI car.

After giving her statement and answering a long list of questions, Sean had assured her that Anthony would never be a threat to her again. From a few things he'd let slip, maybe on purpose, they'd be questioning the people who'd helped to protect Anthony and do his bidding. She wouldn't be sorry to hear of any of them ending up arrested.

That was all great, but really, the only thing that mattered was that she had her little boy back. Cooper had changed Tyler into his pajamas and put him to bed. She was grateful her son had slept through tonight's events.

"You ready to take your son home?" Grayson said as they stood in Tyler's room looking down at him.

"So ready."

"Thought you might be."

"Let me pack up some things for him." She left Grayson to watch over him while she got a large suitcase. She packed his clothes and favorite toys. Anything else he needed, she'd buy. She wasn't stepping foot back in this house again.

Cooper drove them to her apartment. When they arrived, Cooper took the suitcase, and Grayson carried Tyler, who woke up as they entered. He yawned, blinked several times and then stared at Grayson.

"You play with me, Richie?"

Grayson smiled sweetly at her son. "Not tonight, bud. I think your mommy needs some Tyler time."

"Mommy?" He glanced around, and seeing her, he reached for her. "Mommy."

That was the sweetest sound in the world. Grayson

handed him to her, and she wrapped her arms around him. She had her boy back.

"I'll call you tomorrow," Grayson said.

"No, it's better if you don't." The words a goodbye. She forced a smile. "Thank you. I'll never forget what you did for us." Something flashed in his eyes as he took in her words. Sadness, she thought. Sadness was what was in her heart.

It was killing her to be so cold and unfair to him. She owed him so much more than a mere thank-you, but if she didn't send him away now, if she let him stay one minute more, let him say anything to her, she'd lose her resolve. Their time would be over when she had Tyler back, and that time had come. It was what they'd agreed to. All that mattered now was her son. That was how it had to be.

"Be happy, Harlow," he said, then followed Cooper out the door.

And just like that, he was gone.

If this was what she wanted, why were tears streaming down her cheeks?

# Chapter 36

Two weeks had passed and no phone call, no text...nothing from Harlow. Grayson had started dozens of texts to her over the past seven days, then had deleted them all. She'd told him up front how it was going to be. He'd just thought things had changed.

The Feds had confirmed that the gun from Pressley's safe had been the one used to kill George Pickens. Although Delgado had been the one to commit the murder, it had been at the direction of Pressley. Delgado was talking, hoping to cut a deal, and it seemed the man knew all Pressley's secrets, even things Harlow hadn't been aware of. At the prosecutor's urging, the judge had refused to set bail for both men. Pressley would never be free again. She was finally rid of her ex, and Grayson had hoped knowing that would bring her back to him. Guess not.

Damn, he missed her. There was an ache in his chest that refused to go away. Was that love? He didn't know. Maybe not yet, but he'd been getting there. He put his feet on the railing and stared at the ocean. Since he'd walked away from her, he'd vacillated between just showing up at her door versus honoring their agreement.

Maybe she needed him to show her that he wanted more, or maybe she was happy that she hadn't heard from him.

He'd never been an indecisive man, and he didn't like being one now. It was just that every time he wrote a text or picked up the phone to call her, he hesitated. If he only knew what she wanted.

His gaze settled on a woman and a little boy walking down the beach. They were too far away to see their features, but he could tell the woman was laughing as the boy played the age-old game children loved...*don't let the water touch my toes*.

Would Tyler love the beach? Would he laugh when the water touched his toes? Grayson swallowed past the lump in his throat. How many times during the past two weeks had he imagined Harlow and Tyler here, playing on his beach?

Answer: about every second of every minute of every hour of every day. He wanted to stop watching the woman and boy because watching them hurt for what he couldn't have, but he was unable to tear his gaze away.

As the woman and the boy drew closer, Grayson's breath caught in his throat, and his heart skipped a beat and then another. He dropped his feet to the floor, stood and squinted his eyes against the bright sun. Hope ballooned in his chest. Was it her? If it was, and that she was here, it had to mean she wanted to see him.

When they were close enough to see their faces, time stopped, the crash of the waves against the shore ceased, and the only thing he heard was the pounding of his heart in his ears.

It was her.

And she smiled at him.

Suddenly, all was right in his world.

He jogged down the steps, and she laughed when he almost fell on his face because he missed the last step. He'd gladly do a face-plant if it meant hearing that laugh. He grinned. Damn, his heart was going to beat itself right out of his chest and land at her feet. He'd beg her to keep it because it belonged to her. Now and always.

Double damn, he *was* in love.

"Hi," he breathed when he stopped a few feet from her. *Please don't let me be misinterpreting why you're here.*

"Hi," she said with a shy smile.

"Richie, I came to play with you," Tyler yelled.

"You did?" He tore his eyes away from the most beautiful woman on the planet and squatted. He did not want to be Richie to this boy. "That makes me very happy. But you want to know a secret?" When Tyler nodded, he said, "Richie was just a pretend name. My real name is Grayson. But my friends call me Gray."

"Can I call you Gray?"

"Well, that depends. Are you my friend?"

That got a vigorous nod.

"Then Gray it is." If things went the way he hoped, he'd be a father to this boy, and he almost fell on his ass at the idea of being a dad. Him, a father. Who would've thought? He lifted his gaze to Harlow. She looked down at him with love shining in her eyes. His heart, already half out of his chest, finished the job and gave itself to her, lock, stock and barrel.

No regrets about that. Not a one.

After an afternoon of playing in the ocean, which had included paddling Tyler around on the surfboard, he'd conked out on them. Grayson was glad they'd worn the boy out as he and Harlow needed to talk. Something they hadn't been able to do with Tyler around. After tucking him into bed in the guest room, Grayson took Harlow's hand and led her to the living room.

"You know I'm going to make a surfer out of him, right?" He pulled her down to the sofa with him.

She rolled her eyes. "I figured that out about five minutes after he was on the board. He loved every minute of it."

"But did you figure out how hard it was to keep my hands off you the moment you walked out in that bikini?"

"Oh, I thought your fingers brushing across my bottom was an accident."

He laughed. "Yeah, no." He brought her hand up to his lips and kissed the inside of her wrist. "I thought I was hallucinating when I saw you walking up the beach, that I wanted it to be you so badly that I was putting your face on a stranger. I thought I'd lost you."

She threaded her fingers around his. "I had it in my mind that Tyler would need one hundred percent of me after being left with his father for so long, but it's like he's already adjusted to the change and more than happy with it."

"Kids are pretty resilient. I'm guessing he's happy because he's with his mother now."

"He is. He told me he doesn't ever want to live in his father's house again. Then he started asking when you were going to come play with him. It's been Richie this and Richie that. 'Richie read me to sleep' and 'Richie took care of me when I was sick.' Thank you for that."

"He's a great kid." But that wasn't what he wanted to talk about. "What about us? Is there an *us*?" *Yes* was the only word he wanted to hear. Needed to.

"I'm hoping so. When you left…" She squeezed her eyes shut for a moment before opening them and lifting her gaze to his. "When I made you leave, you took my heart with you."

"Only fair since you stole mine. And just so you know, I'm not giving yours back." Best day of his life. This morning, he'd thought he'd lost her, and now it turned out that he was luckiest man in the world.

She smiled. "Good, because I'm falling in love with you."

What could he do to that but kiss her? Slow and deep, showing her that he was falling, too. He was where he belonged—right here, right now—with her.

# *Epilogue*

It hadn't been as hard as Grayson thought it would to talk Harlow into moving in with him. That she didn't want to be anywhere near Faberville and her memories there had certainly helped. He'd ask her to marry him today if he thought she was ready. She wasn't there yet, so the ring he'd already bought was locked up in his desk. Soon, though.

"Gray, I'm here! We can go surfing now."

He smiled at the boy he loved like his own. "You have fun in school today?" He was going to school for the first time in his life and loved getting to spend time with other kids.

"Yes! I spelled all my words right."

"Excellent." Grayson lifted his hand for a high five, and Tyler laughed as he slapped his small hand against Grayson's. "I knew you'd ace the test." They'd practiced spelling the five words—cat, dog, cow, hat and car—last night until Tyler could spell the word as soon as Grayson pointed at the picture. He'd loved every minute of working with the kid. His boy was a smart one.

"The waves are good today. Go get your suit on."

"Yay!" Tyler took off, running back into the house.

It had been only three weeks since Harlow and Tyler had moved in with him, and he'd known how much he was going to love being a family with her and Tyler. He just hadn't realized how much he was going to love it.

The sound of the French door opening and then closing sounded, and although he didn't turn away from the railing, he smiled. His girl would be next to him in a few seconds, and he tried to guess which bikini she'd have on. Now that she lived at the beach and because he'd made sure she knew how sexy she was in a bikini, she'd gone bathing suit shopping and now had a drawer full. Worked for him.

The red one...no, his favorite, the blue-and-yellow one. It had ties on both sides of her hips that he loved to tease her with, threatening to pull them. When she stopped next to him, her arm touching his, his heart did that happy stuttering thing it did whenever she was near.

He dropped his hand and brushed his fingers over her very fine ass. "Oops," he said, grinning when she laughed. And yep, there were the ties.

"Why do you always pretend your hand finding my bottom was an accident?"

"I love you," he said.

She shook a finger at him. "I'm on to you, Snoopy. That was a diversion tactic."

"Can't get anything past you." He shifted to face her. "But I do love you, kitten, and I really love that sweet ass of yours."

She snuggled into him and pressed her face against his chest. "And my sweet ass loves you."

What more could a man in love ask for?

Liam had gone dark.

He was somewhere in West Virginia, looking for a photojournalist who'd gone missing.

"Should one of us go try to find him?" Cooper said. "Probably me since you have a family now."

Grayson shook his head. "Not yet. Although it's worrisome, he knows how to take care of himself. If he needs help, he'll reach out to us. Let's give him a few more days before we act."

If they didn't hear from him by the weekend, then it would be time to worry.

\* \* \* \* \*